This book should be returned to any branch of the
Lancashire County Library on or before the date

EBU

2 3 SEP 2014

Anthony Hays is a journalist and novelist. He has covered topics as varied as narcotics trafficking, political corruption, Civil War history, and the war on terror.

ALSO BY ANTHONY HAYS

The Killing Way

THE
DIVINE
SACRIFICE

ANTHONY HAYS

CORVUS

First published in the United States in 2010 by Forge, an imprint of Tom Doherty Associates, LLC, New York.

First published in paperback in Great Britain in 2013 by Corvus, an imprint of Atlantic Books Ltd.

Maps by Jon Lansberg and Jennifer Hanover

10 9 8 7 6 5 4 3 2 1

A CIP catalogue record for this book is available from the British Library.

Paperback ISBN: 978 0 85789 066 5
E-book ISBN: 978 0 85789 068 9

Printed and bound by CPI Group (UK) Ltd, Croydon, CR0 4YY

Corvus
An imprint of Atlantic Books Ltd
Ormond House
26-27 Boswell Street
London
WC1N 3JZ

www.corvus-books.co.uk

For

ROBERT DOUGLAS HAYS
(1917–1981)

and

CARL T. TALLENT
(1921–2008)

who sacrificed their youth so that we might be free

ACKNOWLEDGMENTS

Faced with the task of giving credit where it is due for this, the second volume of Malgwyn's and Arthur's adventures, I find that the list grows longer, not shorter. But the length does nothing to diminish the appreciation I feel toward each.

My agent, Frank Weimann, and his assistant, Elyse Tanzillo, are absolutely the best. My delightful editor, Claire Eddy, her assistant, Kristin Sevick, and all the folks at Tor/Forge have been wonderful. As always, Bo and Dee Grimshaw and Rich and Roz Tuerk have proven themselves true friends. Bill and Diane Pyron and their children, Amelia and Atticus, have been a constant source of encouragement. Thanks go to Clara Gerl, my lecture partner with DeVry, for her understanding and support. And no list would be complete without Brian Holcombe, who stood by me through some tough times.

I am forever grateful to Geoffrey and Pat Ashe for their willingness to share their vast knowledge of Arthur and his times as well as their friendship. Dr. Christopher Snyder was always happy to answer my interminable questions about the Britonic Age.

Much of my life has been spent overseas, teaching English

and creative writing at a variety of places. And I am the richer for having enjoyed the friendship of Sonya Mitic, Lela Argus, Anita Reci, Todor Gajdov, Jeta Rushidi, Luizia Zeqiri, Jazmin Triana Durango, and Qenan Saliu in Macedonia. A world away in Tennessee, my classrooms were blessed with students like Tristan Daniel, Kassie Vickery, Allen Farmer, Taylor Holder, and more than I could possibly name here. Dear friends from my days in the Marshall Islands include Carolyn Laws, Max Voelzke, and John Tuthill. In England I enjoyed the hospitality of new friends Diane and Ross Bowman and Jane and Chris Lee and old friends Hazel and Nigel Garwell. I had great times with the folks in Reading at the Thames Valley Writers group, the Southampton Writers Circle, and Susan Down and her fine group in Salisbury.

The publication of *The Killing Way* brought a host of old friends back into my life. My first coauthor and childhood friend, Michael Greene, classmates Kathy Louvin, Mike Card, Jeff Harrell, Cindy Lamb, Dave Rizzuto, Dana Spinks, Steve Ellis, Doug Nall, Woodson Marshall, Sheryl Rennie Hall, Bruce Martin, David Vowell, Randy Tarkington, Matt Fischer, Jenny Roberts, Teresa Vaden, Laura Watts, Joan Howell, Lynn Jones, Jeannie Wagner, Debbie Vaden, Ron Estes, Anjanette Benjamin, and the list goes on.

For ten years, I hung my hat in Savannah, Tennessee. I would be totally remiss if I did not mention Lisa Bevis, Ann Bain, Pat Prather, Jimmy Bain, Steve Bain, Billy Bain, Benson Parris, Diane Qualls, Deb Gray, Donna Davis, Stacy Carnal, and Tammy Cherry. Tommy Tallent, Mary Sue Vickery, and Becky Bain have been far greater and more loyal friends than I deserve. And that's true too of Jana and Kevin Shelby.

And, I cannot forget to mention my newly rediscovered

family, the children of my late brother Robert Joe Hays, Sr. His sons, Joe Hays, John Hays, and Jamie Hays. Their children, Amber, Morgan, Alex, and Katherine Hays. His daughter, Christy Dawn Langford, and her children—Ashley, Ryan, Sarah, and Caleb. And then there are the in-laws, Lisa Hays, Brad Langford, and Samantha Hays. Last but certainly not least, Shannah Vivian Farr, who was like a sister to me all those years ago.

To those who I have inevitably left out, I apologize. Their friendship and support are not diminished by their absence.

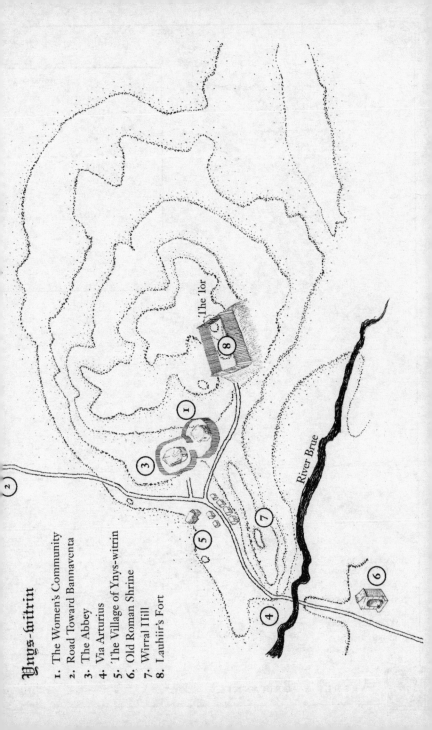

Ynys-Witrin

1. The Women's Community
2. Road Toward Bannaventa
3. The Abbey
4. Via Arturius
5. The Village of Ynys-witrin
6. Old Roman Shrine
7. Wirral Hill
8. Lauhiir's Fort

River Brue

The Tor

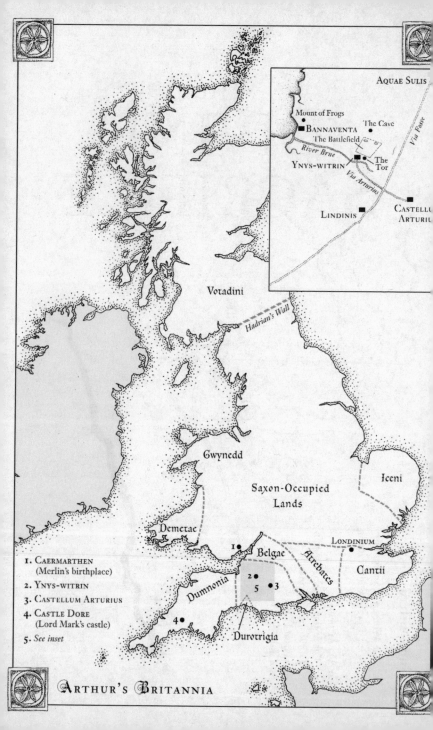

AQUAE SULIS

Mount of Frogs

BANNAVENTA   The Cave

The Battlefield

YNYS-WITRIN   The Tor

River Brue

Via Arturius

LINDINIS   CASTELLU
ARTURII

Via Fosse

Votadini

Hadrian's Wall

Gwynedd

Saxon-Occupied
Lands

Iceni

Demetae

Belgae   LONDINIUM

Atrebates

Cantii

1.

2.
5. 3.

Dumnonia

4.

Durotrigia

1. CAERMARTHEN
(Merlin's birthplace)

2. YNYS-WITRIN

3. CASTELLUM ARTURIUS

4. CASTLE DORE
(Lord Mark's castle)

5. See inset

ARTHUR'S BRITANNIA

THE
DIVINE
SACRIFICE

GLASTONBURY

In the Eighty-first Year from the Adventus Saxonum

The water is high again, transforming the marshlands into sea and turning this ancient place into an island. With gray mist coating the land like a thick fur, I often find my old feet taking me to the abbey, to the old cemetery next to the *vetustam ecclesia*, the original church. With my ninetieth winter upon me, I know more people buried here than those still aboveground.

One grave lies near unto the old church, aye, not far from the well. No marker tells of its occupant. Indeed, if you did not know it was there, it would seem just another bare plot of ground, a hollow place. But that is how he wanted it. Unmarked and therefore unpretentious.

I am not a brother of the abbey. Aye, I am not sure what I am, save an old, one-armed man in a world that does not value such. For a short while, many seasons past, I was a farmer, then soldier, then counselor to the Rigotamos, Arthur ap Uther. It is he who lies between the two stout pillars in the burial ground, interred with my cousin Guinevere. I come to this place often and sit on a rock, wishing that I could speak with them.

Though I am not a brother, my simple hut sits inside the vallum, the ditch that marks the abbey's boundary. I take my meals at the abbot's table; copy an occasional manuscript when my one hand is not too pained. The abbot still seeks my counsel when he treats with the pagan Saxons, who have now spread across our land like a vile disease.

On this day, I thought not of Arthur, of Guinevere, but of the man whose bones lie in the hollowed spot. I knew him, not well, but I knew him. He was a simple soul, too firm in his beliefs to allow for any change, and though he would have willingly died for his beliefs, it was not those that brought him to a violent end. Sometimes the best of us are brought low by the most worthless of reasons. So it was with him. But his was not the only death in that affair. And, it was not the first, but it became the most important.

I remember well the day on which his death began. Beyond the gods cursing our weather, it dawned without any portent of trouble. The most evil occasions often have the most innocent beginnings. That is the way of life. The water was high on that day too, and the Via Arturius, the road running from Castellum Arturius, was muddy, slowing the journey and tiring the horses. But such is not the proper way to tell the tale. And only I am now left to tell it. The others, Arthur, Guinevere, Bedevere, are all gone. But I must tell it in the proper order, to ensure that I leave nothing out. And, as with all days, it began with an awakening. . . .

CHAPTER ONE

"Malgwyn!"

The voice came from the other side of that nether-world whence come our dreams. I ignored its call and rolled over, pulling my fur blanket tighter against me.

"Malgwyn!"

I resisted it still.

"Malgwyn ap Cuneglas!"

I pried one of my eyes open and squinted at Merlin, old and wrinkled, standing there with one of my finest tunics, dyed crimson, in hand. Owain, a little orphan boy who helped us with our tasks, stood next to him, holding my *braccae* and my *caligae*. A smile grew across my face though I wished only to frown. They looked like father and son.

"He is awake!" Owain cried. "Shall I get the water jug again, Master Merlin?" he asked with a smile that betrayed how much he would enjoy dousing me.

"Certainly you should, boy. He used to be a farmer, and farmers are renowned for rising early. I have a theory that rising early allows us to breathe the freshest air of the day. It is time that he went back to his old habits."

Sensing the inevitable, I threw the fur back with my good arm and swung my feet around. "Which old habits are those, Master Merlin? Draining wineskins or killing Saxons?" In truth, I had done more than my share of both. After Saxons had killed my wife, Gwyneth, I turned from farmer to soldier, and at Arthur's side, I reveled in the Saxon blood I spilled. Until I lost an arm at Tribuit. "What will you teach this scamp while I am away, Merlin?"

The old man, whose face resembled a dried grape, wrinkled it further in concentration. "He must learn more about herbs and how to use them to heal, Malgwyn. His education is wholly lacking. Now, come! Don your tunic and breeches. Arthur will be waiting."

I wiped my stump of an arm across my eyes, hoping to clear away the cobwebs of sleep. "Arthur can wait. 'Tis only a two-hour ride to the abbey, and we are not expected before midday."

"Aye, but I think the Rigotamos has a stop to make on the way," Merlin said with a wink.

Pulling myself to my feet, I took the *braccae* and struggled to put them on. "Not on a formal trip," I answered, with enough of an edge to let Merlin know that he was plowing in salted earth.

But Merlin had spoken the truth, I acknowledged to myself as I donned my linen *camisia*. Once, many moons ago, I was a farmer. But the war against the Saxons stole my young wife from me and made me a soldier in the command of Arthur ap Uther, now the Rigotamos, the High King of all Britannia; he was then but the *Dux Bellorum*, the leader of battles, for the *consilium* of lords that held our fragmented island together. My zeal for killing Saxons raised me in Arthur's esteem, and I quickly became one of his lesser lieutenants. But a Saxon sword cleaved my arm along the River Tribuit and took my bloodlust away.

Arthur stanched the flow of my life's blood and saved me, when I wanted nothing more than to die. He took me to Ynys-witrin, where the *monachi* bound my wounds, healed me, and taught me to write with my left hand, gave me something of a trade since farming and warring were lost to me. Death still seemed preferable to all, and I bore Arthur a grudge for my salvation, a grudge that blighted my days and sent my nights reeling into a waterfall of drink.

Ambrosius Aurelianus was then the Rigotamos, having taken office in the wake of Vortigern's disgrace. It was Vortigern who had been betrayed by the Saxons. He had first hired them to counter the threat of the Picts, but the treacherous Saxons turned on Vortigern and swept beyond those lands granted them. The war thus created made the threat of the Picts seem but a minor annoyance, swatted away like a fly. The Saxons hungered for our land, and their appetite was voracious. In the confusion that followed Vortigern's fall, Ambrosius, a native Briton, but one with deep Roman roots, rose to leadership. He brought with him a group of young, valiant warriors, including Arthur ap Uther.

"Oh, did Lord Arthur not tell you?" Merlin continued to chide me. "He has reduced the size of his party. Only you and Bedevere will accompany him."

Owain tied the rope around my waist that held the *braccae*

up. He jerked it tight, too tight, and I yelped. "You should not eat so much, Malgwyn."

I whacked the back of his head for his insolence and turned back to Merlin. "Only two in his escort for a formal visit? What is Arthur thinking?"

Merlin laid my tunic on a rickety wooden bench. "I think that Arthur is reluctant to pay too much attention to Lauhiir. Should he be accompanied by all his nobles, then it could confer upon the little oaf an importance he does not deserve."

Now, that was reasoning that I could understand.

As Owain strapped my iron-studded leather belt around me, I smiled at the memory of the young, oh so earnest, lord.

Arthur, son of both Rome and Britannia, was a soldier above all else, and he fought the Saxons with courage and guile. I fought alongside him, until that day at the Tribuit when a Saxon blade left me bleeding. By the time my wounds healed, Arthur had stanched the flow of Saxons into our lands and positioned himself to become the next Rigotamos.

After a time, I returned to the old village near Castellum Arturius, taking an abandoned hut as my own. Little Owain, a boy of the castle, neglected by his own people, became my assistant of sorts, helping me with little chores. And thus I remained, copying manuscripts for the *monachi*, drinking and whoring, until the night that Arthur came to me and laid the death of Eleonore in my lap, on the eve of Ambrosius's retirement and the election of a new Rigotamos.

I grabbed my leather pouch and checked the contents, my flint and tinder for starting fires, an extra dagger, and a small piece of dark, heavy cloth. I had found it in young Eleonore's hand, when she lay ripped apart in the lane.

Eleonore had been the sister of my wife, Gwyneth. After the death of their parents, while I lay drunk at Castellum Arturius, she turned to my brother for aid, becoming both a beautiful and willful young woman and a serving girl at Arthur's table. Her body was found in the lane in front of Merlin's house, ripped like a slaughtered deer. Arthur came to me to solve the crime. The affair was sordid and nasty, peopled with Druids, true and false, Saxons, and grasping lords, and more deaths followed the first. Among the deaths were those of young Owain's parents, leaving him an orphan in a world bereft of charity. But by luck and a stubborn persistence, I weaved my way through the maze, helping to place Arthur on his throne and keep Merlin safe from the machinations of Mordred, and keeping my own head firmly atop my shoulders. After that, all was different.

I became Arthur's counselor, and I moved into Merlin's house near the main hall in the castle. I had left my daughter, Mariam, survivor of the vicious attack that stole Gwyneth from us both, with my brother, Cuneglas, when I went to war with the Saxons. On my return, I was too lost in shame and drink to retrieve her. She had grown up thinking that Cuneglas and his wife, Ygerne, were her parents. Only during the affair surrounding Eleonore's death did she learn the truth, but even now she lived with Ygerne.

Though I was now responsible for my late brother Cuneglas's family—he died of a head wound some days after the election of Arthur as Rigotamos—it was not appropriate for me to live with them, though I had a yearning that knew no end for

Ygerne, my brother's widow. And, oh, how I wished I could break down the fearful barrier in my own mind that kept me from joining Mariam and Ygerne. Guilt is a powerful foe.

Marriage between widows and their husband's brothers was not uncommon in our land, but the guilt I felt for leaving my daughter with them, ignoring them, overwhelmed all other urges. Ygerne, kind and charitable soul that she was, took Owain too into her home, though he spent as much time with me and Merlin as with anyone. And we needed each other, the three of us. Merlin, whose mind sometimes wandered, needed companionship. Owain needed people who cared about him. I needed people who needed me.

I fingered the scrap of cloth with my good hand, in wonder at the role it had played in making all of that happen. It had led me to Eleonore's killers and a better life; I kept it now for good luck.

"Well, do not expect to arrive at the abbey by the midday," Merlin said in a mischievous tone, "formal trip or not." The old devil delighted in aggravating me. One of the things that bound Arthur and me was my kinship with his mistress, my cousin Guinevere, who lived in a house just off the Via Arturius, the road to Ynys-witrin. The story was an old one and known by but a few. When very young, she had been with the sisters near Ynys-witrin. Headstrong and beautiful, she had joined the sisters to avoid a marriage she did not want. But while there, she met the young Arthur and fell in love with him and he with her. And their love led them to break the boundaries between the sisters and men, and they were caught in an embrace.

Guinevere was driven from the sisters' community in disgrace. But Arthur's rising importance brought the *consilium* to his defense, and he was spared any sanction. Merlin spread the word that she was actually a powerful enchantress and had bewitched Arthur. The story kept people from bothering her, for they feared her magic, and Arthur arranged for the simple house. As the years passed and his prestige grew, he brought her from the shadows into the light of his court as his acknowledged consort. But a king's wife had to be as perfect (in Arthur's eyes) as the king himself, and Arthur knew that her shame in being exiled from the women's community would always be with her. Though things were better, Merlin's rumors of the enchantress followed her still. I had been pressing Arthur to leave the past behind and marry her, but he refused yet, and it remained a sore point between us.

In a more somber tone, Merlin added, "Be careful, Malgwyn. I worry that there is more to Lauhiir's appointment than there would seem."

With Saxons knocking at our eastern door and encroaching on our southern lands, Ambrosius had bowed to the pressure from the *consilium* and named young Lord Lauhiir, the choice of Mark and his faction, as protector of the Tor and Ynyswitrin. Many such lords peopled our land, ruling by brutality and greed. But Lauhiir's father, Eliman, had been a lieutenant to Mark in years gone by. In truth, I liked Lauhiir not, and argued with Arthur about his appointment. To my eye, he was slimy and spoiled, a man who wore fancy clothes to mark his station whereas Arthur wore his station like clothes. But Lauhiir's father had many friends on the *consilium*, and Arthur could not reverse Ambrosius's decision. "Besides," he told me one day, "by having him close to hand at the Tor, I can better keep an eye on him."

I straightened my tunic beneath the belt as best I could with but one hand. "You think there is some evil in it?" I asked Merlin.

"Evil is a vague thing. Do I think it bodes no good for Arthur? Yes. I think with Mordred away on our western border, Lauhiir poses the greatest threat to Arthur's seat. Mordred's head should be gracing a post in the east." Young Mordred was one of Arthur's least favorite cousins. He was sly where Arthur was cunning. Though I had been unable to prove his guilt in the plot against Ambrosius, he had been exiled to our western coast where he could do less harm.

"You are a wise man, Merlin. You know that that could never happen. David, Lauhiir, and Mark would spark an instant rebellion. I did the best I could, but that wasn't good enough to tie the noose about Mordred's head."

At the thought of David, a lord from the northwest, I stopped and frowned. He had challenged Arthur at the election, but lost, a loss he took not well. Aye, he had sought my punishment for striking the boy lord Celyn in some sort of petulant reprisal for his rejection by the *consilium*. Mark was second only to Arthur in strength as a lord. He ruled his lands from Castellum Marcus in the far southwest. Tristan, his son, was serving a kind of enforced servitude at Arthur's castle for his hand in Eleonore's death. He had come to Arthur's castle for the election of the new Rigotamos, representing his father. And, we quickly learned, to counsel a treaty with the Saxons, a treaty he indicated that Mark was intent on pursuing with or without the *consilium*'s approval.

But once there, like many young men, he had fallen afoul of Eleonore's charms and become possessed by the spirit of her beauty. But she rejected his bid and in the violence that ensued lost her life. Although Tristan did not kill her, his actions left her vulnerable to those who did take her life. I had let him believe, however, that he bore the greater guilt.

"But Ynys-witrin is great power to place in the hands of a newly made lord," I continued. "I think that Lauhiir is not equal to it." I did not tell him that I suspected Lauhiir as complicit in the plot against Ambrosius, and that had been at the heart of the matter of Eleonore's death.

"I knew a great lord once," Merlin began, crossing the room and settling slowly onto a stool. "It was long before Arthur was born. One day during the hot season, in the marshes near the water, he was bitten by a small fly. Within days, that small fly had laid the great lord low."

"I take your meaning." And I did, though I still believed that he gave Lauhiir more credit than he deserved. I finished dressing, wishing that it were Kay going with us. In so many ways, he was more aggravating than any of Arthur's nobles, but, despite his temper, I had come to trust him completely. Unfortunately, Kay was off on an official inspection tour of our eastern border forts. Unofficially, he was checking to see what mischief Mordred, Arthur's cousin, had inflicted upon the people when posted to the east. Although Arthur had set Gawain and Gereint to keep an eye on Mordred in the west, he desired that Kay should bring him a report from the east. It was while posted there some moons before that Mordred had let the Saxons into our lands, or so I believed.

Bedevere had been by Arthur's side as long as Kay or longer. A handsome, strong fellow, he was quiet, unlike Kay. While

I had warred as long with one as the other, I could not say that I knew Bedevere well. His father and grandfather had been nobles under Vortigern, and Bedevere had come to Arthur's service while the Rigotamos was still young.

With a face that seemed cut from stone, he carried the look of a man with a hard heart. But the one secret I knew of Bedevere put the lie to that. Once on a scout for Arthur, Bedevere and I took our soldiers into a small village, not too distant from Londinium. The Saxons had been there before us, and we searched among the burning huts and the slain for any that breathed yet. Circling a small shed, I came suddenly upon Bedevere, sitting on the ground, his sword lying by his side. In his arms he cradled a small girl, her hair as blond as my Mariam's, but her life's blood soaking the ground.

The noble with a face of granite was crying. I returned from whence I came, and he never knew I had seen him. As long as Arthur could count on such men's loyalty, he might have a chance in this maze of a world, a chance to do some good among all the greed, jealousy, and evil.

These were the things which held my mind as I finished dressing. Owain rummaged around in our storage pit, looking for bread and cheese. Merlin had already forgotten my journey and was busy working on some odd-looking project at his workbench.

"Father?"

She always did that to me! Like some little water fairy, my daughter Mariam could pop in and out of the house without making a noise. Blond, like her mother, she had a face as fair and pretty as the morning sun, with eyes as mischievous as Gwyn ap Nudd, the fairy king.

"Yes, Mariam."

She edged closer to me and sat on the bench. Touching was still awkward for us.

"Mother says you are to come and eat your morning meal with us before you leave." As always, when delivering a message, she was the soul of severity. "Father, why are you and the Rigotamos going to Ynys-witrin?"

I straightened my tunic before answering. "So that he and Coroticus may argue about the church."

"But why do they argue? Do they not both believe in the Christ?" She was so like my dear Gwyneth, her true mother. Questions, always questions.

Pausing and taking a deep breath, I searched for an answer. How do you explain such a question to a child? She knew nothing of Pelagius and his heresy, of how seriously priests argued over unanswerable questions. Of how a priest could consider the shape of a building a blasphemy and a king could think it an homage and both could truly believe they were right. So, I made a joke.

"They argue over whether to sacrifice a little girl or a little boy to bless the building. I have voted for a little girl, and I know just the one."

Mariam giggled, which was good to see. "No, you don't, Father. You would not have saved me from those awful Saxons if you thought I would make a good sacrifice. And those who follow the Christ do not believe in human sacrifice."

"True," I agreed. "Now, run to your mother's and tell her I will be there in a minute."

She left with the smile still on her face.

"You should spend more time with her, Malgwyn. It would do you good and Ygerne would, I think, welcome it."

A heat rose up in my neck. "Do not worry about what

Ygerne would welcome! She is my brother's widow, and he is but a few months in the grave! Besides, as part of Arthur's household, she will want for nothing."

Merlin cocked his head at me. "I meant that Ygerne would welcome that you spend more time with Mariam."

I grunted and prepared to stomp out of the house as I could think of nothing clever to say. But then the door burst open and a man, wearing a rough brown robe, his face red from exertion, half tumbled and half ran into the house.

"Malgwyn!"

"Ider?" He was one of the brothers at Ynys-witrin, younger than most others.

He was panting heavily, and even the shaved strip from ear to ear, his tonsure, was red. He paused long enough to catch his breath, but when the words came out, they chilled me. "You must come quickly! Brother Elafius is dead, and the abbot wants you immediately!"

Chapter Two

"Did he die by violence, Ider?"

The young brother was sitting on one of our stools and gulping water from a jug that Owain had hurried to him. He shook his head. "It did not appear so to me, Malgwyn. But the abbot sees something strange in it."

"Elafius was an old man, Ider. His death was bound to come soon." I still did not understand why Coroticus had sent Ider to speed our journey. I remembered Elafius well. He was a kindly old fellow, skilled in the healing arts, but an irritating and argumentative *monachus*. He was truly ancient, and I would not have been surprised to have heard of his death anytime in the six years past.

Arthur stomped in before I could respond, and Ider rose to bow to him, but the Rigotamos waved him back to his seat. "We are preparing to leave now. Coroticus knows we are coming today. Why this haste?"

"My lord, I know only that the abbot did not expect you until the evening meal. He sent me to hasten your departure, or at least that of Malgwyn. Please, Rigotamos, the abbot is in a terrible state! Give Malgwyn his leave to depart now."

This morning, before Ider burst in upon us, as Merlin and Owain abused me for a lazy sluggard, I was intended to ride with Arthur to Ynys-witrin. My old friend Coroticus, the abbot, was still battling with Arthur about his cruciform church in the castle. Arthur called it worshipful, reminding the abbot that the cross was a recognized symbol; Coroticus called it blasphemous, but offered no real rationale for his opposition. We all knew his motive; he wanted Arthur to reduce the abbey's taxes. Arthur would not. Without the abbot's blessing, Arthur had called a halt to the church's construction. And now it was but a muddy foundation in the middle of the castle, caught between two stubborn men.

Our meeting would be the third and the only one held at Ynys-witrin. Indeed it was Arthur's right to demand that all such parleys be held at Castellum Arturius, but this trip was special.

The Tor, a tall, steep hill among the small chain which made up Ynys-witrin, was a critical point in our alert system. So important did the *consilium* deem it that they insisted an armed presence was necessary, claiming there was too much of a gap between Castellum Arturius and the channel. So, Lauhiir had the charge of building permanent defenses there.

A watch fire was also kept at the Mount of Frogs, to the northwest, and it was much more defensible than the Tor, but the place itself was said to be enchanted, the home of three giants. Establishing a stockade there had become a problem. Though I believed not in such things, many of our soldiers did believe in giants and enchantresses and magic. Old superstitions die hard. Finally, Arthur ordered a minor lord, Teilo, to dispatch troops there. I believe some extra lands changed hands in the process. This despite the fact that David and another minor lord, Dochu, had troops closer.

The trip to Ynys-witrin then was for Arthur to inspect Lauhiir's fortifications on the Tor as well as to argue religion and the unfinished church with Coroticus. While I minded not my job of observing Lauhiir, I found arguments about religion unsettling. My own beliefs drifted upon a stormy sea, while both Arthur and Coroticus had firm, strong beliefs in the Christ. That the specifics of those beliefs were often as different as words would allow was of little consequence to them, but kept me confused. More particularly, however, I minded how Arthur used me as a buffer between himself and Coroticus, allowing me to earn the abbot's wrath by couching their differences as the result of discussions with me. "Why just last eve," Arthur would say, "Malgwyn reminded me that the problem with that was . . ." Hence my reluctance to abandon my furs and face the coming journey. Until Brother Ider's abrupt appearance.

Arthur twirled his beard with one finger while wrinkling his brow. "No," he said finally. "We will both depart now." He looked to Owain. "Fetch Bedevere, boy. Tell him that I have ordered our immediate departure."

Merlin, who had been silent until then, left his workbench and faced Arthur. "Something lies hidden in this that I do not like," he said, shaking his gray-bearded head. "Ider, when was Elafius's death discovered?"

"Why, just after the midnight, master."

"Who discovered him?"

31

"I do not know. I know only that Coroticus sent for me and dispatched me here."

I nodded. "It must have been so for Ider to arrive so early this morn."

"Both of you," Merlin said, "be cautious. I see nothing good in this. Send for me if you have need of my services."

Arthur patted him on the back. "We will, old friend. Come, Malgwyn. Let us find out what stirs the abbot from his peace."

"Merlin must have cast a spell for rain," Arthur grumbled as we rode our tired, wet horses along the muddy track. The Rigotamos was a tall man, solidly built, with chestnut-brown hair and a long, flowing beard. His fingers were curiously at odds with his body, being short and stumpy. One had been taken by a Saxon spear, but the others, protruding from the wool wrapped around them, were rough and red. A true believer in the Christ, he was also a magician at balancing the demands of the *consilium* and his devotion to justice, a devotion that most called a weakness.

"Be easy, Ider," I told the young *monachus* whose eyes had spread wide at the mention of Merlin and spells. "The Rigotamos jests." Though the peasants and townsfolk still believed that the old man was a sorcerer, he held no magic in his heart, just a bag of tricks that gave the illusion of magic. His pouch held herbal cures, and nuts, sometimes candies for the young. And, in truth, he had put them to good use in the past. Mostly, now, he was just an old man with a wandering mind, sharp and penetrating at times, fogged and clouded at others. But, we treasured him all the same.

Still, I sensed in Ider an uneasiness in such company. "By your leave, my lord," he began in a stutter. "I would speed my own return to prepare the abbot for your arrival."

Arthur glanced at me, his eyes hiding well those thoughts behind them. "As you will, Brother Ider. Tell the abbot that we will take our noon meal with him."

With that, Ider prodded his horse into a slippery trot as if he could not leave us behind fast enough. "Better," Arthur observed. "Now we can speak without caution."

"This journey could have waited until the summer," I pointed out, looking down and seeing how my horse's hooves sank six inches into the thick brown mud. The Romans had planned one of their solid, cobbled roads here, and they had been responsible for clearing the lane on which we rode. But threats from elsewhere in the empire had stolen both interest in another road and the funds to construct it. So, we were left with a path nearly impassable in wet weather.

"No," Arthur answered, shaking his shaggy head. "In truth Elafius's death would have called us forward, or at least called you forward, regardless of when we had planned this visit. And the sooner Lauhiir understands that I will keep my eye turned in his direction, the better he will behave."

"He is a petulant child," Bedevere said, his voice gravelly and deep. "Better you should spank him than coddle him."

"If necessary, old friend, I will do what must be done."

And Arthur was clever when it came to politics. His family traced its roots back to Roman senators, or so he claimed on those few occasions when he actually spoke of them. The Rigotamos was curious with regard to that. He said little of his family, in a time when family meant rank, wealth. I knew, though, that while his ancestry might have gotten him his first post, his rise in power was due to his own actions, his own victories, at which his cleverness rose to the fore again.

He fought with brains, with common sense. Where Lord Mark would send a hundred men headlong into an assault against the Saxons, Arthur would use fifty men skillfully and achieve the same result.

"And what of Coroticus and the church?" I asked. "Will this be the final tale on that?"

"Of course not," the Rigotamos answered with a smile in his eye. "Coroticus will never give up his one point of leverage. He demands lower taxes in exchange for his blessing on my church. That, I will never agree to."

In truth, Arthur was no friend of the clergy. As a young noble, he collected taxes for the *consilium*, and he earned the wrath of priests and *monachi* by not taking their bribes, forcing them to pay their taxes, something that endeared him to the *consilium* but did little for his standing with the church.

We met few travelers on the muddy road, almost impassable in places, rising and falling with the gentle slopes along the levels. Most moved to let us pass. Some bowed to Arthur; a few reached to touch him. I never understood that. It was most remarkable. I had seen many lords in my life, but Arthur was the only one that the common folk wanted to touch. Well, aside from those that wished to hang their lord for his cruelty. Arthur's dealings could seem as cruel as any, but he used that weapon selectively and never without cause.

As we neared the bridge across the River Brue before arriving at Ynys-witrin, we happened upon a group of merchants, their wagons loaded with wares, headed toward the little village outside the abbey. I rode ahead of Arthur and Bedevere and approached the group.

"Fair morn to you!" I greeted.

One of the merchants, a chubby man with greasy hair and beard, turned and eyed me with a fierce look, probably expecting something other than a well-dressed, one-armed man. One-armed, aye, one-legged men were not unknown, but almost none were well-to-do. Most were beggars, shunned by the people as cursed. His eye was quick enough to catch the Rigotamos and Bedevere in the distance though.

"My lord, how may I assist you?" His voice was as greasy as his hair.

"Why come you to Ynys-witrin? Is there some festival?"

"Have you not heard, my lord?"

"Heard what?"

The man's eyes grew wide. "Why, I would think the Rigotamos's councillors would have heard." I was growing quickly tired of this man.

Placing my hand on the hilt of my sword, tucked snugly in my leather belt, I smiled down at him. "If I knew, I would not be asking. Do not test my good manners." The world would not miss one less merchant, and insolence to Arthur's counselors was insolence to Arthur.

His eyes grew wider still and he gulped. "No harm meant, my lord. Patrick is said to arrive from across the sea today. With Patrick and the Rigotamos both here, it becomes a festival."

I groaned. And the merchant hurried to catch up with his wagon, splashing its way through the mud.

Patrick!

This trip was ill-fated from the start. Patrick, though some called him "Patricius," was the last thing we needed. Born to a local official in the last years of the Roman time, he had been stolen by the Scotti across the water when he was but a boy.

After many years, the stories told us, he escaped and made his way to Gaul where he became a priest and had quickly become one of the most famous and important. He allied with Bishop Germanus in the Pelagian matter and earned great respect among the clergy.

Pelagius. Would that I had never heard that name. Pelagius had been a priest of our lands who had aspired to greater rank in the church. I tried to remember what I knew of Pelagian-ism, what the *monachi* had said in passing.

He had been a man of our lands, a deeply religious man, who traveled far and wide, yea even unto Rome itself. He was a man of great stubbornness, a man of stout beliefs, who ar-gued that all man needed, for eternal life, were good works, not God's grace. Rumors abounded that he had gone far to the east, beyond the Holy Land. Said to be a tall, friendly man, he refused to accept certain of the church's teachings. I do not profess to be a learned man of religious things. All I can say for certain was that Pelagius claimed that man had complete free will and could choose between good and evil for himself. If I understood correctly, God's grace and the sacrifice of the Christ had little meaning according to Pelagius. His beliefs made little headway with the church fathers, and he was eventually forced to flee, some said to the far east.

Patrick owed much of his power to his support of Bishop Germanus in the Pelagian affair. When a young *sacerdote* named Agricola, the son of a British *episcopus*, had openly championed Pelagius, Germanus and first Lupus, and then Severus, were sent to end the heresy. Patrick, himself a much younger man than now, gave homage to Germanus, earning the great man's thanks and garnering a great deal of power for himself. And he was not shy about displaying that power. A great busybody, he frequently interfered with lords and their followers. Fortunately, he spent most of his time with the Scotti and rarely visited our shores. Until now.

The signs were all against us. From the strange summons on the death of Brother Elafius, to the sudden appearance of Patrick, to the hidden threat posed by Lauhiir. The old people would have barred our departure, threatened us with the ancient gods. I pondered telling Arthur about Patrick as he and Bedevere drew near.

As if he were reading my mind, he hailed me. "What news, Malgwyn? Why this torrent of travelers?"

I grimaced. We were almost at Ynys-witrin and the word of Patrick's arrival would not profit Arthur so late in our journey, so I decided to let him find out for himself.

"The country folk are turning your visit into a fair, my lord."

Though he nodded and seemed satisfied with the answer, his eyes narrowed ever so slightly. I knew him too well and the look he gave me boded ill for the future. With that, we urged our horses into the stream of people in the lane.

The great Tor at Ynys-witrin was part of a chain of hills, of islands most of the year. Rainwater swelled the great channel to the north and the lowlands around Ynys-witrin flooded often. Only a narrow strip of land joined the island to the rest of Brittania, and it was across that strip that the Via Arturius led, right along the base of the little tor called Wirral, and on to the abbey itself. Though, at some times, the water reached up and closed that route as well, turning the great tor and the little hills into a true island.

In days past, the old folk said that the sea itself came up to the tor. When I was yet young, my father took me once and showed me where the Romans had built wharves for the big ships to come up the river. They were still there, at the edge of Wirral, though few ships made the journey anymore, and they were in poor repair.

As we drew close to the causeway that linked Ynys-witrin with the Via Arturius, I saw the silhouette of a single tree, a thorn tree, at Wirral's summit. Coroticus swore that Joseph of Arimathea, he who gave a tomb for the Christ, came to this spot from Judea with twelve companions. Exhausted, he planted his staff and it took root, growing into the twisted, gnarled tree I could yet see. I knew nothing of the truth of it, but I know that it bloomed during the winter, around about the time that the old Romans held their Saturnalia festivals, and, as my father used to tell me, the Druids held one of their rites.

As I say, I could not judge the story's truth. I only knew that the old tree on Wirral Hill always seemed lonely to me, and somehow sad. If this Joseph did indeed come here from the lands of Judea, many thousands of miles away, he must have been as the thorn tree, a solitary and lonely figure in his own way, twelve companions or not.

I breathed deeply, holding in my chest the smells of a place that was special to me in both good and bad ways. Never, in all of my travels with Arthur, had I found a place such as this. Wood smoke flavored the air, but somehow it mixed with another, purer, cleaner air and acted as a balm to my soul. Explanations for this were weak and assailable. Yet it was true.

The village of Ynys-witrin consisted of a single road that snaked around the gentle slope beneath the abbey and up the hill beside it. The houses were all wattle and daub, an oak frame with a mix of straw and mud and cow dung between the timbers. The odor in wet weather was not pleasant, and it left the road smelling like a herd of cattle. And this day was wet.

I saw quickly that word of our arrival and that of Patrick had truly spread. Our journey had taken but about three hours, and much of that because of the mud. It was a distance of but ten Roman miles. In drier weather it would have taken an hour less. A man afoot, avoiding the sloppiness of the road, could often travel faster, as fast as four miles to the hour if he were unburdened and disciplined in his march.

Merchants with their carts lined the sides of the roads and were tucked between the handful of houses in the village. They sold pottery, wine, *cervesa*, brooches, linen, and wool. Colorful banners of red, white, blue, green draped from their carts. The lookers were many, but I saw few buying. We had little coinage in our country, some old coins of Honorius and Valentinian that were still traded, and occasionally new coins from Rome and other places that came in through our western ports. Even the tin and lead mines were not really producing anymore, though one of Lauhiir's charges had been to make the mines active once more. So, we traded as we could, used coins when we had them. Taxes were collected in both coin and produce. Aye, that was one way Arthur kept his table furnished. But of late, with the countryside recovering from the Saxon raids, times had been hard.

"You should have brought a proper escort, my lord," Bedevere chastised Arthur.

"I did not know that there was to be a festival here. Now, I cannot risk sending either one of you for more troops."

"Do I detect fear in the Rigotamos's voice?" Any man but

myself, Kay, or Bedevere would receive a strong rebuke, but Arthur allowed us freedoms that others did not enjoy. But only in private, never before the people.

He frowned at me though. "Kings are but men, Malgwyn. And men die easily. I am not yet ready to enter the next life. Much is still left to be done in this one."

I looked around, noting the people as individuals and not just a crowd. As I suspected, I quickly picked out a little figure lurking on the edge of a group pushing against a merchant's cart. "Llynfann!"

Like a trapped rabbit, the man crouched, his head whipping quickly around, searching out the man who called him. He saw Arthur first and nearly bolted, but then his eyes caught me and my missing arm. Something of a twisted grin marked his face, and he strolled toward us.

"My lord Malgwyn!" With a cocky smile, he trotted over to us, bowing with great majesty to Arthur.

From the corner of my eye, I saw Bedevere reach for his sword, but my good hand held his. "This one is a friend of mine."

"From your days hefting a wine jug?" Arthur grumbled. In truth, Llynfann looked more like an evil rat than a respectable citizen. But looks often belied the inside of a man.

"From the day that Kay and I kept Merlin's head attached to his shoulders," I shot back.

Arthur raised his eyebrows at that. "So this is one of Master Gareth's men."

Then it was Llynfann's turn to show his surprise. And for a second, the little thief shrank a little, fright returning to his eyes. He was part of a band of *latrunculi*, living deep in the forests and hills between Castellum Arturius and Ynys-witrin.

Gareth, their chieftain, and I knew each other from a nasty affair here at the abbey. My work in that matter had kept Gareth from the executioner's axe. A friendship had been born at that time, and, in the matter of Eleonore's death, Gareth and his men had come to my aid not once, but twice.

"Master Llynfann, I have need of you," Arthur said. He had a way of making the humblest peasant feel as lofty as a prince. "Make your way to my fort at all possible speed. See the commander of my horse soldiers. Tell him that I require a troop of horse, immediately. Show him this, but then keep it for your own purse." He reached into a little pouch hanging from his saddle and pulled out a bright gold coin. With a flick of his wrist, he tossed it down to the thief.

It was handsome payment for the errand. And it would ensure that Arthur's command was heeded. Only the Rigotamos could afford to spend so much on such a task. Seeming an inch taller, Llynfann saluted Arthur and darted back down the road.

"You will never see your escort on this journey, I wager," Bedevere predicted.

"Have faith, Bedevere. Even the most disreputable men can rise high if given the chance." He laughed, slapping me on the shoulder.

"My thanks, my lord, for your confidence," I answered sourly. "Come. Coroticus awaits us."

The community of the brethren at Ynys-witrin was an imposing sight, nestled into the slope of a large hill. Surrounded by a circular *vallum* ditch topped with a timber palisade, the complex consisted of a number of austere wood huts grouped around the old church plus a larger dining hall and Coroticus's own hall, a recent addition to the site, and a kitchen. Most of the smaller structures were cells for the *monachi*, but others housed the herbarium, scriptorium, and places for other work.

Such communities were relatively new in our island. Before, you might find an isolated hermit or two scattered here and there, on land not coveted by a lord, asking only to be left alone so that they might worship the Christ in their own way. But slowly, over time, the hermits gathered together, finding solace in forming a community. At this time, other than taking a daily meal together and contributing to the vegetable garden and other chores, they were free to pursue their own interests much of the time. Before Coroticus arrived to lead the group, they did not even pray together. Now, he had set some order, a meal and two prayers as a community, and I suspected he planned even more.

The old church at Ynys-witrin always mystified me. Always. A simple structure of wattle and daub, it was the centerpiece of the settlement. No one knew for certain who had built it or when. The *monachi* had old scrolls that said Joseph of Arimathea had built it all those years ago when he came to our island. But whether the old church we saw was the same as what he built, or just built on the same site, I knew not. That it had seen more seasons than Arthur, Bedevere, and myself combined was obvious.

Arthur was always after the abbot to repair it, but Coroticus argued that to do such would desecrate a sacred place. Arthur then suggested covering the entire structure with lead to protect it. Coroticus reminded Arthur that the lead mines were not yet productive. Such was one of the many disagreements between them. A burying ground lay near unto the church. Farther east sat the timber hall of Coroticus and the monastic *vallum*, the ditch and mound that marked the abbey's boundaries.

Near unto twenty brothers lived at the abbey. Ynys-witrin was the most ancient of such conclaves. Beyond the *vallum*, a five-minute walk from the abbey and just north of the apple orchard, lay the community of sisters, a collection of some fifteen women who had pledged their lives to devotion and study of the Christ. This was the place where my cousin had first met Arthur; this was the community that cast her out in disgrace when their liaison was discovered.

But the leader of that group was dead now, and a new woman had been brought from Brittany. I knew little of her but that her beliefs were said to be somewhat strange, and Coroticus was said to have opposed her appointment. Yet, Dubricius, the archbishop for all of Britannia, desired her appointment and so it was done. I thought little more about the women as we passed through the gate into the abbey precinct. It seemed unlikely that we would have reason to visit with them on this trip.

"Welcome, Rigotamos, to Ynys-witrin!" cried Coroticus, wearing his rough brown robe and the plain silver cross, the badge of his office, dangling from a heavy chain about his neck. On either side of him were two of his primary assistants, but that was the whole of the gathering. Behind him I could see the brothers scurrying about the abbey grounds, going about their tasks.

"Malgwyn, Bedevere," he continued. "Please also accept my welcome."

"Coroticus, what was the hurry?" I asked. "We were to be here today at any rate, and, forgive me, but Elafius will still be just as dead."

The abbot's eyes hardened. He did not like anyone talking glibly of the dead, and he knew that I knew that. "I was not certain that Malgwyn would be with you. This is a situation that calls for his special talents. And it is a sin to mock the dead."

"Enough, Coroticus," Arthur interrupted, his dislike of the abbot marking every word. "You demanded Malgwyn. He is here. Show us this dead man."

Coroticus swallowed deeply, and I saw the lump in his throat rise and fall. A man of just a few more years than I, he was the son of a powerful merchant from Aquae Sulis. His father's money had bought him the abbot's seat more so than his devotion to the Christ. But in many ways that was a good thing. Coroticus was raised in the world, unlike most of the brothers, and he understood things ungodly as well as those of God.

His manner gave me pause. "You truly think some violence has been done to Elafius?" I had imagined that Coroticus was just being cautious, or devious, for some reason of his own. Either was possible.

Coroticus ignored my question and turned his attention back to Arthur. "I thought, my lord, that you and I could meet while Malgwyn took care of that affair. And with Patrick here . . ." The abbot's voice drifted off.

"Patrick?" Arthur whirled around to me. "Patrick is here?"

"You did not know?" Coroticus did not hide his surprise well.

I put on my most practiced innocent look and shrugged. "This is news to me." In truth, I assumed that Patrick posed a bigger problem for Arthur than for me.

Coroticus dropped his head and shook it. " 'Tis a long

story, my lord. Perhaps it would be better if I explained it all to you while Malgwyn works, as I suggested."

"No. What concerns you enough to bring Malgwyn also concerns me. Take us to the corpse."

Arthur's demand took me by surprise. I thought it would be as Coroticus suggested. They would begin their meeting while I looked into the death of Elafius. Though, from all I knew and had been told, it was almost certainly a normal death, if death can be called that.

"Of course, my lord. I will take you there myself."

Coroticus and his assistants spun about and led us across the grounds, between the old church and the cells for the brothers, to a building I had visited before. The last time, I had gone to see the remains of the boy, the one murdered by Brother Aneirin.

Coroticus had just become abbot. I had been at the abbey for a few weeks, long enough to have met and assessed the brothers, yet not long enough for the great wound that was my arm's stump to completely heal. A scream tore me from my bed one night, and I arose to find that a young boy, a new initiate, had been killed in his hut. All fingers pointed to a little thief named Gareth. Something in Aneirin's eyes in earlier days and his insistence on Gareth as the culprit made me study the puzzle more closely. One night later, the little thief had escaped and Brother Aneirin was found dangling from a beam.

Though publicly Coroticus blamed Gareth, privately all about whispered that it might have been Aneirin. I had no need to speculate. I knew. I sighed. 'Twas always sad for me to see death in so young a body, especially when it was by violence. It had been that incident, more than anything else, that had set me on my current path in life.

This building was longer and deeper than the cells. It served as a preparation house for the dead, before they were laid in their graves in the cemetery. Only a wooden table stood in its center. Little else marked it save some clean linen for wrapping the body and some dried flowers and herbs. The building was not often in use. The poor folk could not afford the fee for a service, so only the nobles and wealthy merchants made use of it.

In our world, most nobles and merchants, indeed most high-ranking clergy, were the sons and grandsons of men who had prospered under the Romans and held civil or church office, as *decurions* or *presbyters*. In truth, even Patrick's father was said to have been a *decurion*. But Patrick's case was a little different; his kidnapping as a boy stole him away from the luxuries his father's station could provide.

A *monachus*, a boy really, stood in the doorway. He was of the nervous sort, constantly wringing his hands, his eyes flitting about. "Abbot, I have watched carefully. No one has passed."

Coroticus patted the boy on his arm. "Be at peace, son."

Lying on the table was the naked body of an ancient man, his bones poking through his age-bleached, wrinkled skin. I had known Elafius well during my days at the abbey. We were not particular friends, but I respected his knowledge of herbs and their uses. He had charge of the herbarium and often visited me with extracts of willow bark and other medicines.

Inspecting his body, I saw no real marks, though there was little light in the cell. Where his body touched the table was dark, very dark. I had seen it before and guessed it to be the settling of his blood after he breathed his last.

"Why am I here, Coroticus?" I asked. Nothing obvious

46

sang of foul play. He was just an old man whose time had come.

The abbot pulled his robe from about his neck nervously. "When he retired last night to his cell, Malgwyn, he was fine. He showed no sign of distress, save aggravation with the new abbess."

"I did not know that she had been around long enough to cause aggravation."

Coroticus waved a hand in dismissal. "It was nothing to cause concern."

"I still see naught to cause you to send for me."

"His cell, abbot." The young boy found his voice.

"What of his cell?" I asked.

"You should see it before you judge my reasons for summoning you."

"Why did you not take me there first? This was a waste of time!" My fury was more the result of the long trip in the mud than anger with Coroticus.

"No, I wanted you to see first that he had no marks of violence. Then you will understand better what you see in his cell." Despite my glare and that of Arthur's, Coroticus was firm.

Arthur turned to the young *monachus*. "See that our horses are stabled. In a few hours, Illtud will be arriving with a larger escort for me. Arrange for them to be fed."

"Now," I said, turning to Coroticus, "take us to Elafius's cell."

Saxon raiders. That is who seemed to have swooped down upon Elafius's cell. Though the *monachi* were forbidden to have personal possessions, the old man's hut was cluttered with man-uscripts and herbs, tossed about carelessly. A chair was knocked over, lying across the bedding. It looked as if the room had been searched, perhaps. "Where was Elafius found?"

Coroticus pointed to a place on the hard-packed earthen floor. "Here, slumped on the floor. He looked as if he had collapsed."

"I wish you had not removed him before I arrived."

"He had to be prepared for burial, Malgwyn."

"But you have not yet prepared him, merely stripped him of his robes and laid him out on a table."

"It is a beginning. You arrived sooner than I thought."

"And you want me to study his death and find if there were some evil in it, yet you deny me those things I need? Never mind." I turned to Arthur. "My lord, I suggest that you go and take your meal with the abbot. I shall stay here. Later, when Elafius's cell has told me all it can, I will join you."

At that, they left me to my chores. I eyed the cell once more. It was as if a whirlwind from the gods had struck. The simple table and chair allowed in each cell were both turned over. Some small vials lay broken and scattered on the floor, their contents staining the earthen floor black. The furs of his bedding were shoved into one corner.

I stood where Coroticus indicated they had found Elafius. Slowly, carefully, I turned in a circle, my arm extended outward. The cell was small, but not so small that I could reach across from wall to wall.

If a man became seized of some illness suddenly, how would he act? It was a question of some interest. Would he flail about? Would he simply fall quickly and quietly to the ground? Would he collapse in some kind of spiraling heap? And if he did, could he have created the kind of destruction I found there? I did not see how. To create the havoc I saw, he would have to have suffered some horrible pain, thrashing about helplessly, not stricken suddenly unconscious and falling in a heap.

The documents lay spread across the cell, in no identifiable pattern, I thought. Then I noticed something odd. The documents all lay face up, with none covering another, at least not much. The writing was visible on each. That such a circumstance could happen by accident seemed unlikely.

I righted a stool and sat on it, studying carefully the carnage before me. But was it carnage? Something about the scene disturbed me.

Carefully, I got to my knees and studied the documents. They made little sense to me, writings on metallurgy and other technical subjects. Many were the subjects covered by the documents copied by the brothers. While most were religious, some touched on other matters, plants, herbs, cooking, farming. I had, myself, copied a treatise on the stars by a woman named Hypatia of Alexandria. Coroticus had me do it because the work was considered blasphemy by the bishop, and he wanted none of the *monachi* to know that he possessed a copy. He said that Hypatia was a learned woman of Alexandria, but also a pagan beauty that bewitched men and made them worship her. Christians had stoned her to death and torn the limbs from her body. Coroticus spoke of Christian charity, removing her from the miserable existence that was her fate, but I always thought this incident an odd form of charity.

What puzzled me most was that the sheets were all faced up, as if someone had been reading them. Studying the scene,

I noticed that Elafius's bedding, his furs, were crammed into a corner, as if purposely jammed there, not accidentally tossed there by the thrashing of a dying man.

I realized then that someone had searched the dead man's cell. But I saw no method of telling if it happened before Elafius died or after. Logic told me afterward, but did the same man who searched the cell kill Elafius as well? Or, perhaps, Elafius caught the intruder searching and paid with his life. I could not make that judgment. Indeed, it could have been Coroticus himself who had searched, looking for some reason for the old man's death.

But then I saw an empty vial partially hidden beneath one of the parchments.

CHAPTER THREE

I snatched the vial up. Empty but for a few drops of a dark liquid, it was of the small sort, suited for holding extracts of herbs or leaves. My eyes roved the hard-packed dirt floor, but I saw nothing that could have been stored in the vial. But then, under the edge of a parchment leaf, I saw a partially smashed red berry. And not just any berry. A yew berry, from those trees we used to make our hunting bows. A few yew needles were also sprinkled across the floor. I sniffed the residue in the vial.

Quickly, I searched the floor, but other than two or three more berries, there were no other signs. I did not like this, not at all. My mind was suddenly fogged by a mass of thoughts, like to that of snowflakes riding the wind. Yew berries, at least the seed, are poisonous to man and beast as are the needles. Indeed, many horses and cattle fell to them. An extract of yew berries and needles was equally deadly. And the poison strikes quickly, fatally. No one knew what it did to a man. No one had survived a dose of them. Some said the extract of the seeds and needles had other uses, but of that I knew little.

But poison was a woman's weapon, or so it was believed,

and this was a community of men. And, besides, Elafius was a doddering old man, unlikely to have fallen afoul of a woman.

My heart was racing and the snowflakes of thoughts pounded my skull in a blizzard. Did Coroticus know of the yew? Is that why he called for me? Yet Elafius worked in the herbarium. It would be normal for him to have them, perhaps. Or would it? Who had searched the cell? For I was certain that was how it happened. I began to realize that regardless of what Coroticus knew or did not know, his actions in summoning me were at least grounded in reason. And many, many questions were yet to be asked.

I rose and backed into the corner where Elafius's furs were bunched to study the cell from yet another angle. As my feet shoved the furs yet farther into the corner, I caught a glint of something shiny and silver. In amazement, I bent over and plucked a silver *denarius* of Valentinian from the ground. This was the most amazing find of all. *Monachi* were forbidden to possess coins. And I had never seen a coin of Valentinian quite like this one. It was inscribed "I promise to serve five years" in Latin. An odd inscription for a coin, I thought. Why did Elafius have this coin? Or had his murderer dropped it?

And it was bright, shiny. Not worn at all. Sometimes we saw such coins in the far west of our lands, when merchants brought them in, but they were few, very few.

Too many questions. My stomach growled. I was hungry, but I knew that I had to see Elafius once more before he was buried. Besides, knowing Arthur and Coroticus, they were arguing over some obscure element of the church.

I sent one of the young *monachi* to watch over Elafius's cell and headed back to the building for the preparation of bodies.

As I crossed the muddy ground, I noticed a very young, very round *monachus*, obviously new to his service as his scalp gleamed whitely where his tonsure had been newly cut. Above pink, cherubic cheeks, his eyes followed me hawkishly, brazenly, and I wondered who this fresh face could be.

"Ider!" I spotted the young *monachus* hurrying on some chore. He stopped and ran to my side.

"Yes, Malgwyn?"

I almost chuckled at his eagerness to please. "Who is that *monachus* there?"

Ider's face screwed up into a frown. "That is Gildas. He is newly come to Ynys-witrin. Coroticus owed some debt to his father and took the boy in."

So, this was Lord Celyn's brother. "Why does he look as though he swallowed sour wine?"

"He has not learned the lesson of humility. Indeed"—and Ider shook his head sorrowfully—"I doubt that he shall ever learn it."

I nodded in agreement. A lack of humility seemed to be a family trait. "Come with me. I must examine Elafius's body once more."

With Arthur and Bedevere busy elsewhere, Ider was visibly more relaxed. "Of course, Malgwyn. I would be honored."

And so he fell into step with me as we trudged across the muddy ground. Ider had come to Ynys-witrin only in my last months there. He had been such a fresh-faced youngster, so devout and eager to learn the ways of the *monachi*. I often wondered what drove these boys to so imprison themselves at such a young age. They had hardly sampled the world, and yet they entered into a life of deprivation without giving themselves the chance to explore that world. I knew that many of them were second sons, unlikely to inherit more than their father's reputation. So, service to the Christ was a respectable calling.

"What think you of Elafius's death, Malgwyn?" Ider shook me from my musings.

I paused before answering, sidestepping a heap of horse dung but landing my foot in a puddle the span of a hand deep. The splatter of water attacked Ider's robe.

"I think little of it at present," I finally answered, shaking the muddy water from my *caligae*. "Tell me of Lord Lauhiir. How long has he been here?"

"Just a fortnight. He sent some of his men and workmen to improve the Tor for his arrival. They eat much meat there, Malgwyn." Ider shook his head, and I laughed a little. We all ate meat, but not much. It was too rare a food, and the *monachi* kept their diet simple, mostly bread and vegetables. The amounts of meat that graced a lord's table would have caused sour stomach in any *monachus*, except Coroticus, that is. His table held as much meat as any lord's. But such were the differences between abbots and those who served them.

"If that is the worst of his sins, then he is truly blessed," I answered as we came to the door of the hut. "Please, Ider, attend me a moment. I will not be long."

The young, pale-faced *monachus* nodded eagerly. "I would learn from you, Malgwyn."

"Learn what? Learn writing? You are a *monachus*; 'tis the brothers who will decide what work would suit you best."

Ider's face turned red. "No, Malgwyn. I would learn to solve puzzles as you do."

"Then," I said with a chuckle, "you yearn to spend your days in frustration." With that, I entered the hut once more.

Nothing else had been done with Elafius; he lay as we left him. This time, though, I knew what to look for.

"Light that candle," I instructed Ider.

"But 'tis still light," he complained.

He spoke truly, but what little light filtered through the unchinked walls of the old hut and in through the door were hardly sufficient to read a holy text. I needed to read the holiest text of all, a human body. "Just light it."

Ider did as he was instructed, and quickly the small cell was filled with a yellow, hazy glow of light.

Once again, I faced the wrinkled white skin, shrunken now; he looked older and but a pale shade of himself. This time there were no shadows to hold secrets. His back from head to foot was dark though. I had seen such in dead bodies on battlefields before. I knew not its cause, but I knew it happened at some time after death.

I looked first at the place where his jaw connected with his skull. The finger impressions were obvious, on both sides. "Bring the flame closer," I directed. Just as I thought, a palm print could also clearly be seen on his forehead. In the dead, I had seen that bruises, marks, were more vivid than in the living.

Waving Ider back, I stared at the cold body and thought for a long while, matching images from his cell with the marks on his body. Books strewn about, as if someone searched there. A silver *denarius* where it should not have been. The marks on Elafius's body. The yew needles on the floor of the cell.

Suddenly I jerked from my reverie, almost knocking Ider back into a wall. I grabbed the dagger from my waist and saw that its edge was not as sharp as I needed. I turned to Ider. "Bring me a knife."

His eyes widened like those of a frightened young deer. "A knife?"

"Ider! We cannot help Elafius now. But by desecrating his body, we may make some sense of his death."

Still he hesitated.

"The blame will be mine. Now, fetch me a sharp knife from the abbot's kitchen."

The young *monachus* scampered away as I continued to ponder. Someone strong had held the *monachus*, forced his mouth open and poured yew extract down his throat. But for that to have killed him, he would have had to swallow a goodly quantity. I knew enough of battle wounds to have seen men's stomachs split open and their last meal come spilling out. Now, I would do it to find the cause of a man's death, not to kill him myself.

"What is this nonsense?" I turned to find Coroticus standing imperiously in the doorway, with Arthur looking amused behind him. "You will not cut this poor man's body open! It is being prepared for burial. I will not have you desecrate it further."

I laughed at him and scratched my half-arm. "If I do not, good abbot, then you will never know what happened to Elafius."

"I already know what happened to Elafius," came a strangely familiar voice. I looked beyond Arthur and saw the chubby young *monachus* Gildas, his freshly shaven tonsure shining in what little sun God provided on this miserable day.

Turning, I looked at him. His face wore a smile born of thinking himself too smart. "And how did he die?"

Gildas stepped forward. "He was killed by the woman Rhiannon, from Gaul. I heard them argue about the divine

56

sacrifice. Obviously, she killed him. She is a stout woman, unlike poor, ancient Elafius."

"And how did she accomplish this feat?"

He shrugged. "She strangled him, I should think."

I turned to Arthur with a look he knew too well. Turning to Coroticus, he ignored Gildas and entered the fray for the first time. "Give him the knife. I will place my faith in Malgwyn, not this child."

Coroticus wanted to argue. I could tell by how his lips stretched into a thin line. But he trusted me as well, and he dared not dispute Arthur. "Give him the knife," he ordered Ider, who looked pained at being caught between such powers.

I took the knife, not as sure of myself as I once was, and approached the old man with some fear. For a man with my reputation, it was an odd feeling. But I reminded myself that the old fellow could feel nothing, and so I slit his belly, about where I reckoned his stomach was located.

I cut carefully, amazed that no blood spilled from the wounds. Fascinated with the things I found, the different creatures that inhabit our flesh, I saw the one I sought. With the greatest of care, I sliced it open and found the remnants of his last meal. Vegetable pieces mostly. And a few yew needles. Perhaps a small handful of a black liquid that I took to be yew extract. We all knew how yew needles rendered a man senseless. But there seemed hardly enough to do even that.

Motioning for Ider to rearrange the lamps, I checked the other organs, not knowing exactly what I was looking for. I worked my way up his torso, looking for anything, something, to account for his death. Reaching behind his ears, I cradled his head and immediately felt something amiss.

I rolled it to the right and left and it moved too freely.

Something caught inside his neck. His neck was broken. That was how old Elafius had died.

"Who is this Rhiannon?" I asked, still staring at the pulp from Elafius's stomach.

"She is the new abbess. From Gaul," Coroticus explained. "She has some uncommon views. Well"—he hesitated—"somewhat uncommon for our lands but common enough in Gaul."

I grunted. "Rhiannon" meant "holy" in our ancient language, an appropriate name for a woman in the Christ's service. "And they would be?"

"Might we move outside?" Coroticus asked uneasily. His was not a path strewn with bodies. That much was obvious.

Our little troop left the cell and poor Elafius behind. Once in the gray daylight, the abbot seemed to return to a proper mood. In the distance, I could see the *vallum*, the ditch and fence that separated the abbey grounds from the surrounding lands. *Monachi*, brown-robed and ascetic, scurried about the grounds on some errand or other.

"Rhiannon was used to the practice of women serving at the church services, giving the holy bread to those who would take communion. This is not something that we or the church in Rome accept, only in Gaul. And, yes," Coroticus admitted, "Elafius argued with her over it, many times since her arrival."

"They argued violently, most violently, but especially the very worst yesterday eve after the meal," Gildas interrupted. I had seen such as this little scamp before. Secure in their position by virtue of wealth or influence, they thought themselves above all. And their ambition knew no bounds.

Arthur turned toward the young *monachus*. "The next time you speak without my bidding, young man, you will do so from a pit in the earth, filled with rats. Now, leave Master Malgwyn to his work."

I suppressed a smile. Gildas had several brothers, all older than himself, one of whom Arthur had personally killed. The others all led factions that would not join the *consilium*, and Arthur had no love for them. That Coroticus allowed Gildas into the abbey spoke more of his father's purse than his politics.

With some reluctance, I turned to Arthur and the abbot. "Elafius's neck was broken. Of that, there is no doubt. How it came about, through design or by accident, I cannot say."

"How do you accidentally break someone's neck?"

"By trying to force his mouth open and pour yew extract down. His neck must have been broken as they poured the yew, for some of it made it down to his stomach. Dead men cannot swallow. The yew was meant to poison him. Yew will do that to horses and cattle. We know this well. Either those who held him were too rough or the old man's neck was easily snapped."

"Are you certain of this?"

I thought of the silver *denarius*. But I knew from experience that this was not the time to reveal it. "I am certain this is how he died. I know that more than one was involved. Perhaps the woman recruited others to hold him while she poured the poison down his throat. Perhaps it was an attempt to make her seem guilty. Either way, the woman bears questioning if nothing else."

"A-hem!" Coroticus cleared his throat. "She is the head of the women. She was sent here because of her great devotion to the Christ."

"She was sent here because of her family's influence," Arthur snapped. "When the troop arrives, send them to arrest her. Otherwise, not a word from any of you. Especially"—and he glared most effectively at Gildas—"you."

Arthur turned to me. "You have seen all that you require?" he asked.

I nodded. "I have seen enough."

"Then join us as we confer with Patrick at the abbot's great hall."

"And what of Lauhiir?"

"He can wait. It will do his ego good."

With that we trudged across the muddy ground to Coroticus's great hall, almost as large as Arthur's seat at Castellum Arturius. The timber hall stood on a line with the old church to the east, beyond the cemetery and the cells of the *monachi*, which ran to the north, into the edge of the slope. From where we stood, we could look down slightly on the row of timber shops that marked the village.

Coroticus fell in step with me, leaning in close to my ear. "Malgwyn, Rhiannon could not have killed Elafius."

"Why?"

"She is a stout woman, I grant you, but she is not the murdering kind. Yes, she is strong in her beliefs, but she is gentle as a lamb."

"People, even gentle people, can be roused to violence if their beliefs are challenged strongly enough."

"Not she."

His strong support for the woman made me question his relationship with her. In those days, though abbots and *monachi* were forbidden the pleasures of the flesh, many ignored the prohibition.

With that he fell into a silence as Arthur glanced back at us.

"Coroticus," he bellowed. "What temper is Patrick in?"

"He is in a foul mood, my lord. Though ancient he may be, he is stout as a bull. And just as loud."

I chuckled quietly. Obviously, Patrick's visit was as welcome to Coroticus as to Arthur. Patrick did not like leaders such as Arthur, Christian though they might be. He considered them all false believers. His hopes for bringing our peoples together lay not with kings or lords, but through the Christ. Yet even in that single purpose, the fathers of the church seemed to have no consistency and much controversy. It was no wonder I regarded them with a skeptical eye.

"And what brings the great man to such an anger?"

"He has heard there is Pelagianism among us. And once he arrived here, Gildas whispered in his ear about Rhiannon and her Gallic beliefs in the divine sacrifice."

"Is it not enough, Coroticus, to worship the Christ and his Father? Must you always be fighting so fiercely over such nonsense?"

Shock and amazement rolled across the abbot's face. "Malgwyn! 'Tis not nonsense. These are very important affairs."

By then we were approaching the great hall, and Arthur was looking about for me. I saw Bedevere standing close by, whispering in the Rigotamos's ear, probably warning him about some part of Patrick's rage.

Lucky men, we were. Though not enough time had yet passed for our little thief to make his way to the castle, I scanned the area for any sign of our reinforcements. None. I took a deep breath before drawing abreast of Arthur. We had but ourselves to defend against the roaring lion.

"My lord Arthur!" Patrick's cry echoed off the wooden walls. He stood, without help, though he looked ready to topple over at any moment. That much, I knew, was an act. Patrick, it was said, was stronger than any two men, but affected frailness as the situation suited him.

Arthur, tall and strong, bowed before the old man, using his shield with its red cross, to hold himself up. "I give homage to the great Patrick, defender of the Christ, and keeper of all that's holy."

This took the old man aback. He had a mole on his right cheek and sharp, piercing black eyes. He recoiled, as if offended, but we all knew he wasn't. "I am touched by the Lord Arthur's praise, and surprised by it. My feelings about such lords are well known."

Another man would have hazarded a sharp sword with that remark, but Patrick was not an ordinary man. His rise from slavery among the Picts to his training as a *presbyter* to his return to the land of his enslavement had made him more than a legend; he was a symbol to Christians from Rome to the far northern regions of our island.

Arthur rose to his full height and bowed his head. "You have not met me, *episcopus*. I defend the Christ with more than words. I defend him with action."

I glanced at Coroticus; he was relieved that Patrick's attention was focused on Arthur.

"Then you are different from your fellows. That much is certain. But do you speak only words, or do you speak with a sword?"

I watched as Arthur took the old man's measure. "Which would bring me the greatest esteem in your eyes?"

Patrick smiled. "So, you seek to say only what will please me?"

"Is that not what you expect?" Arthur circled the room, taking his time before continuing. "I speak when that is the weapon needed. I pull my sword from my belt when it is called for. My sword becomes more and more necessary as the Saxons continue to invade the western lands of the Durotrigii and the Dumonii and the other lords of the *consilium* less ruly."

I noticed a tightening of the lips on the fat little *monachus* Gildas. His brothers were among those unruly lords. At least the living ones were. But his father's wealth brought him no esteem with Patrick, who had sacrificed much to serve the Christ, so he kept his counsel and said nothing. Perhaps he was not as stupid as I thought.

Patrick saw us not. He was focused on Arthur, nodding in what I took to be approval. "I see that the stories they tell of the Rigotamos are, at least, partially true. I am well pleased. When I wrote to the soldiers of the tyrant Ceredig, it seemed that I was talking to myself. Bloodthirst. Greed. Those are the only things true *tyranni* understand."

My stomach began rumbling. Apparently, Arthur and Coroticus had eaten while I was seeking answers in the matter of Elafius. I was about to go off to the abbot's kitchen and see if any scraps were to be had when Coroticus asked the question we all wished answered.

"Is that why you are visiting us, *episcopus*? To meet the Rigotamos and judge him?"

Patrick smiled and shook his wrinkled old head. "Matters of greater consequence than yet another *tyrannus* have brought me on my journey. The *monachus* Elafius sent me a message of a disturbing situation here at Ynys-witrin. It seems that Pelagianism has returned to haunt our church. And now, the young *monachus* Gildas tells me that a Gallic woman is taking a role in the divine sacrifice. This is an outrage and against our beliefs."

"Why did you not seek out our *episcopus*, Dubricius, himself?" I spoke for the first time. "It was he who brought her here."

The old head reared back in surprise at my question. "Who are you to question me?"

"Malgwyn is my counselor," Arthur interrupted.

"And mine as well," Coroticus hurried to add.

I was pleased that they spoke. Their recommendation gave me at least some standing in an unfamiliar situation.

"You are Malgwyn the scribe?"

"I have been many things in my life. Scribe is one of them."

Patrick nodded. "I have heard of you. Travelers tell me that you helped stem the rising tide of the Druids, that you helped hold the people for the Christ."

I shook my head. "I unmasked false Druids only. My intentions and motivations had little to do with the Christ."

As he cocked his head at this honesty, a lock of Patrick's white hair fell across his wrinkled forehead. "Your earthly intentions and motivations count for little. The Christ guides us to do his work through our hearts."

I wanted to laugh, but I knew this was the wrong setting. "As you wish."

Patrick nodded as if this were exactly what he expected, total acceptance of his word. He narrowed his eyes and scanned the gathering. "Now, bring unto me the *monachus* Elafius, so that we might explore this problem of Pelagianism. I do not see him here."

"You know Elafius, *episcopus*?" Coroticus asked, as surprised as the rest of us.

"Of course. Elafius is the son of a neighbor of ours from

Bannaventa. He is a childhood friend of mine. Do you think that I would abandon my mission so readily and hurry here on just any complaint? I trust Elafius as I would my own blood."

"Did Gildas not tell you?" I had to deflate the little *monachus*, though I knew that Patrick would not take it kindly. "I would think he would have told you immediately."

The old bishop looked at me, again surprised. "What is the matter?"

"Elafius is dead."

Coroticus and Arthur were not happy. Bedevere hid a smile behind his gloved hand. That Elafius had been in secret correspondence with Patrick about problems at Ynys-witrin brought yet a new element to the old *monachus*'s death. It gave me much to ponder. But if Patrick came to see Elafius, he should know that his correspondent and, it now appeared, old friend was dead by someone's hand.

"Is this true?" Patrick spun quickly, belying his age. Coroticus was red faced. Obviously this was the first he had heard about Elafius writing Patrick or of Elafius knowing Patrick.

"It is true that Elafius is dead. Of Pelagianism at Ynys-witrin, I know nothing."

Something in Coroticus's face made me doubt his words. I had never seen him lie; at least I had never known that he was lying. He had withheld information from me before, and I knew he could quibble, but this time, the timbre of his voice shuddered just a little. His eyes grew a bit too large. That he was lying, I was certain. About what he was lying, I had no idea. Too many possibilities floated about the hall.

"With all respect to you, *episcopus*, but we are not in your care. Your lands are across the waters with the Scotti. Problems at Ynys-witrin belong to me and to our bishop at Castellum Marcus. From whence springs your authority to hold sway over the *monachi* of Ynys-witrin?"

The question was bold. Although Coroticus was right in asking it, few men would have had the courage to question Patrick's authority anywhere on any issue, such was his renown. Who among us had sacrificed as much as Patrick, the son of a *decurion*, stolen by Scotti raiders and made a *servus*? Then, after he broke free, he devoted his life to the Christ, returning to save those who had enslaved him. Such sacrifice comes not from a common man. And with those sacrifices he had purchased great power in the church, more power than all the coins of Honorius could buy.

Which brought to mind the *denarius* in my pouch. I ceased listening to the argument between Coroticus and Patrick. It took no great wisdom to know that ultimately Patrick would win. Our *episcopus*, Dubricius, was a man of good family and little spine, except one for maintaining those things that his station afforded him. He enjoyed the finer things of life and kept his hall near that of Mark's in the far western lands. Wines, pottery, such luxury goods were still imported there and still relatively cheap.

No, Coroticus was fighting a desperate battle against overwhelming odds. I would counsel immediate surrender. Patrick would have his way.

The *denarius* in Elafius's cell was another matter. I wished to draw it from my pouch and look at it, but knew that I could not. Now was not the time to tell Patrick that not only was his boyhood friend dead, but that he had broken his vow of poverty. My mind was then drawn back to my growling belly until one voice rose above all others.

"ENOUGH!"

Arthur. The Rigotamos. Weighing in at last. He stomped between the feuding clerics and planted his *caligae* firmly on the floor. "Coroticus, you know that even though you have your own bishop, should Patrick consult with him, the outcome would be the same. Patrick would be empowered to investigate the matter."

"And," I added, more to see the reaction than anything else, "the more you object, the more it appears you have something to hide."

Then, something strange happened. A great relief seemed to come over Coroticus, as if he were unburdened of some heavy load. I watched as the lines on his face almost literally disappeared before me. Coroticus had been protecting something or someone, and now he had been freed of that chore.

"I bow to the wisdom of the Rigotamos, and"—he turned and faced Patrick—"out of respect for all that you have gone through, *episcopus*. I will not obstruct your investigation. I must advise you, however, there are certain questions I may not answer because I gave my word as abbot and as a man of God."

Patrick stood. "This I can accept, because there are many confidences I hold which I would not be willing to reveal. Take me to the *monachus* Elafius. I would see his corpse."

"He is being prepared for burial, *episcopus*," I said quickly. Patrick would not approve of my cutting his body open. "Take a little rest, and he will be ready for you to view him."

The old priest started to argue, but I think it was more out of habit than for any specific reason. After a moment he nodded. "My journey has been a long one. I will go to my quarters. In the evening I would speak to those *monachi* close to Elafius."

"As would I," I said.

Patrick raised an eyebrow at me.

"Malgwyn is inquiring into Elafius's death at my request, *episcopus*," Coroticus said. "The Rigotamos agreed to let him serve as my *iudex* in this matter."

Arthur smiled. He liked it when others used the old Roman titles as did he. Arthur's father had also been a *decurion*, like Patrick's. *Decurion* was a title that covered a number of offices with a number of duties.

Now, confronted by two powers of the church, Arthur was out of his element, and he needed to establish himself as a force. This marked his first encounter with Patrick, and he needed the old man to leave with a good impression of him. Arthur believed in the Christ too strongly to be classed with the other *tyranni*.

"No problem of the church goes unheeded at my court," Arthur assured the old bishop.

Patrick rose, his simple robe catching on the stool. He pulled it free with no little effort and patted Arthur on the arm. "I am pleased with you, for now, Rigotamos. I will arise in time for the evening meal."

We all watched as the old priest shuffled from the hall, his two assistants flanking him.

Suddenly, the trio was brushed aside as three soldiers burst into the hall.

"My lord Rigotamos!"

The troops had arrived.

Chapter Four

As Patrick and his men collected themselves and departed, with Patrick mumbling something about "typical *tyranni*," Arthur's three soldiers strode farther into the hall, their swords clanking from their belts.

They were three of the younger soldiers—I could not recall their names—excited, by the looks of them, to be called to the Rigotamos's personal service. Three of a kind, I thought, all lusting for the glory and riches of battle, unaware that Arthur hoped his fighting days were behind him.

"We are here, my lord," the tallest of the trio said.

Arthur barely glanced at them. He was in deep thought about something.

"My lord?" The boy obviously did not know his place.

Finally, after a few more silent seconds, Arthur waved a hand at them. "Leave the other men here to serve me. You three go quietly to the women's community and inquire as to Rhiannon, the abbess. When you find her, take her into custody, politely. Bring her to me here. If I hear that you have harmed her in any way, you will find no sanctuary from me. Am I understood?"

All three swiftly nodded.

"Then go."

They saluted after the Roman fashion and left.

"What is it, Arthur?" Something was troubling him, and since only he, myself, Bedevere, and Coroticus were there, I could hazard being so familiar.

He turned and stared at the abbot with those dark, piercing eyes of his. "You lied to Patrick, old friend. I have heard you argue, hide, misdirect, but I have never heard you lie before, and you do not do it well. Whatever is happening here does not bode well for you, or for Ynys-witrin. Do not let the abbey's safety depend upon your lies. Lauhiir is not as I am. If he senses weakness, he will exploit it and most fiercely." Arthur surprised me. He gave voice to the very thoughts I entertained.

For the first time in all the years I had known Coroticus, he found no words to answer Arthur. He hid his chiseled features by dropping his head down into his brown robes.

Arthur jerked his head at Bedevere, signaling him to go outside and take charge of the escort.

Coroticus hurried after the burly soldier, murmuring something about seeing to Elafius's burial. Gildas, standing quietly in a corner, started to say something, thought better of it and followed the abbot out.

"Tread carefully here, Malgwyn. This story seems to have its share of twists and turns. If this woman, Rhiannon, is responsible, our problems may just be beginning."

"With the church?"

"And others." Then, after that cryptic pronouncement, Arthur swept from the great hall, leaving me alone.

With nothing to do until the woman was taken into custody, I made for the kitchen to see if any scraps could be found.

One thing that could be said of Coroticus is that he did not cheat his guests on food. Nor did he pay much attention to custom. By tradition, *monachi* were not allowed to eat the flesh of any animal that walked on four feet. But, since the abbot entertained distinguished guests, I found servants preparing pork and lamb for the evening meal. They cooked the meat on an iron spit, hung above a large stone, a hollow carved from its center where wood was kept burning. The meat popped and sizzled and filled the kitchen with tantalizing smells that made my hunger all the more real.

On a sturdy wooden table, I found some cheese and bread and eagerly ate. The servants paid me no mind. First, in my crimson tunic, they knew I was part of the Rigotamos's party. Second, some of the older servants remembered me from my long stay some years before.

As I cast about for some wine to wash down the food, one of the older servants, a man named Deiniol, approached me.

"Malgwyn. It is good to see you again. You do not visit often enough."

"I have little reason to wander this way now that I serve Arthur, and I have no need of religion." Before serving as Arthur's counselor, I had scratched out a living copying manuscripts for the abbot. It was while recovering from the wounds that cost my arm that I learned from the *monachi* how to write.

"You heard about old Elafius?"

"Aye, that's one reason I am here."

71

"It had to be that woman, Rhiannon." Obviously, word of my discovery that Elafius was poisoned had spread quickly. Deiniol did not hide his distaste for the lady. I was becoming very intrigued. She had only been at Ynys-witrin for two or three moons. A short time to become so disliked.

"Why say you so?"

"They argued most fiercely, Malgwyn. Every day it seemed, Elafius and Rhiannon found themselves in another argument."

"What, exactly, did they argue about?"

"The divine sacrifice. Women in the church. Rhiannon has very strong opinions, as did Elafius. They argued last night in the great hall. Patrick had not yet arrived, but Elafius boasted that he had sent for him and expected him at any moment."

That was something, I thought, Rhiannon would not welcome. Patrick was a traditionalist. As for myself, I did not believe it mattered who served the divine sacrifice, as they called the ritual that symbolized the Christ's sacrifice on the Cross. Aye, there was alchemy involved in that ritual. Once, I heard Coroticus and others argue over whether it was really wine and bread or changed miraculously into the body of the Christ. I am a simple man, and could not grasp their meaning, but it sounded as outlandish as some of the beliefs of the Druids.

"Could she have killed him, old friend?"

Deiniol thought for a moment. He pursed his lips and a bit of cheese clinging to one lip fell to the ground. "Only if it was poison, Malgwyn. She is not the kind to take a man by the throat. Aye, she is strong, but that calls for a cruelty that I do not think she possesses. And Elafius was stouter than he would appear. That she would wish him dead, yes. That she could choke the life from him, I doubt."

I thanked Deiniol for his thoughts, and stole away with some bread and cheese, wandering from the kitchen out toward the old church. A pair of the *monachi* were digging Elafius's grave near the church, and I found myself drawn to the site.

Taking refuge beneath a tree to the south, I ate my food and watched quietly as they turned the sod. Few men were buried on the battlefield, and that is where I had seen most of the dead in my life. Their carcasses rotted, glutting the ravens, until nothing was left but bones. But at least Elafius would have the dignity of a burial, a Christian burial.

Such burial practices had changed, aye, even in my lifetime. In times past, we worried not about what direction we buried the dead, but now those who followed the Christ insisted that the bodies be buried facing the rising sun. What difference that made, I do not pretend to know. But Coroticus was adamant about it.

So, Elafius was dead of a broken neck. Of that I was certain. But why the yew extract? Was his neck broken accidentally? These "whys" were the only questions left to be answered. But they were large questions. Major questions. Certainly he did not drink the extract by himself. Marks on his body indicated that someone had held him and forced him. Who? To that question, I could not find an answer. I did not yet know the woman Rhiannon. So, I could not say as yet whether she could have done this deed. And the silver *denarius*, where none should have been? That was a question too.

Whoever killed Elafius also had searched his belongings. That did not seem like the actions of a woman angered to murder by religious beliefs. That fact spoke of someone who knew what they were looking for, and it was something specific. I tried to recall those manuscripts flung about—treatises on herbs, questions of theology, metallurgy. Just an assortment you might expect to find in the cell of a *monachus* who worked in the scriptorium.

The food filled my belly nicely, and I turned from the problem with Elafius to other concerns. Patrick's inquiry was likely to last some time. He was a strong man, strong in his beliefs. If he found this Pelagianism thing roosting hereabouts, he would cut it out as one would cut out an arrow. He would not care who else was cut in the process.

Though I had spent many months at Ynys-witrin, healing from my wounds, I learned little of the Christ and this religion. It was a strange faith, anchored in belief in a man said to be the son of God. Coroticus preached that to believe in the Christ was to be granted life eternal. Somehow, I was not sure that was truly a reward. Life had been difficult at the best of times. An eternity of that seemed more curse than blessing.

I shook my head to clear it. Such things were beyond my ken. My chore was to focus on Elafius, to discover what mischief had been done to him. And to ferret out what it all portended for the abbey and Arthur's domain. Those things, and not the fate of poor Pelagius, were my problem.

Brushing bread crumbs from my beard, I rose as the *monachi* finished digging Elafius's grave. My belly was not full, but it was eased. At that moment, I wished that it were my head, not my stomach, that found comfort.

"Malgwyn!"

I looked up to see Ider racing across the burying place.

"Malgwyn, the soldiers have returned with Rhiannon. She has been taken to Coroticus's hall. Three of her women fought with us and tried to stop us. We took them as well."

"We?"

"Well," the young *monachus* said with a red face, "I tried to help as best I could."

"I'm sure you did." From the sounds of it, Arthur's orders had not been strictly followed. If Ider were correct, they were not quiet at all. All of Ynys-witrin must know of it now.

I rubbed my forehead with my one hand wearily. Nothing seemed to be going right. And we had yet to visit the renowned Lord Lauhiir, a task that thrilled me not. First things first, I thought. Better to confront the lady without Patrick than to hear her story for the first time with his interference.

On any other day, I might have spent my morning playing with my daughter, Mariam, and taking my noon meal with my dead brother's wife, Ygerne. She and I had become good friends in the months since his death. I had begun to wish that I had found her before my brother, but such was not to be. I was old and one-armed, not fit for a woman as good as Ygerne. Of that much I was certain.

But instead of the simple pleasures of home, I found myself following after Arthur and straightening out messes.

I heard the horses' hooves before I looked up and saw them.

Soldiers, in purple tunics, two riding abreast. Their hair was long and flowing, sweeping behind them as they bore straight down on me.

Stopping dead in my tracks, I watched as they paid no attention to my crimson tunic, sign of my service to the Rigotamos. Only my quick feet took me from their path as they gave no ground. I stumbled and fell to my knees, scraping one on a stone and covering my knee in mud.

"Out of the way!" one of them shouted, already past me. They pulled their horses up short in front of the old church.

Heat radiated up my neck and my eyes grew wide in anger.

As they dismounted, I took a stone the size of my hand and hefted it. The pair was laughing and talking, their backs to me. With a skill born of practice and necessity, I flung the rock with my left hand and was lucky enough to strike one of them in the head, dropping him in his tracks.

The other whirled around, reaching for his sword, and came for me.

But by that time, I had my sword in hand and gave it a quick tilt upward, inviting him to come forward. I saw then that this was barely a boy, a mewling upstart of a boy to be certain, but a boy nonetheless. Fright showed in his eyes, and he glanced quickly left and right. And saw no allies.

"Do you not recognize the tunic of the Rigotamos's household?" Killing him would do no good, and the child must learn sometime.

He went pale as a corpse, pale as poor Elafius. "I'm sorry, master. I did not know."

"No, you young whelp, you did not think. Your Lord Lauhiir should train his soldiers better." At that, I turned and gave him my back as I walked into the abbot's hall.

The soldiers had indeed taken Rhiannon into custody.

I walked into the hall amid the screams and shouts of a tall but slim and buxom wench, her arms held by two soldiers who were barely managing to keep their grip.

"Release her," I ordered. "She is no prisoner."

And the dark-haired woman, now free, turned to see her benefactor. Oh, she was a handsome one. Though Ygerne had been filling my thoughts, I cannot deny that the fire in her eyes sparked a rumbling in my loins. By Arthur's God, she was a beautiful woman!

"Who are you?" Her predicament had apparently not sunk in as yet.

"I am Malgwyn, counselor to the Rigotamos, and *iudex pedaneous* in the affair of Elafius's murder. The Rigotamos ordered that you be brought here to be questioned by me. If you choose to blame someone, then blame me."

"I will. Should I choose."

The Rigotamos entered with Coroticus. Arthur stayed silent, knowing that it was my duty to perform. Coroticus looked ill.

"As you most certainly know by now, Elafius is dead. It is known also that you argued with him. I wish to know why you were arguing."

She tossed her long tresses back and laughed. "That you must ask that question exhibits your stupidity, not your sagacity."

Ahh, this was one for the parchment. Our lady Rhiannon, head of the women's community, was truly a formidable woman. But I would not take her challenge. "Answer the question, woman, or you will be under arrest, bound and gagged."

"And you think this would be the first time? You are a simple man."

Arthur was about to say something, but I stalled his assault with one of my own. I laughed. Laughed at her. "Woman, if you think you are the first to call me stupid then your own idiocy surpasses mine."

And that shut her up. And it gave me a chance to take her measure more fully. She was a tall woman, nearly as tall as myself. Her long hair was a light brown, the kind you often saw on Gauls. Her lips were full and her eyes a deep hazel. Though her gown was loose-fitting, I caught a hint of a fine figure beneath it. She was indeed a beauty, and I wondered if that accounted for Coroticus's protection of her. Under other circumstances, I would have volunteered to be her protector.

I could tell from the slight smile at the corners of her mouth that she enjoyed my retort. "You are called Rhiannon. Whence came you?"

"Braga."

I nodded. Braga was a large settlement in Gaul, the one-time home of Nimue, a serving girl whom Arthur won in battle and who now worked in the kitchen of his castle. She was a pleasant child and had proven helpful in the past, and I made a note to ask her of this Rhiannon if the chance arose. I doubted, though, that I would be seeing the castle again until this affair was settled. "Why came you here?"

"The sisters had need of someone to guide them. I answered their call."

The answer lacked a key ingredient, I silently noted. If Gaul was her home, *why would she leave*? I sensed something missing in her voice, or something hidden.

"You argued with the *monachus* Elafius last night. Why?"

"If you are asking if I killed the old fool, the answer is no."

Behind me, I heard Arthur chuckle.

"Woman, you would try the patience of any man! But I will have answers to my questions, or I shall still be here asking you questions through the next full moon."

The outburst seemed to take some of the steam from her bravado. "Ask your questions. I will answer."

"Of what did your argument concern?" I asked for the third time.

"The divine sacrifice."

"What was at issue?"

"Whether a woman could properly serve a function in that

78

ritual. Elafius said no. Where I come from, it is custom. I saw no reason to change my beliefs because an old *monachus* objected."

"Coroticus did not object?" From the corner of my eye, I noted the abbot begin to speak, but Arthur's hand on his arm silenced him.

Rhiannon caught the move as well and she smiled slyly. "Coroticus chose not to interfere with the conduct of the women's community. He has much to keep him busy here among the *monachi*. The practice is not unheard of here in Brittania, and he is wise enough to know that he cannot control all things."

This didn't sound like the abbot that I knew so well. He prided himself on keeping his thumb pressed down on all under his purview. Such was the abbot whom I knew. I glanced in his direction again and he avoided my eyes. Arthur, I saw, had noticed his avoidance as well. He frowned at me, his forehead crinkling, as if to say, *Let it lie until later.* The Rigotamos had no desire to embarrass Coroticus in front of others.

I turned back to Rhiannon. "Please account for your movements last eve, after the evening meal."

She smirked. "Such is an easy tale to tell. I retired to our community beyond the *vallum*. You may ask any of the women. I checked on them all before I took my rest."

I chuckled inwardly. Such women would lie to protect their mistress. I did not judge them harshly or prematurely. When challenged by an outsider, those in such a community were more apt to rally around their leader than not. The *monachi* at Ynys-witrin would certainly lie for Coroticus rather than face his wrath. Hence I was not disposed to relieve Rhiannon of the cloak of guilt laid upon her. Nor could I place too great a faith in Gildas's accusation. It was based on youthful emotion and ambition, not logic.

"Thank you for your time, my lady," I said finally.

"You have no more questions?" she asked, a hint of disappointment in her voice.

"We know where to find you. When I have delved further into this matter, I am sure there will be further questions. Be not disappointed, abbess. Our interest in you has not wavered."

She turned to go, hesitated, and turned back to me. "Were I you, Master Malgwyn, I would speak to Lord Liguessac as well."

"Why Lauhiir?" I looked to Arthur, who had his eyebrows raised as if to say, "Why indeed?"

"He has consulted with Elafius several times since his arrival at the Tor."

"Were you aware of this, Coroticus?" I spun and faced the abbot, but his features showed total surprise.

"No. I had no idea." His voice gave a hint of the lie.

I turned back to Rhiannon. "Do you know the substance of these conferences?"

She shrugged. "How would I? As you have pointed out, I was not close to the man, and I'm certainly not close to Lauhiir." At that she turned away and left the hall.

"My lord, two of your men?" I asked Arthur. He motioned for them.

"Follow her," I instructed. "I want to know where she goes and who she talks to. Be quiet about it. Try not to make a spectacle of yourselves."

These were older men, men I knew. They nodded quickly and slipped out of the hall.

"Was that necessary, Malgwyn?" Coroticus complained.

I turned to face him. "If you find that ants are ruining your grain, do you just step on the ones that you see, or do you follow them back and kill the whole colony? If she is involved, I doubt that she alone is guilty. She may lead us to others. The problem is, my lord abbot, I do not know what is or isn't necessary in this affair. 'Tis better not to take chances. The lady may be as innocent as a lamb, but we cannot know that as yet."

Coroticus nodded slowly. "You have changed, Malgwyn. You act with a certainty you once did not possess. It is a welcome thing. See that this confidence does not turn into arrogance."

"Malgwyn may be guilty of many sins, Coroticus," Arthur said. "But arrogance is not among that number. I have wagered my crown on him and he did not disappoint me. You called for him. He did not seek this affair."

While I had hated Arthur for many moons, I no longer bore him ill will. Aye, we were settling into something like our old rapport, when he was *Dux Bellorum* and I one of his captains. As Rigotamos, he was proving as capable a governor as he was a general. And while I no longer commanded a troop of horse, I had moved even higher in his esteem, taking my place alongside Kay and Bedevere as one of his closest confidants and counselors. We had come so far.

"Why did you call me? You sent Ider galloping down the lane to hurry me along, and yet, now that I am here, you seem reluctant to place your faith in me."

"Let us move this discussion into my private chambers. What I would tell you is not for all ears."

Without another word, Arthur, Bedevere, Coroticus, and I slipped through the door into the small suite of rooms at one end of the great building. Once there, I watched as Coroticus's shoulders slumped. Gone was the erect bearing. In its place appeared a tired man with little confidence.

"To answer your question, I sent for Malgwyn because I did not know that he would be coming with the Rigotamos, and I needed his peculiar talents. Elafius was dead, and I did not need to desecrate his body to see that it was by the hand of another."

"With respect, Coroticus, just knowing that he died by another's hand does not make clear the questions of how and why such was accomplished."

He took a step back and nodded, almost as if chastised.

"Why are you so intent on absolving Rhiannon of any guilt? Are you bedding her?" In my experience men displayed an inability to think a woman was guilty of anything for only two reasons. Either they were bedding her or they wanted to.

"You are a hard man, Malgwyn. You spare no one in your quest. Be careful that you do not make more enemies than friends."

"A good man, Coroticus," Arthur replied, "makes a dozen enemies for every friend that he can claim. Such is the price of being honorable."

Coroticus slumped into a chair. A thin trickle of sweat ran down his graying temple. "No, Malgwyn. I am not bedding her. I will admit to wanting to, but my belief in her innocence is staked to another cause. She is a good woman and her faith in the Christ is strong. In the short time she has been here, she has taken firm control of the women's community and it has grown. That counts for much, and if some of her beliefs are contrary to my own, that is no reason to think her guilty of murder."

"That is tolerant of you, my lord abbot," I conceded. "I suspect that Patrick will not share your tolerance."

"Patrick is yet another crisis to deal with. His time would be better spent saving souls in the land of the Scotti, not here trying to root out Pelagianism."

"Is there Pelagianism here?"

Coroticus shrugged, but I detected something false in his movements. He was hiding something yet.

"Well, is there?"

"My *monachi* are free to believe as they wish about certain things. That is how I keep this community of believers functioning."

I sighed. An answer without an answer. Such is why I hated nobles and abbots. They have been a bane to my existence for more years than I can count. Always talking but never really saying anything. Even Arthur was guilty of this at times, when things were especially tense.

"So," I deduced, "you do have followers of Pelagius here."

"In a manner of speaking." Coroticus continued to speak in vague terms.

I gave up.

"Well, that's an issue for you and Patrick, not me." I turned to Arthur. "Perhaps, my lord, it is time to visit Lord Liguessac."

Arthur nodded. "Bedevere! Gather our troop of horse. We go to the Tor."

"Malgwyn?" Coroticus called to me.

"Yes?"

"Tread carefully with Lauhiir. He does not take well to questions."

Then, it was my turn to shrug. "I care not for what he takes well to. Both our commissions come from the Rigotamos. In that, we are equals. If he cannot understand this, I will teach him."

"You were more pleasant as a drunk," Coroticus remarked.

"And you were more honest before you became an abbot," I countered.

At that, we swept from the hall and began to make our way past the women's community to the summit of the Tor.

CHAPTER FIVE

The Tor at Ynys-witrin was as tall as it was mystical. Viewed from certain angles, it was visible as far away as Arthur's castle. Viewed from a different angle, it was invisible. No one had yet figured out why this was true, but we knew it was.

Great legend and great mystery shrouded the peak. Some said an ancient and holy treasure was buried somewhere on its heights. Others talked of hideous monsters lying in wait within the hill. Tales so ancient that even Merlin did not know their source told of a *mundus*, as the Romans would have it, on the Tor. Such a place functioned as a doorway into the underworld. I did not doubt that there was a cave beneath the Tor, but such cold dark places often excited people's imaginations. Why, some even said that the Tor was the home of Gwyn ap Nudd, the fairy king.

More important, the Tor served a critical function in Arthur's alert and message system. Watchfires linked Dinas Emrys, the castle of Ambrosius, with the Mount of Frogs, then the Tor at Ynys-witrin, and thence to Arthur's castle.

Now, it was to be the fortress of Liguessac, son of Eliman. He was more commonly called by his nickname, Lauhiir or

"Longhand." Arthur was forced by the *consilium* to give Lauhiir dominion over the Tor, despite the fact that I considered him part of the conspiracy against Ambrosius Aurelianus and Arthur's claim to the throne, that plot which took my brother Cuneglas and young Eleonore from our midst. At the critical moment, however, I had no evidence with which to convict him. And one did not accuse nobility of treachery without evidence, not if one valued his head.

So, instead of being exiled or condemned, Lauhiir was given command of a critical link in our defenses. Arthur was of mixed feelings. He preferred having Lauhiir close to him, but worried at the possibility of further betrayal. One message from Dinas Emrys or the Mount of Frogs not passed on could cause the collapse of our defenses. To that end, at my urging, Arthur had posted four horsemen at the Mount of Frogs to stand ready to speed any emergency messages to Arthur's castle.

On the lower part of the slope that lay at the end of the long, narrow shoulder of the Tor, Lauhiir had begun construction of his gatehouse and defensive ditch with a wooden palisade. A well, an old Roman well, lay just outside his new wall, and I nodded in understanding. There was no water on the summit, and carrying such up that steep slope was difficult at the best of times. But Lauhiir was building his own hall on that summit, a sign of pride more than practicality. I had to compliment him though. He had constructed a long rope hoist that, when manned at a number of way stations, could see any burden hauled to the top. I noted too that the hoist was handled by *servi*, *servi* with an unmistakable Scotti look to them. This puzzled me a little. *Servi* were gained in battle mostly, but we had had no set battles with the Scotti in many years. The only other way to obtain *servi* was to buy them, but this many *servi* bespoke a wealth that I did not think Lauhiir possessed. I sighed and shrugged. Perhaps his family had given them to him.

Now, we climbed the winding path that led to the summit, where signs of ongoing construction were plentiful. From all appearances, Lauhiir had laid into the project with a vengeance, and building was furious on the south and east sides. A timber hall was rising at the same time that rough-cut stone and logs were forming a rampart around the entrance. On three sides, the approach to the Tor was defended by steep slopes. Wisely, Lauhiir was allowing the Tor's natural slope to act as a barrier and only building gateways where they were needed. The slope was so steep that a handful of spearmen could hold off three times their number.

As we arrived at the temporary gate, I noticed a crew of metalworkers, hammering away at a makeshift hearth and another smelting tin from tin ore. A group of village folk carried big baskets and lined up near the hearth before one of Lauhiir's men. He would tip each basket over, eye the contents, and then count out a coin or two from a pouch next to him.

Tin was one of our great commodities, one the Romans had treasured and exploited. Our campaigns against the Saxons had kept us from reentering the tin trade. But Lauhiir's commission from the *consilium* dictated that he immediately begin further mining and smelting. Naturally, he would receive a share of the profits, as would Arthur and the other lords.

I remembered then the documents on metallurgy in Elafius's cell. And Rhiannon's revelation that Lauhiir had been conferring with the *monachus*. Could Elafius have been engaged in some manner by Lauhiir to help with the tin mining? Could something have gone wrong in their relationship? Something so wrong that it called for Elafius's death?

Shaking my head, I tried to drive the thoughts out. I was too ready to believe ill of Lauhiir, too prejudiced by my recent dealings with him. That trail lay too near the path I would wish it to be. Such affairs were seldom resolved with the easy solution, a point I often made to my friend Kay.

As we passed through the gate, I saw Lauhiir talking with some workers and studying some designs. Despite his long fingers and hands, he was neither tall nor short. A large paunch pushed at his tunic, and a faint sheen of sweat covered his face, giving him that oily appearance I would forever associate with him.

"Is that the best you can do?" Bedevere shouted. I snapped from my musings. Lauhiir's guards had apparently given Arthur a sloppy, half-mocking salute, and Bedevere was upbraiding them for it.

To my amazement, the pair of guards did not bother to respond. Indeed, they gave our little party their backs in the supreme sign of insolence. Then, suddenly, a tubby windstorm blew into their midst, scattering them with the flat of his sword, laying both of them low.

Lauhiir jammed his sword back into its sheath and bowed majestically before Arthur. "Forgive them, my lord. They are young and ignorant. I welcome the Rigotamos to my new home."

So, Lauhiir, who had once been one of Arthur's most fierce critics, was going to play the subservient noble. This might prove to be an interesting trip after all.

Arthur dismounted, followed by Bedevere and myself. "I accept your hospitality, Lord Liguessac."

And so began the obligatory bowing and scraping by Lauhiir. Bedevere and I followed in Arthur's wake as he walked with the young lord inspecting the construction projects under way. At the very peak of the Tor was the great watch fire, used to send signals on to Castellum Arturius. With the sun riding low in the sky, you could see the glow of the fire at Arthur's watchtower far to the south. In times of trouble, it would burn a deep red from some mixture of Merlin's. He had also manufactured a concoction that would turn the flame a bluish-purple. All of these mixtures were distributed to Arthur's watching posts, and each of them had a specific purpose or message they conveyed.

On high ground at the east of the summit, a timber hall was taking shape. Down one slope were the gnarled branches of an old apple orchard. I suspected that Lauhiir had been burning some of the wood from there, as I could smell its fragrant scent, hovering over the Tor.

The hearth had been built and three of the walls had been erected. To the south, already in use, were the metalworkers' hearths. Lauhiir was very ambitious. Some five hearths were manned by teams hard at work. Men manned the bellows, keeping the fire hot as other men, having pounded the tin ore into a powder, thence into balls by adding water, clay, and straw, were feeding the balls into the fire. Once fired, the brittle remains would be broken open to reveal the smelted tin.

But in truth, we were less interested in the work being done than in Lauhiir's demeanor. As Arthur had said on our trip from the castle, "Any fool can fortify the Tor. Even young Owain couldn't botch that job." So, it was Lauhiir's sentiments that we needed to measure. And I had the added task of judging his involvement in the death of Elafius.

For some reason, I did not feel strongly that he was involved. I did not know why, but the death of an ancient yet simple *monachus* seemed disconnected from the aims of a young, ambitious lord. Having said that, I had misjudged such things before. No one could be excused from guilt in this affair. At least not yet.

At one point, as we made our circuit of the summit, I found an opportunity to begin probing. "How is the mining operation coming, my lord?"

"I have sent the word out that we would be paying for tin ore. Every family hereabouts has a pan for searching the streams," he reminded us. "As you can see, we've begun the process of smelting. It is not complicated, but it is time-consuming. Alas, I will miss the counsel and advice of the *monachus* Elafius. He made himself an expert on tin mining to help me with my work."

I raised my eyebrows. Either the news of the old monk's death had traveled quickly—it was but a thousand yards from the abbey to the Tor after all—or Lauhiir knew much. "In truth?"

"Aye." The pudgy lord nodded glumly.

"You are well informed, my lord."

Lauhiir shrugged. "Some of my soldiers told me. They had spent the night in the village and passed by the abbey on the way here. Elafius was very eager. Our process was organized by his instruction."

"A truly sad loss, then," Arthur interjected. "I did not know that *monachi* were versed in such subjects."

"He studied the documents at my behest," Lauhiir replied hurriedly. Too hurriedly, I thought.

"What led you to him?"

"Why ask you?"

I shrugged. "No real reason, my lord. It just seems an odd coupling for such an enterprise. I knew Elafius fairly well from my days at Ynys-witrin, but I knew nothing of his interest in metallurgy."

Lauhiir considered this for a moment, stroking his beard with those long, long fingers. "Now that you ask the question, I suppose it was that new *monachus*, Gwilym, that first directed me to Elafius."

This was a new name to me. "A young *monachus*?"

Lauhiir laughed heartily. "No, a new arrival, but as old as the forest." Then he leaned in conspiratorially. " 'Tis Gwilym that has brought this visit by Patrick. 'Tis he who has been whispering Pelagianism among the brothers."

Arthur, Bedevere, and I exchanged looks. Why had Coroticus not told us of this? We had questioned him directly about Pelagian influences, and yet he had not mentioned any adherents, even avoided the issue.

Bedevere gave me a questioning look. I knew what he was thinking. Perhaps Coroticus had withheld this information, but what did Pelagianism have to do with the death of Elafius? 'Twas a good question, and one that I did not have an answer to. But that a man such as Coroticus, he who had called me to this task, would hide anything, spoke volumes.

"Surely you knew this?" Lauhiir asked.

"Coroticus has fully briefed us on the situation at the abbey," Arthur replied. "If you do not mind a further question, why did this Gwilym direct you to Elafius in this matter?"

Now it was Lauhiir's turn to shrug. "I think I mentioned at the evening meal one night that I needed help with the tin mining. Gwilym suggested Elafius as a tireless researcher and learned man. The next day I visited with him and learned that the old *monachus* had been correct. He eagerly offered to help. I accepted his assistance."

"Did Coroticus know of your arrangement?"

At this, Lauhiir became red faced, too much so, I thought. It was a simple question, and I thought it appropriate since Coroticus had charge of the abbey and all therein. "I do not know," he sputtered. "I did not feel the need to seek his permission."

"Of course not," Arthur said with a smile, defusing the growing argument in Lauhiir's eye. I held further questions, knowing that Arthur wanted no squabble over authority. Where a noble and an abbot were concerned, Arthur preferred to leave their relative positions ambiguous.

"Oh, Lord Liguessac?"

"Yes, Rigotamos."

"Have you heard from Lord David lately?"

Lauhiir's eyes grew wide, too wide, I thought. "No, my lord. Why would you ask?"

Arthur shrugged. "He sent word to me that he had reports of Scotti raiding north of here, and that he intended to send scouting parties to investigate. I just wondered if they had reached this far south."

"No, Rigotamos. I would invite you to dine with me, Rigotamos," he said, changing the subject, "but until my hall is completed, I have been dining at the abbot's table. He has been very gracious."

"Then we shall be dining with you after all. Coroticus plans a feast in honor of Patrick. It is my duty to attend." Arthur said nothing without carefully considering his words, especially in the presence of such as Lauhiir. By Arthur's words I knew that he had no desire to dine with Patrick. And he cared not that Lauhiir knew.

We began to return to our horses when Arthur hesitated and turned back to our host. "Oh, I meant to ask you when the *consilium* might expect an accounting of the mining you have accomplished to date? I saw a merchant ship at the old Roman port, from the far eastern provinces, I judged."

Lauhiir's face turned red again, but not from anger this time. Rather, his discomfiture came from embarrassment. "I, uh, well, yes, we have sold our initial shipment to a merchant from Judea. I'm sure that I can have an accounting prepared before you depart for Castellum Arturius."

"That will be satisfactory. You may have it delivered to Malgwyn." Among my many tasks for Arthur was to keep track of all documents submitted for his, or the *consilium*'s, consideration.

At that, Lauhiir saluted, spun about and went back to his lair. Arthur, Bedevere, and myself trudged out the western gate where our horses were tied.

"Will we be returning to the castle tomorrow?" Bedevere asked.

Arthur paused and stroked his beard with a gloved hand. "No. Too much is amiss here. The dead *monachus*, his tie to Lauhiir, Patrick, Pelagianism, Coroticus's deceptions. I fear that we are needed, if for no other reason than to support our friend Malgwyn in this matter. As Rigotamos, I can take some of the burden from him in delicate matters. And should he need to cross swords with Lauhiir, we can provide a barrier. By himself, Lauhiir might be more inclined to ignore him. With you and me at his side, Malgwyn will have an easier time navigating these murky waters."

I hated to admit that I needed Arthur, that I needed any man, but he was right. In his castle I operated under his protection. You would think that now that he was Rigotamos, the High King of all the Britons, I could perform my duties throughout our lands, but such was not, and would never be, the case, I feared. While some lords paid Arthur the proper obeisance, others gave only assurances that they would, then turned and did what they pleased.

"So, Malgwyn," Bedevere began in a surprising moment of levity. "How does it feel to have the Rigotamos and a lord of the *consilium* in your service?"

"An obedient dog might serve me better," I grumbled, struggling into the saddle.

"An obedient dog cannot condemn someone to beheading," Arthur pointed out.

"True, but neither can a dog condemn me to beheading if I displease it." A thought struck me. "My lord, how well do you know the young *monachus* Gildas?"

Arthur shook his shaggy head. "Not well. I know his family better. Aye, I was forced to kill one of his brothers, Huaill, for piracy in our waters. Their father, Caw, refuses to pay obeisance to the *consilium* even yet."

"Do you pay any heed to what he says?"

"Why should I? He is a child, spoiled by his father, disregarded by his brothers, who could only find a home with Coroticus, and then only because his father paid for it."

"You are harsh in your judgment."

"I am harsh only when it is deserved. He will scheme and connive and cause Coroticus unknown trouble. What he needs instead is a good spanking. Trust me, Malgwyn. Hear little of what Gildas says and believe less. But you have had your experiences with his family."

"Me?" I had no idea what he was talking about.

"Remember the upstart noble that tried to prevent me from taking up the sword?"

"The boy noble? Celyn?" Then I remembered.

"Aye! He is Gildas's brother, the only member of that family that pays any allegiance to the *consilium*, but I suspect that he serves more as a spy for his father than as a true lord. Why do you suffer him?" Sometimes, Arthur's logic seemed as no logic at all.

"Ambrosius and I discussed him. In truth, Ambrosius believed that it was important to keep at least one channel of communication open to Caw. I did not and do not believe that we will profit from it, but I bowed to the Rigotamos's wish. Now, it is a deed done." He stopped and ran a hand through his long hair. "To reverse it now would show disrespect to Ambrosius."

"Why care you for that?" My frown could not have been more severe. "Ambrosius is Rigotamos no longer. You"—and I grasped his arm with my hand—"You are the Rigotamos. Celyn's brother Huaill fought against you, forcing you to kill him. No other man would give heed to the same concerns that trouble you. Banish him from your court and worry yourself no more."

"Malgwyn, you must understand. I do not intend to be like other men. If we are to have a united land, then the Rigotamos's crown must have respect. Overturning decisions made by the past Rigotamos does nothing but diminish the office. And to rule by fear is easy. To rule by the common consent of your peers and the people is not easily accomplished. But it is that kind of respect that is lasting. And it is that kind of respect that the Christ would smile upon."

I released his arm slowly. "I know that I often seem impatient for you to act, Arthur. But sometimes men such as Caw must be struck down simply to get their attention. Some men respect only strength and brutality. It has always been this way. My fear is that in your quest you will appear weak to those who would strike you down."

He cast those deep, probing brown eyes at me, and his face stretched into a half-smile. "Then they would be mistaken and I would deal with them appropriately. Remember this always, Malgwyn. I will do what is necessary when it is necessary." He paused and let the smile become large and welcoming. "We are not so very different, Malgwyn. You act very much as I do. If you truly believed that brutality and direct action were always the best way, you would have killed Mordred in the affair of Eleonore."

"I could not prove his complicity, my lord," I said, hanging my head.

"Exactly, Malgwyn. You believe in justice. You believe in doing what is right, no matter how. In that we are as one."

With that, we edged our horses down the uneven, terraced steps back toward the abbey, Coroticus, and Patrick.

Feasting with Coroticus was quite unlike dining at Arthur's hall. While I had stood in amazement at the kind and variety of the foods offered at the Rigotamos's table, Coroticus was even more generous. Platters of oysters, still in the shell. Pork, chicken, fish. Wine from Rome and Gaul. But the vegetables were delightful. The brothers kept gardens, and now, in the midst of the growing season, Coroticus's table fairly groaned beneath their weight.

However, while Coroticus's feast offered greater variety, Arthur's hall was less filled with ceremony, or rules. At least on this occasion. I had eaten at Coroticus's table when it seemed little different than Arthur's. But, with Patrick present, Coroticus had implemented new rules, including scripture reading while we all ate.

After welcoming one and all (but especially Patrick), and saying a blessing for our meal, Coroticus gestured for us to begin eating, which was fine by me. At Arthur's table, I usually failed to enjoy my meal because I was paying special heed to conversations going on around me. Part of my duties for Arthur was to be aware of all that went on at his feasts, who spoke to whom, what they talked about. I was constantly on my guard.

Still, there was something eerie about the silence at Coroticus's feast. The only sounds, beyond the crackling fire, were the smacking of lips and teeth as food was eaten, and the droning of an old *monachus* as he read Latin from a scroll.

Patrick seemed pleased by Coroticus's piety and adherence to the accepted conventions, pleased and reluctant to show it. I judged him tough and savvy and unwilling to acknowledge strength in any man other than himself. Such was the failing of many powerful men.

The meal gave me time to consider what I had learned so far, as little as it might be. On the one hand, I had Elafius, an elderly *monachus* and one famed for debating religious practices with Rhiannon, head of the women's community, killed by a broken neck. Indeed, Elafius was apparently many things—theologian, metallurgist, and owner of a silver *denarius* when such was forbidden by the church.

Then there was Lauhiir, newly appointed lord of Ynyswitrin. That he had aims opposed to Arthur's was accepted. But whether those aims had a hand in Elafius's death was still a lesson to be learned, as well as Rhiannon's involvement if any.

Too many questions befogged the landscape. For a man whose war reputation rested on knowing the ground and exploiting it, a mist-shrouded battlefield was a true challenge. Even my friend Coroticus was not acting as usual. When you cannot even trust the actions of your friends, judging those of your enemies becomes far more complicated.

I sighed, almost too loudly. No such situation was without its difficulties. That much I had already learned in Arthur's service. That and other things, such as behaving at court, treating with nobles and commonfolk alike. In different clothes, that is. I had learned how to change from "Mad Malgwyn," the drunken crackpot who lived on the edge of the castle, to Malgwyn, counselor and scribe to the Rigotamos. Such had not been an easy path, but most nobles remembered my guile and passion in fighting the Saxons in the days before my great wound at the River Tribuit. And those memories served me well when my abilities, my courage, were threatened.

Now, as I looked along the tables, I realized that I had chosen a good path, if one fraught with dangers and intrigues. I had been given a second and third chance to prove myself in this life, and for that I was grateful.

And even as I thought these things, the sound of dishes being retrieved from the table filled Coroticus's hall with clatter. Among the common *monachi*, severity of diet was as much a tradition as scarcity of personal possessions. But with Patrick here, our abbot was not afraid to show his well-supplied table, and the *monachi* were granted a reprieve from their ordinary fare of bread, soup, and vegetables. Patrick seemed more impressed with the silence and readings than the abundant food though.

With the dishes taken away, Patrick cleared his throat. Now was the time for business to begin. "Good Malgwyn. Have you reached any conclusions about the sudden death of Elafius?"

"I have had little time to inquire as yet, *episcopus*."

He raised an eyebrow at me. "That is disappointing. Perhaps too much is made of your reputation for resolving such matters."

"Other men assign me my reputation. I make no claim to be any better or any worse at these things than any other man."

Patrick nodded. "Such is a facile answer. You did not spend the day lost in drink, did you? I would expect no less from a counselor to a *tyrannus*."

The sound of a chair thrown back shattered the silence in the hall. Arthur.

I did not look at him, merely raised a hand to stay his anger. "Great *episcopus*. All in our *patria* sing your praises. You are called the guiding light of the Christ west of Gaul."

The old bishop narrowed his eyes. "What profits you to remind me of this?"

"I profit nothing from saying this or from inquiring after the death of Elafius. The Rigotamos profits nothing either. We have endeavored only to do our duty as we see fit. We do not insult you with outrageous claims. Rather we celebrate your strength and courage in the worship of the Christ. Do we not deserve the same consideration?"

I sensed rather than saw Arthur relax. By chastising Patrick for his rude behavior, I had turned not only the attention away from us but away from Elafius. For the moment.

Coroticus sighed deeply. "Malgwyn, you forget yourself."

But Patrick, his face suddenly a marvel of sadness, waved a wrinkled hand. "No, no. Good Malgwyn is right. You must forgive me. I am an old man, one filled with passion for all things concerning the Christ. Often I let my zeal overrule my gentler emotions."

"Not at all, *episcopus*. The fault lies within me," I conceded. "You see, I am not the devoted servant of the Christ that you are. Aye, it is a constant source of embarrassment to Lord Arthur for he is as great a believer as you, regardless of how you may view *tyranni*."

"Then perhaps I should make it my personal goal to bring your soul to the Christ." He was not asking a question. He was making a statement. I fought to control my eyes, as they desired nothing more than to roll in exasperation. I knew without looking that Arthur and Bedevere too were fighting a chuckle. My eyes dared not even venture to Coroticus, he who had spent hours trying to claim me for the Christ.

"Now," Patrick continued. "Send for this woman, Rhiannon, who, young Gildas tells me, believes that women should take part in serving the divine sacrifice."

"Are you certain that it's wise to enter into such an inquiry after such a tiring day?" Coroticus asked.

At that Patrick's face screwed up into an expression of frustration. "I am certain, abbot, that I can brook no further delays in this matter. I have traveled a great distance to study this problem. All I find once I arrive are your protestations of assistance and your obstruction of my task."

Had I been in Patrick's position, I could not have stated it better. That much was certain as well. We had been intent on blocking his path, were still intent on masking his way. But did it have to be such? Why were we so resistant to Patrick?

"My lord *episcopus*?"

"Yes, Malgwyn," he said fretfully.

"I have a proposal."

"Speak."

"Though you are very much my senior, we are both too old for all of this debating. Each of us has his purpose, his focus. I suggest that rather than fight each other, we cooperate, share our results. Pool what talents God may have granted us and see if we can unwind this spider's web together."

"A *coito*?" Patrick's lined face took on a thoughtful look.

How like Patrick! A *coito*. I had once heard Arthur use the term and asked him what it meant. In the old days of the Roman republic, Arthur had told me, it described the way that consuls arranged to share power with their colleagues. Sometimes one would handle external affairs, the other internal. Other times there would be a senior partner and the other junior. When Arthur mentioned it, he had been approached by a member of the *consilium*, shortly after his election as Rigotamos, and pressured to divide the kingship as the consulship had oft been split centuries before. Naturally, he declined.

But I was inclined to join together with Patrick. He knew the religion of the matter. I knew the politics and something of the personalities as well. Together we might be able to unravel this tangle. Arthur would not like it, but I was making a career of doing things that Arthur did not like.

After several seconds, Patrick nodded slowly. "It is agreed. I will share with you my findings and you will inform me of yours. In this way, we leave far less to chance." Patrick paused.

"I would not do this thing with many men, Malgwyn. But you have a grace about you, a sense of the Christ's hand watching over you. Some men like you are blessed."

A flush rose in my cheeks.

"I do this to speed my inquiry, my lord bishop, not from being led by the Christ." I saw no reason to operate under false colors. "You have knowledge and a quick mind to aid me, so I will use you."

"Malgwyn!" Bedevere burst forth at my bluntness.

"I think that the *episcopus* appreciates honesty in men of all stripes."

For his part, Patrick had already forgotten the exchange. "Malgwyn may not publicly proclaim the Christ, but who are we to say that His hand does not guide Malgwyn yet? Each man makes choices for his own reasons. I require only that the end result of those reasons be in the glory of God."

"I require that the end result of those reasons be to the glory of the truth, which, as my dear friend Coroticus would say if he were not so tongue-tied, are one and the same."

"And he would be correct," decided Patrick.

I rolled my eyes. I personally knew several truths about the church that they would not want revealed. Everyone hides things. This is a fact of life. The issue becomes the importance of what they are trying to conceal. The more important the secret, the more they will lie to hide it. The more they lie, the more their lies get tangled and stumble over each other, entrapping them. It was such things that I looked to for guidance in finding the truth. And since my talents seemed to lie in that direction, whether I favored it or not, that was my charge from Arthur, to seek the truth.

"I am now ready to see this woman, Rhiannon. Bring her

before me and stop these incessant delays!" And Patrick headed for the door.

"*Episcopus*. As the abbot has noted, it is quite late. Perhaps we should begin tomorrow? Your journey has been long, and this day's events have surely added to your weariness."

Patrick honored me with another of his severe looks. "For a man prized for his industry, you seem very reluctant to apply yourself."

"My lord, tired minds often forget to ask the right questions and often fail to recognize important information. Believe me, I have experience in this."

The old man frowned, but nodded. "Very well. On the morn then. Now, if you will excuse me, Coroticus," Patrick began, and then, cocking his head to one side, he added, "And you, Lord Arthur," almost as an afterthought.

"But of course, *episcopus*," Coroticus stammered. "Whatever you wish."

Patrick began walking again slowly, almost painfully it seemed. Followed closely by his two *monachi*, he headed for the door. Halfway there, he paused, not bothering to turn, and spoke. "Good Malgwyn?"

"Yes, my lord."

"I am told that you have a fondness for strong drink."

"Not as much now as some time before."

"I will expect you to keep your mind clear in this matter. You will upset me greatly if you resort to that again. Place your faith in the Christ. Lean on him."

I did not answer him, merely watched his back as he continued out of the great hall. When he and his followers had safely departed the hall, I turned back to Arthur, Bedevere, and Coroticus.

"Are you sure that was wise, Malgwyn?" Arthur asked.

I shrugged. "This affair is too confusing. It is unlike the deaths at Castellum Arturius. Here there is no logical motive, no obvious goal. Almost anyone could be guilty of this crime. Lauhiir had had some secret dealings with Elafius. Rhiannon had argued with him over religious matters. My good friend Coroticus is hiding something. No, no," I said with a wave of the hand as Coroticus started to interrupt. "Your protestations will fall on unwelcome ears, abbot. I am not asking you to divulge that which you would hide. At least not at this time.

"We have accusations of Pelagianism, the whimperings of that dolt Gildas. Aye, we need Patrick to help us sort through all of this. I do not doubt his honesty, though I do not share his devotion to his cause. We both seek the truth for different reasons."

"You do not think him a part of this affair?" Bedevere asked.

"How could he be? He was not here, arrived only today as we did. No, Patrick is an honest man, though I like him not. Zealots always worry me. But he will do what he says, of that I have no doubt.

"And now, my lords, if you will forgive me. I need to take my rest. Coroticus, where shall I sleep?"

"I have prepared beds for you and Bedevere in one of my private chambers. The Rigotamos will have his own room here in the hall, next to yours. Is that acceptable?"

I waited for Arthur to consent, but personally I was pleased. During my long stay at the abbey some years before, I was assigned one of the spare, cold cells built for the *monachi*. Coroticus did not refuse himself the pleasures of the flesh nor the comfort and luxury his station could afford.

While I mused about these things, Arthur nodded his acceptance of the arrangements. Bedevere, as was his habit, said nothing, deferring as I did to Arthur.

One of the servants came and showed us to our chambers. We crawled onto our respective furs, silence reigning in the room. I trusted Bedevere; I had always trusted him. He was renowned for his loyalty, his discretion. But he was a quiet man, and he seemed to brood over some old tragedy. I was much closer to his fellow, Kay.

I lay there awake for a long while. After a few moments, I could hear Bedevere's even breathing. Outside, an owl spoke to me across the night. A whiff of the damp lands surrounding the abbey drifted through the hall, as the sounds of the servants cleaning up receded into silence. For a while.

And then I sat up. A scuffing sound came from the great hall, quiet, almost too quiet to be heard.

Someone was slipping through the feasting room, someone who didn't want to be heard. I looked across the room to the dark lump that was Bedevere, but he was yet asleep.

Then, the door to our chamber creaked open.

Chapter Six

I threw back the fur covering me with my one arm and slid myself into the darkest corner of the chamber. Bedevere was snoring, loudly. I strained to catch the sound of our intruder. Doing so made me feel a little silly. It could simply be one of the *monachi*. Or one of the servants. But something told me it was not. Something spoke to me and said that the explanation was not that simple.

The wooden door to the chamber eased open. Had I not been awake, I would have heard nothing. A dark shadow of a figure entered, almost floating above the floor, it seemed, edging up to my bed and kneeling down beside where I should have been.

Before I could discern his intentions, another dark figure flew through the air in a single move, sweeping the intruder from the floor and against the wooden wall with a crash.

"Quickly," I heard Bedevere say. "Who are you and what do you want?" So much for thinking he was asleep.

I saw the vague outline of a candle on a table. Searching blindly in my pouch, I found my fire-making materials and, deftly though I had but one arm, had the candle lit.

The intruder had not answered Bedevere, but his heavy breathing filled the room.

In the dim glow of the candle, I saw, finally, who it was. Llynfann, my favorite little thief. "Bedevere! Release him!"

My old friend turned, and even in the dim candlelight I could see disbelief on his face. "Malgwyn, he stole in here to do you some mischief!"

"I did not, my lord," Llynfann said with a quiver in his voice. "I came to fetch him."

"Fetch me for whom, Llynfann?"

"The lady, Malgwyn. The lady of the woods."

Bedevere looked at me in confusion. "The lady of the woods" was a name applied to my cousin Guinevere, Arthur's consort. Those, like Llynfann, who lived in the forest knew her only as "the lady of the woods." During the events surrounding Eleonore's death, it had been Llynfann who guided Kay and myself through a midnight-blackened forest. Aye, without Llynfann and his bandit leader, my old friend Gareth, that affair would have ended quite differently.

"Why should Guinevere wish to see you now?"

I frowned. "She is my cousin. We are friends. The question should be, why does she want to see me so urgently that she used Llynfann to fetch me?"

"As you like," Bedevere conceded. "But why?"

"The only way to find out is to answer her call."

"Shall I alert Arthur?"

I considered the thought. "No, better that I find out what she needs first. If need be, we can easily send for him. Come, let's be away."

107

Fetching our horses almost took longer than the journey to Guinevere's cottage. A candle burned in the window, glowing dully through the wavy Roman glass. I suspected that the builder had robbed an old Roman villa for the glass as few craftsmen made it now. Llynfann had accompanied us at my request. I did not know but that his services would be required again.

The door swung open and a flash of long blond hair showed as my cousin motioned us in. Once inside, she hugged me and nodded to Bedevere. "Malgwyn, why comes Bedevere with you?"

"We were staying in the same chamber, and your messenger was not as quiet as you would have hoped him to be."

She laughed, and I relaxed. If she could find something to laugh at, then perhaps her summons was not that serious.

"Why have you called for me, cousin?"

At that she stopped laughing, took on a somber look. She glanced again to Bedevere from the corner of her eye.

"You may say whatever you wish. Bedevere is assisting me in this affair."

Guinevere nodded. "I feel awkward, Malgwyn. I had a visitor earlier, the woman Rhiannon. She believes that you will try to blame the *monachus*'s death on her."

"Why does she think that?"

"She believes that Patrick will insist on her guilt. After all, she admitted to arguing with Elafius, the old fool."

I raised my eyebrows. "Did you know him?"

"Of course. I often visit the women's community. I still have friends there. And I know many of the *monachi*. Elafius was a disagreeable man."

"And why did Rhiannon seek you out?"

Guinevere shrugged. "I had met her recently. After you questioned her, when she returned to the community, one of the other women told her that we were cousins."

"What did she want with you?"

"What do you think? She wished me to plead her case before you."

"She told me she did not do this thing; why would she need her case pled before anyone?"

"She fears Patrick."

I nodded. "She should. Patrick and I have decided to ally ourselves in this matter."

At that, Guinevere's eyes showed little surprise, telling me that word had already spread of our alliance. "Malgwyn, have you lost what little is left of your mind? You do not even believe in the Christ, and you've joined with the most famous *episcopus* in all Brittania."

"Cousin, this affair is not simple. Elafius was not your typical *monachus*. And I do not believe it is as simple as Rhiannon killing him over some religious difference. Too many questions are left unanswered by that explanation." I held up a hand as Guinevere began to protest. "Guinevere, Coroticus is hiding something. Lauhiir is hiding something. I'm told that a *monachus* named Gwilym is hiding something. I need to understand the religion in all of this, Pelagianism, the divine sacrifice, Rhiannon's role. I am likely to miss such important information because of my ignorance. Patrick can help prevent that."

My beautiful cousin shook her head, sending her long, flowing hair flying about her. "Malgwyn, I do love thee. You are very nearly all the family that I have left. And I respect your skill in these matters. But I fear you have made an error by joining forces with Patrick."

Something in the look in her eye put another thought in my mind. "Is that your fear, or Arthur's?"

"Both." And the voice surprised both Bedevere and myself. Arthur.

"But we left you at—"

Arthur smiled. "Do you think that I am incapable of moving quietly?"

I shook my head. That had been one of Arthur's special talents as a military leader. He could move great bodies of horse more quietly than anyone I knew. Slipping from the abbey would have been no more trouble for him than arising in the morning. "But you seemed earlier not to desire a visit with Guinevere."

Guinevere cut him a glance, a hint of irritation flashing in her eyes.

"Can not a Rigotamos have even a few secrets from his closest aides?"

I hung my head, appropriately chastised.

He stepped out from the next room and lowered himself into a wooden chair. "I am worried, Malgwyn. Guinevere speaks for us both. While I believe in the Christ, you know and all know that I have not been a friend of the church. Patrick knows this too. And he has an undying hatred of nobility. *Tyranni* he calls us."

"Rigotamos, I serve you. But I serve truth as well. You had no hand in the death of Elafius. Guinevere had no hand in it. Bedevere had no hand in it. And whether we like it or not, Patrick had no hand in it. I believe that Patrick seeks the truth as well. I do not understand Pelagianism, and I do not understand what causes men to act so passionately about questions that cannot, to my mind, ever be resolved.

"Yet, I sense that this affair is tightly bound up with religion. I do not know how. It is for his understanding of such things that I turned to Patrick."

"Malgwyn, he would like nothing better than to embarrass me. By embarrassing you he accomplishes the same purpose." Arthur was pleading with me. He knew that on some things I could not be commanded.

"So, it was really you that arranged for my cousin's summons."

"No, Malgwyn," Guinevere interrupted me. "Rhiannon did come to me. She is afraid that she will be blamed for this thing. And she is afraid that Patrick's beliefs will sway him against her."

This was something new for me. When I had sought the answers to other affairs, I had sometimes had people try to sway me one way or the other. But never had this many people pulled me in so many different directions.

My stump of an arm ached, but I did not know if it were from the old wound or the lateness of the hour. I was disappointed in my cousin and Arthur. They should know that I would seek only the truth. Something inside of me sought only what actually happened in an affair, not what others would wish had happened. I did not know where that great drive, that great urge, sprang from. I only knew that it controlled me.

I sat down and hung my head. "Rhiannon may be innocent. And she may not be. I do not yet have enough information to clear her or convict her." I raised my head and focused my eyes on Arthur and Guinevere. "But you both know that I will follow the evidence wherever it takes me. I did not especially care for Elafius when I lived at Ynys-witrin, but no man deserves to die before his time. Death is too much a part of our lives as it is. And murder, to me, is a disturbance of the true order of life. Someone helping it along is an insult to that life.

"And mark this. I will be the one deciding who is to blame in this affair. Not Patrick. Not Lauhiir. Not Guinevere. Not Arthur."

Arthur's power seemed to rise up in his throat and threaten to choke him. But, with Guinevere's hand on his shoulder, he swallowed deeply and nodded.

"You knew he was stubborn when you first went to him, Arthur," Guinevere softly chided.

"Aye, he is stubborn. And carries himself as an unruly pup. But—"

"But," Bedevere concluded, "he is a master at these things. Do I have to remind you?"

"Be of good cheer, Rigotamos," I said after a moment. "At least your crown is not resting on this."

That showed how little I understood about the powers at work in this matter.

I awoke the next morning, still as muddled in my thinking as I had been the night before. Bedevere was already up and about his business. I sat up and leaned my back against the wall. Had I made a mistake in allying Patrick to my cause? He was most certainly a man of great biases. I had made the move almost in desperation. But such a move, once made, could not be retracted.

With a shake of my head, I used my one hand to push myself to my feet. Self-pity was something that I thought I had put behind me. Obviously there was no cure for such a disease.

The sun had already risen in the east. I could smell food

cooking in the kitchen building. A cock crowed somewhere in the distance. It was a lonely call, less a greeting to the new day than a plaintive cry, one that sent a shiver of memory along my back.

My earlier sojourn at the abbey was a dark time in my history. The loss of my arm had seemed the last rung on a ladder that led only down. And I had blamed Arthur for leaving me alive when I had nothing to live for. I closed my eyes and shook my shaggy old head. Falling into self-pity was a danger for me, an ever-present one. Merlin, my friend and companion of recent months, sometimes gave me a concoction of valerian root to forestall these bouts of melancholy. It helped in some strange way, and Merlin took no small pleasure in that, as I was always teasing him about his "cures."

But in truth, the only cure for my inner doubts and fears was my daughter, Mariam. A smile lit my face as I pictured her bright features.

"You are the man Malgwyn?"

The voice startled me from my reverie. I looked to the door and saw a truly ancient *monachus*, his face as wrinkled as Merlin's, his towering but spare frame clothed in the same brown cloth sheltering his fellows.

"Do I know you?" I straightened and tried to place his face, but to no avail. He had not been among the brothers when I had lived with them.

He shook his head as a tired smile marked his lips. "No, our lives have not yet overlapped." With a grace unexpected in one his age, he slid further into the room. "I have been told that you seek the murderer of the *monachus* Elafius."

I nodded. "And you are . . . ?"

"I am Gwilym."

My eyebrows rose automatically.

"You have heard of me then."

"Your name has been mentioned in my inquiries." The sparkle in his eyes intrigued me. I had not expected him to present himself so readily. Indeed, a part of me half expected him to be at the heart of whatever was yet unspoken in this affair. "I have been told that you are whispering Pelagianism in the community."

Those lively eyes sparked more brightly. I guessed that he had not expected so direct a question. Ofttimes, I felt that we danced around too much, attempting politeness at the expense of truth.

"You do not waste time."

"I am not as young as I used to be. Wasting time is the privilege of the young. So, *do* you champion Pelagianism?"

"Might I sit? If you are old, then I am ancient."

I motioned to a chair.

He moved slower than Patrick, but with just as much grace. "Yes, I have spoken in favor of Pelagianism. To say so causes little harm since you would have discovered it eventually anyway. I would not call it 'whispering,' though. I made no secret of it."

His candor brought a smile to my lips. Would that more of those I questioned were so forthright. "You know that Pelagianism has been denounced by the church fathers in Rome?"

"Of course," he conceded, still wearing that same smile. "But that does not keep me from believing as I like."

"Did you argue with Elafius?"

"Of course. Elafius was a strong opponent of Pelagianism." He said that term as if it rolled strangely off his tongue.

I searched my mind, trying to remember what I could

114

about Pelagianism. Something about free will and original sin. I had committed too many sins in my life to remember the first. But I had spent enough days at the abbey to know that my sins were not the ones in question when it came to Pelagianism. He and Augustine were perpetually at odds. But even Augustine granted that Pelagius had been a likable man, even a good man. He had disappeared when I was but a child, some said to the far eastern lands.

For me, this was so much idiocy. But I knew that religious men took such things seriously. Was it enough to spark a murder? I still could not fathom that. Especially the manner of Elafius's death. It was such a haphazard, clumsy affair. I believed that it had taken two people to kill the old *monachus*. At least. One to hold him down. One to pour the yew extract in his mouth. But why go to so much trouble? And then breaking his neck. Obviously the manner of his death was important. But why? Was there something symbolic about the yew extract that I was not seeing? Why not a simple sword? Why not a dagger across his throat?

And who stood to profit from the old *monachus*'s death? Murder was always about profit of some kind. It was always about gain.

"Do you have other questions?"

Startled, I realized that I had forgotten about Gwilym. I judged him to be about Patrick's age, perhaps a bit older. It was odd for such an ancient *monachus* to arrive at the abbey.

"Whence came you here?"

"Gaul," he answered quickly, too quickly, I thought. Gaul. First Rhiannon and now Gwilym. I wondered.

"Were you acquainted with the new abbess in Gaul? You both arrived here about the same time."

"I have known Rhiannon all of her life. Her father was a close friend of mine."

"So you came from Braga as well."

He shook his old, bald head. "I came originally from near unto Caermarthen as did Rhiannon's father. But when the first colonies went to Brittany, we went as well. Our paths diverged. He chose the life of a farmer and I chose service to God. Later, I returned to Braga and learned that Rhiannon was also serving God. She was offered the post here, and as I have no family of my own, I came with her."

"So you have spent your life in Gaul?"

"I have traveled much in my life. But it would seem that all those roads led only to my *patria*, the land of my birth. I find a certain comfort in that."

"What say you of Rhiannon's insistence on women serving in the divine sacrifice?" I doubted that she might still be involved in this affair, yet I worried that I was thinking with my loins and not my brain.

Gwilym took a deep breath. "My understanding of the Christ and his teachings says that women should be prized as much as any man. Yea, there are yet manuscripts which say that the Magdalene was a disciple, and the one most beloved by the Christ. If this be so, how can it then be said that He would have denied women a role in His faith?"

The one answer ready on my tongue was that women were a lesser sort, a weaker sort than men, but I had seen too much in my life to really believe that.

"Since you have traveled so widely and yet still hold views that Rome has long since denounced, can I presume that you knew Pelagius? Perhaps studied under him?"

He cocked his head. "What makes you think that?"

"Your continued belief in the teachings of Pelagius, in the face of the church's denunciation, speaks to a personal loyalty."

"You are indeed a perceptive man. Coroticus told me of this. Yes, in my youth I knew Pelagius, and it was my honor to accompany him on some of his travels."

"But this is not something you have shared with the rest of the *monachi*."

Gwilym smiled. "Do you read minds, Master Malgwyn?"

"No, but it would only make sense. To preach Pelagianism is one thing; to be known as a colleague of Pelagius is something else entirely."

"You understand much."

"Did you argue with Elafius?"

"I did. Many times since I arrived. He was most annoying."

"How so?"

"Age usually teaches us how little we know. That is where true wisdom lies. Elafius thought he knew everything. He had no wisdom, only knowledge. Knowledge without the wisdom to use it properly is dangerous."

"Was Elafius dangerous?"

"Perhaps, to someone. But not to me. I thought him sad."

"Did you see him the night he died?"

"Only at the meal. Then he went to his cell and I to mine."

"Did he seem disturbed? Did he act differently than normal?" I felt, rather than knew, that Gwilym knew more of this affair than he was revealing.

The old *monachus* did not answer at once. He considered the question carefully. "He seemed distracted that evening, as if something occupied his mind. But he was a secretive man, and he would not speak of it to me were he not so."

"You did not like him."

"I think I have said that."

"I find this most frustrating, Gwilym."

"And why is that, Master Malgwyn?"

"I have the feeling that everyone knows something they're not telling me about this affair."

"A conspiracy?"

"No, Brother Gwilym. I think everyone has a different bit of the story. But for whatever reason they are all being quiet. I fear there may be too many secrets for me to ferret out this one."

"It is said that Lord Arthur trusts you above all other men, trusts your judgment, your wisdom."

"In some matters, perhaps. I have known the Rigotamos for many years, warred with him as one of his captains. You learn who you can trust in such times."

"Then you will not want to disappoint him in this affair. It will prove unfortunate if you do."

This was something new. While no one was offering much information, no one had yet hinted that Arthur was vulnerable in this matter. I believed until that moment that it was most probably bound up in religion. That was one of the reasons I had turned to Patrick.

"Why say you this?" I inquired.

"Because nothing and no one is as it seems."

"Including you?"

Those lively eyes sparkled at me. "Most especially me."

I laughed then, but it was the laugh of a frustrated man. "Then how do you propose I proceed?"

"With equal measures of caution and suspicion, I advise. Know that the reason some will lie to you has nothing to do with your quest, it is to protect secrets of their own unrelated to Elafius. I have lived many years, Master Malgwyn, and I have learned to discern the difference between truth tellers and liars. You will encounter few of the former and many of the latter."

"That is most discouraging."

"Be that as it may, I sense from you a stubbornness that will not be swayed. This bodes well for your task."

"You speak in riddles."

"I speak as honestly as I dare."

"And if everyone I question is as forthcoming as you, Arthur will be dead of old age and I not far behind him before I ever get to the root of this matter."

Then the old *monachus* did something I did not expect. He reached out a wrinkled hand, touched my half-arm almost tenderly, and fixed his gaze on mine. "You have faced death, and he did not make you tremble. I think he will have a hard time conquering you."

I shrank back. "Are you a seer, or a madman?"

He laughed, drawing his hand back. "Neither, and both. But more than those things, I am a judge of men. Arthur chooses well in whom he places his faith."

With a bewildered shake of my head, I realized that I had learned all I was going to discover here. Gwilym would keep his secrets a while longer. And I suspected that he had no hand in Elafius's death. I could not be certain, but I did not feel him strongly in that affair. "Go about your business, Gwilym. And I shall be about mine."

"Gwilym! I am so glad that I have found you." Coroticus had joined us.

The old *monachus* rose and bowed to the abbot, who looked strangely uncomfortable with what was, truly, his due from the *monachi* as their leader. "Yes, lord abbot, how may I serve you?"

I found the look Gwilym gave Coroticus rather odd as well, almost a confirmation of the abbot's discomfort. "Well, uh, I was hoping that you could do an errand for me."

"Anything, my lord abbot."

"Please walk with me then, and I will explain it to you." And Coroticus took Gwilym by the arm and led him through the door and away.

I shook my head. Never had I seen the abbot so solicitous with one of the *monachi*, even aged ones like Elafius. This new *monachus* would stand more study.

CHAPTER SEVEN

A few moments later, and I was standing in the path between the abbot's kitchen and the great hall. *Monachi* and *servi* scurried by, carrying large amphorae, the kind that held wine, up the path from the village. I guessed that they contained wine from the far east. Coroticus and his bishop on the western shore were devoted to the vintages from that region. Although I knew that Coroticus had never been to Jerusalem, I also knew that early in his church career he had traveled to Rome. It was there that he gained his taste for fine wines.

Two *monachi* were hurriedly digging a grave in the cemetery near the old church. My stomach gnawed at me, but I knew it wasn't from hunger. Or perhaps it was, a hunger born of the paucity of information in the death of Elafius.

I still could not fathom who stood to profit from the old *monachus*'s death. Had Lauhiir been up to something with Elafius that he would not want known?

And now I was allied with a man with whom I was absolutely uncomfortable. I drew abreast of the old well beside the chapel, the one called the Mother Chapel, and took the opportunity to sit on a rock next to it.

I noticed then that the men carrying amphorae went not to Coroticus's kitchen, but continued on toward the Tor and Lauhiir's encampment. And behind them came even more men, carrying amphorae and skins, wrapped bundles. It was a virtual caravan of goods.

"Good man?" I queried of one of the workers, wearing the tunic and breeches of a common laborer and carrying a lighter load than many of the others.

He stopped and looked over at me. "Aye, master. May I help you?"

His words burst forth with enthusiasm. He would be helpful. No suspicion tainted his words. That was a telling factor.

"For whom are these supplies intended?"

The man shrugged. "Some for his lord abbot, but most for the new lord on the Tor."

I waved him on, and his weary steps carried him on his journey. What was it Gwilym had said? Nothing was as it seemed? Lauhiir had neither the money nor treasure for such purchases. So, how then, could he pay for these things?

The parade of amphorae and parcels continued past me. Two of the *servi*, tiring of the task, set their loads down next to one of the wooden huts to refresh themselves. I stared at the pile of goods, wondering again where Lauhiir had got the money to purchase such luxuries. As I watched, I saw a shadowy hand slip from the door of the cell, snag one of the parcels, and silently slip it inside. I grinned.

After a few moments, the *servi* took up their burdens and resumed their chore. I rose and walked idly up to the door, suddenly snatching back the fur door and grabbing a squealing, howling Llynfann by the scruff of his neck.

"Master Malgwyn!" the little thief stammered. "I was doing you no harm!"

"You are a thief, my little friend. You harm anyone stupid enough to leave their valuables near you. But right now, I have need of you."

I released him and he straightened his tunic.

"How may I serve you, master?"

"I need your especial talents. I need to know where these goods come from, the ones that Lauhiir brings. And I wish to know how he pays for them."

Llynfann knitted his brows together, not a difficult feat since his thick brows painted almost a single dark line across his forehead. "You do not ask for much, Malgwyn."

"The more difficult the deed, the more coins will clink in your purse."

He nodded then and smiled a ragged-toothed grin. "For you, Master Malgwyn, I would do anything. Else, Gareth would slit my throat."

"Ahh," I said with a smile. "You're more interested in saving your own neck than being of service to me."

He shrugged. "What does it matter as long as I do your chore?"

"Excellent point. Find me when you have news."

And the little man darted away, lost from sight within seconds.

With that chore under way, I grabbed a soldier from Arthur's troop and sent him to fetch Bedevere and the young *monachus* Ider. I resumed my seat and watched the *monachi* scurry back and forth about their duties, and I pondered the seemingly endless procession of questions that plagued my mind in this affair.

Who had reason to kill Elafius? That was at the heart of the matter. I knew the how, and I was fairly certain I knew the when. But it was that ever-present question of why that worried me like a nagging wife. Why should it profit any person, man or woman, to murder the old *monachus*? That was the one thing I couldn't fathom.

As I pondered these questions, I saw that the soldier had accomplished his mission swiftly. Bedevere and Ider were already striding across the grounds toward me.

"Master Malgwyn," Ider sputtered. "You have need of me?"

"Yes, Ider. You will speak to all of the brothers. I need to know if any of them saw Elafius or anyone else about that night, especially around his cell. I must account for every second from the time the evening meal was ended until the morn, if possible." Ider's eyes grew large. "This is a task within your abilities, Ider."

He nodded and gulped. Bedevere, as was his nature, said nothing, just fixed me with a bemused smile.

"For you, old friend, I need you to circulate amongst Lauhiir's men, asking the same questions. In particular, I need to know if they saw any sign of Rhiannon. She claims to have gone back to the women's camp after the meal. I need to know if this is true. Also, my little thief, Llynfann, will be looking for me. If he can't find me, he may come to you. Keep him safe."

"But Malgwyn," Ider interrupted. "How would the soldiers know aught of Rhiannon?"

"You think that Lauhiir's soldiers go without women?"

"Malgwyn! They are religious women!" Ider was aghast.

"And religious women do not desire men? Grow beyond your innocence, Ider."

"The boy is young, Malgwyn," Bedevere softly chastised me. "But what of you? While Ider and I are doing your work, what will you be doing?"

"I'm going to confer with my new partner, Patrick, to see if his inquiries have produced anything of value." I noticed the look in Bedevere's eyes. "You do not trust him?"

"Malgwyn," Bedevere began, hitching his breeches and sitting on a rock. "We have known each other many years. I watched you closely in the affair of Eleonore. You have always seemed to have a clear path before, a well-planned journey that would take you to the truth. But in this matter, I do not sense that. I see you floundering, like a man in the river who cannot swim."

He was right. And I knew it. I turned to him. "In Arthur's castle, I know the rhythms of life as well as my own heartbeat. When something goes wrong in that rhythm, I can sense it, feel it. I have learned over the years to detect truth in the same way. When I hear a lie, most times, it jars me like a club to my chest. In truth, Bedevere, everyone that I have questioned in this affair, but you, Arthur, Guinevere, and young Ider, has lied to me. Aye, even Coroticus and Patrick. It is as if everyone here has a different secret to hide. Gwilym told me as much himself, though I think he is privy to more secrets than just his own. When faced with such a situation, I have no alternative but to change my methods."

"That may be the most I have ever heard you say, Malgwyn." Bedevere chuckled. "So you are off to question Patrick in the guise of conferring with him? Do you think he will be so easily fooled?"

"Never fear, old friend. I do not underestimate Patrick. He could not have survived so long among the Scotti without being clever."

"More than clever, Malgwyn. Perhaps tricky, and even deceiving."

"I will heed your advice, Bedevere."

I found Patrick washing his face in a decorated red bowl outside the wattle-and-daub cell provided for him. I took the chance to appraise him from afar, this man who had become a legend in the church. His frame was spare, but his arms, thick with cordlike muscles, spoke of a man who knew hard work. At an age when most men turn frail, Patrick moved with the strength and certainty of men half his years.

"My lord *episcopus*!" I announced my presence as I drew near.

Patrick stopped his ablutions and wiped his wrinkled face with a piece of cloth. "Master Malgwyn. Will you join me in prayer." It was not a request, but a statement.

"No." It was a test, a chance to see how the old man would react to being contradicted.

To my surprise, he turned away from me with a smile and lowered himself in a chair. "You are either a man of strength or a spoiled child. Your history, as I know it, would argue against the latter." He adjusted his robes and motioned to a stump beside him. "Please, sit. Let us treat as men of the world. Men such as we need no Arthur or Coroticus to observe our actions."

I nodded. This was Patrick's conversation. It took me but seconds to realize that.

"I came from near these lands, you know. Bannaventa, near

126

the coast. My father was a *decurion* named Calpornius, and we had both a town house and a large estate, some of which my grandfather, Potitus, had given us. It was a beautiful place, a good place for a child." Patrick's eyes were focused beyond me, toward the mist-covered Tor rising high above us. "I was a poor student, Malgwyn. And I knew not God. In truth, we were all slipping away from the Christ. Old shrines to the Roman gods were being rebuilt, renewed. The departure of the legions left everything confused. Men who had once owed their positions and wealth to Roman patronage were now faced with a future that did not include Roman protection."

"I can only imagine, *episcopus*." I knew not what else to say, indeed, it seemed he expected nothing from me.

"Did you know that I was only sixteen winters when the Scotti kidnapped me from our estate? I was a mere child. But I was child enough to do much harm. In the space of an hour, I committed a grievous sin. And it was shortly after that that I was kidnapped and taken to Hibernia. I told only one other person of it. I have always wondered if my servitude were a penance for my sin."

I wanted so badly to ask the old priest what his sin had been, what wrong he had committed. But for whatever reason, Patrick had decided to confide in me. In my heart I knew that it was wrong to venture any questions. I took a careful look at him, put aside my prejudices and tried to appraise him as a man. And I noticed what I had missed when I saw him as just another obstacle in the road. He was an old, tired man, and the wrinkles in his face mapped the burdens on his soul.

"Tell me something of your history, Malgwyn. How came a simple man such as you to the service of a tyrant?"

Before I had really looked at him, I would have met his

request with carefully worded derision. Now, I simply began. "I was a farmer, *episcopus*, with a wife and child. They were murdered one day in a Saxon raid while I was gone to market with the other men of our village. Vengeance drove me to Arthur's men.

"I showed a talent for warfare and killing, and Arthur made me one of his captains. Until a Saxon at the River Tribuit separated my arm from the rest of me." I lifted my half-arm in demonstration. "Arthur saved me and brought me here. The brothers made me a scribe and I made myself a drunk. Then, not long ago, Arthur saved me yet again and made me his counselor."

Patrick turned to me and chuckled, something I had not seen him do before. "Malgwyn, do you realize that you summed your entire life up in less time than it takes for me to wash my face?"

"It has not been a very eventful life, *episcopus*."

And at that, Patrick laughed a full-bellied laugh and slapped his knee.

"I am glad to be so entertaining, *episcopus*." His reaction did not really upset me as much as it surprised me.

"Malgwyn, if we are to be colleagues in this matter, please call me 'Patrick.' You have told me of yourself. Now tell me of Arthur."

"What would you have me say?"

He looked to the sky not in frustration or exasperation, it seemed, but simply in contemplation. "How do you feel about him?"

"Is that important for you to know? I do not think Arthur bears any guilt in the death of Elafius or the spread of Pelagianism."

He nodded. "No, but his shadow lies heavily across the land. Even in Hibernia, I hear of the great Arthur, his strength, aye, his compassion. These are not traits that I normally apply to *tyranni*. Coroticus tells me that you have not always been with Arthur, that for a long while you hated him. But then you suddenly emerged as his champion, ferreting out a conspiracy against Britannia and the church. I have seen enough of you to know that, sober, you are a man of caution, a man of intelligence, and not a man easily frightened or cowed. So, I must know why a man such as you chooses to serve a *tyrannus*."

I studied that face once again. It was stern, yet not hostile. He would have his answer or I would be pestered with the question and little work would be done. I remembered a phrase in an old manuscript I had copied for Coroticus. "You proceed from a false premise, Patrick. Arthur is not a *tyrannus*. You use too large a brush, and hence you paint too many men with your accusations. Are there *tyranni* among us? Of course. Most of the members of the *consilium* are but *tyranni* striving to appear noble. We have *iudices* in our larger towns and they are unjust. You have priests who are not holy. But you have priests who are good and godly men. We have *iudices* who are just. Some members of the *consilium* are noble and good men— Bedevere, Kay, and most especially Arthur. You cannot view the world in such absolutes, Patrick. All is not good or evil. Whatever god or gods created this world, it was not done in absolutes."

"Do you deny that good and evil exist?"

"No, but I would say that all men are capable of good and evil. Good men sometimes make decisions that result in evil. Sometimes evil men make decisions that result in good."

Patrick shook his head slowly. "You live in a confusing

world, Malgwyn. And though I am not the shrewdest of men, I note that you have carefully skirted appraising Arthur as I requested."

I hung my head. He might think himself not very shrewd, but there was little that he missed. "Arthur is . . . Arthur. He is a unique man, at least a unique man to hold his position."

"And how is he unique?"

I considered the question. "He has a conscience. He cares about something more than the heft of his purse. Arthur cares about the lives of his people."

"Malgwyn, you will forgive me if I do not accept your word with my whole heart. I have been observing nobles such as your lord Arthur for many, many seasons now. I have heard several claim to care for the people, but they were words only. I have seen these *tyranni* slaughter women and children in a border village of a neighboring lord and call their actions necessary to protect their own people. Can you tell me that this is just? That this is godly?"

"No, I cannot tell you that. But I can tell you that it is the way of the world."

"I am not a wise man, Malgwyn. I have often wondered why God chose me to minister to the Scotti. For He knows what suffering they have caused me. And He knows that there are many other men smarter than me. But if one accepts your words, that this 'is the way of the world,' does it yet relieve us of our responsibility to try to make this a better world?"

I stood swiftly, a frown spreading across my face. The old man's protestation that he was not wise was at the least self-serving and inaccurate. He had driven the talk in this direction because he knew that if I disagreed with him, I was putting the lie to my own actions. The damp weather gave body to the manure used in mudding the cell walls. It was an appropriate odor.

"Be at ease, my new friend," Patrick counseled. "Please sit. We are not enemies, and I find much to like in your Lord Arthur."

I planted myself back on the stump and waited for Patrick to begin again. And once more, he looked not at me but into the distance.

"I tell you this, Malgwyn, because I feel that I can trust you. I have encountered few men who are so universally respected, especially few men who have also been so universally pitied for being a drunk.

"I am engaged in a battle, Malgwyn. The church fathers in Rome are attempting to take my life's work from me."

"Why?" Patrick's work was known far and wide, as the Briton who had brought the pagan Scotti to the Christ. He was the kind of man around whom legends were spun.

"I told you of a great and horrible sin I committed as a youth, and of my best friend whom I confided in. He kept not my confidence. Officially, it is that sin, they claim, that keeps me from being qualified as a bishop. Unofficially, they believe I have become too powerful in the church. They fear me, and what they fear they remove."

An understanding struck me. "You did not come here in search of Pelagianism at all. You came here to speak to Elafius about this sin of yours. Elafius was your best friend, the man who betrayed you to the church, and you came seeking revenge."

He turned toward me then, the wrinkles in his face seeming

131

deeper somehow. "No. Elafius was the brother of the girl I killed, and I came seeking his forgiveness."

I was fifteen years old, young and fanciful. We had few needs then; the Roman withdrawal was just completed and our larders were still full. Except for the occasional raids by the Scotti, we felt safe and secure. My father and grandfather were still important men in our town. Indeed, my grandfather, Potitus, was a presbyter and my father a deacon. During the Roman time, they had been engaged in the collecting of taxes, and with the Roman army leaving us, they too were at somewhat of a loss. My older brothers and the servi handled the farm work. My mother and sisters busied themselves with the management of our town house and villa. I had few duties except to be young and have fun with my friends.

My closest friends were Elafius and his sister, Addiena, and my dearest friend of all, Tremayne, son of our neighbor Trahern. Elafius, Tremayne, and I were all of nearly the same age, but Addiena was somewhat younger. We chased each other and played games, fished, hunted.

That summer we had not yet seen all the changes that would soon take place. The elders knew, but they put on a cheerful face and went about conducting their business normally. An undercurrent of fear was palpable but we played anyway; uncertainty in our elders was something we did not want to acknowledge.

I was old enough to understand the changes that were happening to me physically. At our country estate we had animals. I was not the smartest child, but I was not stupid either. I knew how those urges in me could be served, but I had no practical understanding of the matter. That summer, as I was going to meet my friends, I happened upon two of our servi in a barn. I saw them and then I understood the coupling. The woman seemed to enjoy it as much as the man. They did not hear me and I did not disturb them.

Elafius, Addiena, and Tremayne were to be waiting for me at a little spring on the far side of our estate. People rarely ventured there, and it was a good place for children to play. But when I arrived, Addiena was alone.

I saw immediately where this story would lead, and though Patrick was speaking softly, I glanced around nervously, but no one else was near. We looked for all the world like two colleagues in rapt discussion. I yet started to caution Patrick, but his raised hand stopped me before I made a sound.

She turned and looked at me as I approached, and she smiled. Addiena was such a pretty child, long brown hair and already the beginnings of a mature form. She favored games where she would hide and we would find her, if we could. She had a quick laugh. Seeing the servi had stirred strong emotions in me. Seeing Addiena made me wonder at what the servi found so pleasurable. And I resolved to take this chance to find out. I will not tell you the rest except to say that she was frightened by this new game I was showing her, but I had gone beyond being able to stop the demon in me. I tried to force myself on her. She began screaming and I covered her mouth, tighter and tighter, frantic now because I knew that Elafius and Tremayne would be drawing near. And then she stopped struggling, stopped screaming, stopped breathing. I swear to you that I stopped breathing too as I looked down and fully understood the horrendous thing I had done. The shame and the horror soaked me like a chilling rain, and I shivered beneath the hot sun.

I leaped to my feet and ran as fast as I could back home, praying that neither Tremayne nor Elafius had seen me. I rushed inside the villa and straight into my father's arms. He asked me what was wrong, and unable to think of anything else, I told him of seeing the servi. I was out of breath and he assumed that I had been confused by what I saw. He laughed and told me that we would need to talk later.

In a few hours, Elafius, his father, Tremayne, and a few other men appeared at our villa. They told of how Addiena had been found, strangled, abused. I could not hold back my tears, though I believed that they would know immediately that I had done this thing. But all believed it was because I was distraught. Except Tremayne. He just looked at me oddly and said nothing.

In the community, speculation was that some rogue or servi *had done this deed. The men, organized by my father, mounted their horses and patrolled the countryside. On the third day, they found traces of where a Scotti raiding party had put in on the coast, some miles away. Although they were able to trace their movements to a point not far from where Addiena had been killed, it ended there. Her death was ascribed to the Scotti raiders anyway. It seemed the most likely story.*

A fortnight later, Tremayne and I were walking across the field, near the spring where Addiena had died. Tremayne was a good lad, my best friend. His father was a decurion *just as mine was. We had been born the same year and raised as neighbors. I was somewhat larger than he, and he had an inquisitive nature that had escaped me. Indeed, Tremayne was smarter at fifteen than I have ever been.*

"I saw you that day, Patrick," he said to me. "What day?" I asked. "The day that Addiena was killed. I glimpsed you running away, but Elafius did not see." I was shaking inside, and a cold sweat bathed me. I could lie, but Tremayne would see through it. He stopped and sat in the grass. "Tell me what happened," he said. And I did.

"Patrick!" I stood aghast, the only thoughts running through my head those of a husband who has seen a wife so ravaged. Perhaps the church was right, perhaps a man with such a past had no place in Hibernia. I dropped my head and shook it. "*Episcopus*, I have a hard time reconciling the man before me with the monster that could force himself on a child!"

For his part, Patrick did not beat his breast or bray at the world. He said simply, "We were all children then."

Something in the simple way he said it told me much about how long and how deeply his transgression had haunted him. Rather than dwell on the deeds of decades past, I tried to focus on the here and now.

"And this Tremayne is now the man who has betrayed you to the church fathers?"

"He kept that secret for many years. What circumstances occasioned this betrayal, I do not know. He too has had his difficulties with the church over the years."

I thought Patrick was being a little too understanding and I said so.

"It is how I am, Malgwyn. But Tremayne's betrayal was just a fraction of my own. I betrayed my friendship with Addiena and Elafius. And that betrayal is far worse than any visited upon me by Tremayne. Just a few months later, I was taken by Scotti raiders and sold into slavery in Hibernia. I often wonder if Tremayne would have kept his silence so long had I not been taken. I was six years under the control of my Scotti masters. By the time I escaped and made my way home, too much time had passed and Tremayne had left home to find his way in the world. Elafius was already in the Christ's service."

Then it was my turn to look off across the land, its curves still shrouded in mist. "I have, in my time, traveled to Bannaventa and the surrounding countryside, Patrick. Nowhere in my travels have I heard of a man named Tremayne. Where does he live now?"

And Patrick smiled. "He entered the Christ's service before I did, after studying in Gaul, but he changed his name as so many do when they enter into such a life. I strongly doubt that he has any involvement in the present affair here. He was a headstrong youth and angered the church fathers greatly. His has not been an easy life, and I know not what has become of him, or even if he be still alive."

"Why come here to apologize to Elafius now? Surely it would have been better had you done it much earlier."

Patrick shrugged. "In truth, I was not sure where he was. He studied some little bit in Gaul, but I always suspected that he would return here, to his homeland. His letter about Pelagianism gave me a reason that even Dubricius could not find fault with. Bishops are very protective of their territory. And I have drawn their wrath before when I chastised a *tyrannus* here who raided into Hibernia and killed Christians."

"Then why would Dubricius not complain now? Of this Pelagianism."

"I believe that Dubricius has always been a secret follower of Pelagius. But Pelagianism is so overwhelmingly opposite to what the church believes that Dubricius does not dare to appear to support it. Remember that they sent Germanus to combat Pelagianism twice, once with Lupus and once with Severus. And I happen to know that Severus is in Britannia now. Indeed, Malgwyn, it is Severus who is leveling these charges against me. He is a driven man. It would take little to get him to wage a new crusade against Pelagianism. He was the darling of the church when he stood with Germanus. I suspect that now he seeks to regain some of that glory. Dubricius cannot be sure who else Elafius wrote to, so it behooves him to suffer my presence here, thus allowing him to give the appearance of fighting Pelagianism while, in actuality, ignoring it himself."

I studied the old *episcopus* carefully. "Affairs between lords are treacherous, my new friend. But I never dreamed that they could be as devious and duplicitous within the church."

Patrick stood, smoothing his robe. "Then you have much education ahead of you, Malgwyn. Come, let us begin our day's work."

"A moment, *episcopus*. Why did you tell me all of that? You had no need. I am no one, just a simple man, counselor to a king who cannot claim that his household is as one on any issue. A man you had never met before yesterday."

"Because I sense in you a man in whom trust can be placed. Because after I leave here, I shall appear at a special commission at Castellum Marcus before Dubricius and Severus and others, where my continuance as *episcopus* of Hibernia will be decided." He stopped then and turned to me. "I have a *confessio* written out, and I wish you to take it should something happen to me."

"But Patrick, choose one of the *monachi* who wait on you. You know them, and they are of your faith."

"That is why, Master Malgwyn, I have chosen you. Do not worry. I do not plan on missing the meeting at Castellum Marcus. But, were something to happen to me . . ." He reached down into a bag, retrieving something. "Take this scroll," he said, handing it across to me. "It is my *confessio*, much as I have given it to you already." I took it without eagerness.

Patrick stopped for a moment and looked around our Ynyswitrin. "Should God visit my death on me here, this would be a pleasant place for my earthly body to await the resurrection. But put no marker for me, no sign of where these old bones lie. That will suit me best. I have attracted enough attention in life to satisfy one in death."

All I could do was nod. And we continued to navigate the remainder of the path up to Coroticus's hall where we would hold court that day. "Tell me something, Malgwyn," Patrick asked after a moment. "Did Elafius suffer much?"

I thought of the hands and fingers that held him, those that gripped his jaws and forced them open. And then I lied. "No, *episcopus*. His was a quiet passing."

Patrick nodded absently. "I am glad. As a child, Elafius was a giving, caring person. He knew no strangers, and he would give them anything they asked. Why do you think he was murdered?"

That was a question I had been pondering much. "He knew something that was important enough for men to kill him. Now, whether this same information was important to you or to Arthur, I do not know."

"Why not important to the abbot?"

"He could be as easily murdered as Elafius. The person that needed Elafius silenced was not afraid of Coroticus. What Elafius knew or what he represented was far more dangerous; his secret has implications far beyond Ynys-witrin."

Patrick stopped in his tracks and spun around. "How know you this?"

I halted before him. "Think, *episcopus*, your arrival has been heralded here since you set foot on the coast. Swift runners brought news within hours that you were headed this way. Arthur's arrival has been common knowledge even longer."

"So. What does this tell you?"

"Elafius was murdered suddenly, in somewhat of a hurry.

He needed to be eliminated and something he had in his possession had to be taken."

"You can read minds, it seems?"

"No, his cell had been searched hastily by the time I arrived here. Someone was looking for something and they did not have the time to be pretty about it.

"My guess is that it was your arrival that hastened Elafius's death."

"Why say you so?"

"The Rigotamus has been scheduled to visit for more than one moon. Your visit was only known for certain a few days hence. The search of his cell was something done in extreme haste. No plan had been laid beforehand."

"What brings this talent to you?" Patrick asked. "It is a valuable one and one that you should cherish."

"I have no idea, *episcopus*, but it is with me." I stopped and held the door to Coroticus's hall open to him.

He laid his hand on my shoulder as he passed through. "It is a special gift, but one that may make you the mark of assassins."

"I have harbored such thoughts myself," I grumbled in his wake.

"I will defer to you in this matter, Malgwyn. Your experience is better suited to an inquiry of this sort. Rooting out Pelagianism is one thing. But this is now a murder inquest, and that is more properly your territory."

He was right, but I was surprised at his willingness to cede authority. Though I knew that finding Elafius's killer was unlikely to preserve his bishopric, Patrick did not seem a man willing to cede any authority for any reason.

CHAPTER EIGHT

We arranged ourselves at the front of the hall. I turned to the four soldiers left by Arthur for my use. They were common soldiers, not officers, and each carried a small round shield, a spear, and a cloak rolled into a bundle and wrapped across his body from shoulder to hip, a hip that universally held a dagger. "Bring us the woman Rhiannon," I instructed one of the men. Two of them saluted and headed out of the hall.

"Shall we begin with this woman, this Rhiannon?" Patrick asked.

"Yes, *episcopus*," I said. "There is much of this affair wrapped around religion, it seems. I have taken her measure as a person. I would hear your thoughts of her as a person of God."

Patrick nodded. Now that his secrets were revealed, he was still as devout in his beliefs, but I sensed an ease with me that had been missing before. The soldiers gone, Patrick turned to me. "Your anger was not at Arthur, my new friend. Your anger was at all the killing you had done, but which had not wiped away the anguish from your soul. You had killed and killed Saxons and yet they came. Your men lay around you dead and still your beloved wife had not risen from the grave. You wished to die. And Arthur kept you from that, but your anger was at yourself for all the killing you had caused." He spoke softly, without a hint of chastisement.

"You are a very, very perceptive man, Patrick. But I have come a long way along the road that you have laid out."

"But you have not come to the Christ. He can take your burdens from you."

"Please, *episcopus*, I have the greatest respect for those who have chosen that way. But I am not one of them."

"Yet," he added with a smile.

I returned the smile, feeling comfortable before the old *episcopus* as I had not before. "Not yet."

"Then perhaps I should take this time to work on that."

I rolled my eyes as he began.

Rhiannon was just as fetching today as the day before. Her long hair flew violently about her shoulders, and her robe seemed to stay on only by God's mercy, so excitedly did she cast her arms about.

"Do you think that I have nothing else to do but answer your summons?" she asked me, quite unabashed. She stopped long enough to cast her eyes up and down Patrick. "For a great *episcopus*, he seems harmless."

"The same might be said of you."

The look she shot my way could have pierced the toughest iron, and she moved with a firm step to a wooden chair set in front of the abbot's dais. "Ask your questions! I have work to be about." I was more taken with her than before. I knew she was of my age, maybe a bit younger, but her monastic life had kept many of the lines of age from her face that marked those of her contemporaries. Her eyes fired like nothing I'd seen, and I could readily understand how Coroticus would be tempted.

I kept my eyes averted from Patrick.

"You will be silent, woman!" The impatience was thick in Patrick's voice.

"I know you're an ancient man, but are you so bored that you brought me here just to look at?"

This time even the soldiers chuckled. Coroticus had had some small snacks laid out and she helped herself to some oysters without asking.

"I think you take liberties." I said, trying to bring myself to the task at hand.

Her hand paused on its journey to her lips, but then continued. "Are these your oysters, Master Malgwyn?"

"They are God's oysters," Patrick pointed out. "And He gives us dominion over them."

"Then I am exercising my dominion." She sat back in her chair, smoothing her gown. I was not positive, but I sensed a tremor of concern in her manner. This confrontation caused her greater fear than her first, and she covered for it by her cockiness and lack of respect, and I wondered at the cause. She seemed younger today, and that was odd, but I could not say why I believed it so.

"Have you not resolved the old man's death yet?"

"No." I shook my head. "I was hoping for your help in that. I understand he was your favorite debating partner."

She cocked her eye at me. "I suspect that if you listen long enough you will learn that I was his lover as well."

Patrick grunted. The old *episcopus*'s forbearance was welcome but it seemed it had less time to last.

"Madame Rhiannon, your part in this inquiry will last only

so long as I suspect that you are keeping information from me. The sooner you cease your childish actions and tell us what we need to know, the sooner you can return to your duties with the women's community. Do you understand?" I left nothing to the imagination as I stood and leaned in toward her.

But this one was not easily intimidated. She did not look at me, but threw the now-empty oyster shell to the floor. "Malgwyn, you are a strong man. And that is good, but don't think that just your strength will be enough in this endeavor." To demonstrate her diffidence, some bone hairpins magically appeared in her hands and she went about the task of pinning up the fireball that was her head of hair.

I was tired, no, beyond tired, of people telling me what I was and what I was not. "Tired" was a weak word to describe my anger. Flinging my cloak back, I lunged forward, planted Rhiannon's feet on the floor, sending the bone hairpins flying about the room, and pointed at two of the soldiers. "The abbot has an iron rod for roasting meat. Find it! Then stoke a hot fire in the hearth." I turned and looked into Rhiannon's widening eyes. "I will have answers to my questions or we will feast on your feet tonight!" I spoke strongly, but the nest of her hair tickled my nose and the view I had down her wrap, revealing two wondrous breasts, made my manhood strong also. Her hair was scented with rose water, and I found myself breathing of it deeply. I released her and stepped back.

"Malgwyn!" My tirade had brought Patrick to his feet. "We do not torture people."

I chose now to shock him and all those around us. "You may not. But I do. My commission is to find the killer of Elafius, and you all treat it as a joke. I did not like him, but he deserves better. So"—and I paused and touched each eye in the room with my own—"I will do what I have to in order to make this thing happen."

The soldiers, who were less shocked by such orders, shrugged and left to find the iron rod. I set myself to building a fire in the great hearth. "*Episcopus*, if you will lend a hand and tie Madame Rhiannon into that chair, I would be grateful."

"Certainly, Master Malgwyn." And without another word, he snatched a rope coiled in the corner.

"*Episcopus!*" Rhiannon shouted. I admired her flexibility. She went from insulting Patrick to seeking his protection as quickly as the flicker of an eyelid.

Patrick dropped his head and looked very regretful. "I am sorry, good sister. I have no authority here. 'Tis Malgwyn who wears the judicial robe. At best I am simply a guest."

"Ask your questions," Rhiannon said, the flippancy gone from her voice. With Coroticus absent and Patrick conspiring with me, she had little choice. I nodded to Patrick and he tossed the rope in the corner.

She looked at me with less disdain, and I found it welcoming. I wondered how much of her attitude was a disguise for her own fear. A great deal, I thought. Like everyone at the abbey, it seemed, she had some secret. Even Patrick had one, as I was now aware.

I did not answer her immediately, finding my eyes drawn to the glowing red and orange embers of the fire, the touch of the fragrant smoke sending my nose twitching before it escaped through a small hole in the roof.

"I understand that you have known Gwilym, the old *monachus*, for many years. Is that true?"

Poor Rhiannon. She had been prepared to discuss Elafius, the divine sacrifice, her whereabouts on the night of Elafius's murder, but not Gwilym. Her face could not hide her surprise at all. Her eyes, bright and brown, grew wide. Her fingers clenched the sides of her chair so tightly that her knuckles seemed ready to burst through the skin. She had no ready answer so she told me the truth.

"Aye. What of it?" But her shrug was too late. And she knew it.

"Why did you not tell of this before?"

"Why should I? He did not kill Elafius."

"But he was the one spreading Pelagianism. It was his activities that caused Elafius to send for Patrick. That sounds like he might have had reason to rid himself of an interfering old man."

Her eyes flashed again, but this time with anger, anger that I would accuse her friend of such evil. "No. I have known him all of my life. He is not capable of this."

"He is not capable of murder, but he is spreading Pelagianism?" Patrick entered the fray.

This time the old *episcopus* was the target of her flashing eyes. "Believing in the ideas of Pelagius does not make one capable of murder," Rhiannon snapped at him. "No matter how much you would wish it so, all believers in the Christ have not repudiated Pelagius. There are yet many in Gaul and here in Brittania who believe that he was right and that the church is wrong."

Patrick bounced to his feet with a speed that belied his age. "How dare you! You would steal the meaning from the Christ's sacrifice!"

"Pelagius does not steal anything! He simply says that man alone can either accept or reject salvation. The Christ set the perfect example by sacrificing His all. But man is not dependent on the grace of God for his salvation!"

"You speak rubbish, woman! Salvation is by God's grace

and good works! Hear me, woman. I knew Agricola, and I debated with him and bested him. You are but a child and cannot match his skills, so do not pretend that you can!"

"And you are become an old man in his dotage! Do not pretend otherwise!"

They would have continued like that for hours, but my head was already in pain. God's grace. Good works. Free will. Undiscoverable truths! "Enough!" I shouted, springing to my own feet. My eruption accomplished its purpose as both fell immediately silent, yet fixedly glared at one another. "Can you say with certainty that Gwilym could not have done this thing?"

Rhiannon pursed her lips and looked away from me. "No," she admitted after a long moment. "I cannot. I did as I told you yesterday. I left this community, crossed the *vallum* into my own, and did not return. I know not what Gwilym did after the meal."

She was lying, but whether it was on the question of Gwilym or her own activities I could not determine.

Patrick looked to me. "We must see this Gwilym."

"He is away now," Rhiannon said.

"No, he is not," I said. " 'Twas just this morning that I spoke with him."

Those blazing eyes cut to me, and I sensed something unsaid. "You are of the women's community. How would you know that he was away?"

"Do I not have eyes, great Master Malgwyn? He was leaving the abbey as I was brought here. We passed on the path and spoke."

"About what?"

"The abbot sent him with one of the other brothers to a nearby village to help with a sickness." She almost whispered the words.

I felt the flush of my face as the anger rose. So that had been Coroticus's game when he plucked Gwilym from my chamber! Had Coroticus been right there, I might surely have broken his neck. He knew that we would be seeking the old *monachus* again. For some reason, rather than just obstruct us with his silence, the abbot was taking a more active role in blocking our queries. I remembered Gwilym's warning that he was hiding as much as anyone. Apparently, our abbot knew that secret as well.

"What or who is Gwilym?" I demanded. "Why is he so important? Why is he being protected?" Both Patrick and I leaned in expectantly, though we had no hope of an explanation.

Rhiannon looked first to Patrick with the narrowed eyes of hatred and then to me, her expression less harsh. "I will not tell him," she spat out. "And," she continued more softly, "you, I cannot tell."

"Why can you not tell me? Did Gwilym do this thing?" That he was guilty seemed the only reason for this continuing effort to block my inquest.

She shook her head. "I cannot say, but he is not the kind to do murder."

"Then why?" I was pleading with her. To my amazement, Patrick had stayed silent throughout this exchange.

Tears had filled her eyes by then, and she simply shook her head. As frustrated as I was with her, I took no pleasure in treating her this way. Her cheeks were stained with the shiny tracks of tears. Had she not been a woman of the community, the chalk that most women used to whiten their faces would have been running down her cheeks, driven by the tears. "Go," I said finally.

"Malgwyn!" Patrick sprang to his feet.

"We have nothing with which to charge her, *episcopus*. We have no witnesses that place her near Elafius after the evening meal. I doubt not that the other women will confirm that they saw her in their community near unto the time that Elafius must have been killed." The disgust in my voice must have come through strongly for I noticed Patrick's shoulders droop in resignation. "Go, but we may have more questions for you. Be so good as to not leave the abbey to help in villages."

Rhiannon stood and smoothed her dress. With both hands, she wiped the tears from her face and tried to regain her dignity. "Do what you must, Malgwyn, but I do not believe that Gwilym did this. It is not in his nature."

"Murder is in any man's nature if he is pushed to it."

She cocked her head and looked at me oddly. "If you need me, I will be easy to find." With that she swept from the room.

"I think that was a waste of time, but this question of Gwilym must be resolved," I said. "As of now, he is the only one we know with reason to kill Elafius. I do not think the woman was involved, at least with the act itself."

"Agreed. Then I believe we must inquire of Coroticus. He seems to be engulfed in this affair."

I had no desire to question my friend, but Patrick was right. We had leverage with Coroticus because of the church and his position. And he absolutely knew things that he was not telling us. But Patrick's sovereignty over him was more supposed than real. Bishops were zealous in guarding their bishoprics; they regarded the presence of another *episcopus* as that of an invading king, bent on their destruction.

I did not think Coroticus viewed it as such, but I believed that he would use it to his advantage. I nodded to my soldiers. "Find Coroticus. Bring him here, but do not harm him. Show him every respect. Tell him that the *episcopus* and I *request* his presence."

They left and Patrick turned to me. "Do you believe that Coroticus did this?"

"No, Patrick. I know Coroticus too well. He might stand to the side and allow someone to die. He might direct it to be done. But I do not think he would ever foul his own hands with blood. And if he had wanted Elafius dead, he could have had it done years ago. When I was here, after the River Tribuit, Elafius was just as annoying as anyone." I stopped and pulled on my beard for a second. "That is what bothers me, Patrick. Elafius was annoying. But unless you are a *tyrannus*, that is little reason to kill. If such were sufficient, Arthur would have killed me years ago. A question, Patrick?"

"Certainly."

"Why do you so fervently oppose women playing a role in the divine sacrifice? It seems of little consequence to me."

"Malgwyn, my new friend, it is well-established doctrine that women should play no role in the sacrifice. It would dilute the meaning. The same practice has infected Brittany as well."

"What is it they do that so outrages you?"

"Ofttimes, a *sacerdote* or *presbyter* will travel from house to house administering the divine sacrifice to families. In some regions, a woman is allowed to hold the cup that contains the precious blood of the Christ."

I knew that he was speaking symbolically, although I had heard some of the *monachi* once discuss their belief that the wine they drink somehow becomes the real blood of the Christ once they drink it. Such things were beyond my ken. "And this offends you?"

"It is contrary to teaching and tradition. The Christ had no women among his apostles. So, how could it be proper for women to take an active role in celebrating His sacrifice?"

"When I lived among the *monachi* here, I heard some of them talk about the Magdalene, that she was a favored one."

Patrick frowned. "She was a fallen woman that the Christ raised up, but that was all."

"And you do not think that the Christ—"

"Malgwyn!" Patrick snapped, his face flushing red. "He would not have done such. He had not that need."

I held up my hand in submission. "'Twas just a question, *episcopus*. No offense intended, I swear it."

His complexion returned to normal and the wrinkles softened again. "Women are just a . . . a . . ."

"A lesser sort?"

"That is not my judgment, Malgwyn, but the judgment of Saint Paul."

"Were I you, *episcopus*, I would not voice such beliefs before the lady Rhiannon."

Patrick chuckled, smoothing some of the wrinkles from his face. "No, I do not believe that would be a wise course."

Young Gildas entered the hall carrying a pitcher. "*Episcopus*, I thought you might like some refreshment." He filled a beaker for Patrick, then turning toward me, he hesitated. Patrick sipped from his beaker and smiled at me.

"Please, Malgwyn, join me. A cup of small beer will settle our stomachs and our nerves."

At that, Gildas reluctantly filled a beaker and offered it to me. I think it was at that moment that my future with Gildas became as hard as flint. The gall of the youngster! To place himself as my judge! I would not easily forget his impertinence. Our time of reckoning would come.

The young *monachus* seemed about to say something to Patrick, but he paused and turned the corners of his mouth down into a frown and left without a word.

"Forgive him, Malgwyn. He is young."

"He is too certain of himself for a youngster. I wonder how much of his insolence comes from his father and brothers. They oppose Arthur, you know."

"I know. But I believe that Gildas is not highly favored by his family. I believe that he wishes the church to replace them in his life. So, his devotion to duty must be encouraged. The church needs such as young Gildas."

"The church should find a way to beat the immaturity out of him before I do," I grumbled, sipping the small beer. The *monachi* kept one building for the brewing of beer. Despite my love for the product, I knew little about the process. I knew that they reused the ingredients and it had something to do with a double-bottomed pot. And the succeeding batches were of lesser strength, ending with the small beer that we were drinking. Weak for my taste but satisfying nonetheless.

"You should be more tolerant," Patrick chided me, sipping from his own beaker.

"You are different, much different than your reputation. Aye, than your actions yesterday would attest."

The old *episcopus* winked at me and grinned. "A leader of the church must be stern when necessary. It is far easier to become more pleasant later, after one has established a stern, demanding manner."

I smiled at the admission. "One thing I do not understand. You were made a *servi* by the Scotti for six years, and yet you went back to work among them. Why?"

Patrick stretched his legs out and massaged his knees. "After

I had made my way home, I resolved to never leave again. But I was troubled by visions. I will not bore you with the details, but I soon understood that God was calling me to His service. I had not been religious before, but when I realized that God was speaking to me, I answered His call. I understood too that He wanted me to return to Hibernia and convert the Scotti. But understand me, Malgwyn. I did not do these things for God. It was a gift of God that I could do them."

"*Episcopus*, why would your God or any god send a man back to preach justice and peace to a people who had held him captive? I am sorry, but the miracle to me is that you survived your return at all."

Patrick leaned over and patted my knee. "My God protects me and keeps me safe. He protects you as well."

I did not like all of this talk about gods. It made me squirm in my seat. Lifting my half-arm and waving it at him, I grunted, "Well, He did not mind His business on at least one day."

Half expecting Patrick to begin to chastise me for blasphemy, he laughed a belly-deep chuckle. Since he had confided in me, it was as if his soul were lighter and his worries fewer. Unfortunately, at that moment Coroticus walked in.

For his audience with Patrick, the abbot had chosen to wear his formal robes, rimmed with fur. His fingers held gold and silver rings, and the cross around his neck was not the plain one he normally wore, but a stone-encrusted, golden one that I suspected he had ordered specially made.

Patrick grimaced at Coroticus's apparel. In my short acquaintance with the *episcopus*, I already understood that he was a simple man, prizing simple things. The richness of Coroticus's garb was not sitting well with my new friend.

"You asked for me, *episcopus*?" Coroticus was all innocent inquiry.

Patrick immediately straightened and cast a forbidding look at the abbot. "Why did you send Gwilym away today?" Without preamble, he launched straight into the matter.

In the pause which followed, I could smell the hint of cooking pork drifting up from the kitchen. Mixed with herbs, it flavored the air with its delicious scents. But I could not enjoy the smell. My friend Coroticus had lied to me. I did not understand why.

"May I sit?"

Patrick nodded, and Coroticus adjusted his robes and lowered himself onto the chair.

"Why did you send Gwilym away from the abbey today?" the *episcopus* repeated.

The abbot did not answer quickly. He looked away for a moment, toward the timber walls of his hall. "By what right, *episcopus*, do you ask me such questions? This is not your bishopric. You have no say in how I conduct the affairs of my abbey." All of this he said without looking at either of us. Indeed, his voice held a distant, almost whispering quality.

Patrick studied the abbot carefully. He glanced at me. Coroticus's voice had the sound of a condemned man, a man resigned to his fate. "You are correct, abbot. But Malgwyn holds Arthur's commission as *iudex*. Do you deny his right to ask questions?"

Then Coroticus turned and looked at us both. "If I believed that such questions were valuable to his inquiry, I would not challenge his right. But, as Gwilym has not been formally accused, I saw no reason to limit his movements. And, as the

153

episcopus knows very well, if Gwilym did commit this act, he is protected by this sacred precinct."

"He is protected as long as he remains within its bounds," Patrick corrected him.

Sanctuary. It was an ancient right. Anyone could seek sanctuary within a religious precinct. As long as they stayed within that precinct. They were protected from harm, and woe be unto the man who violated this right.

"Where did you send him? What village?"

"I will not tell you, Malgwyn. And no one else here knows. I respect you greatly, but in this matter, I do not trust you to abide by the rules of sanctuary. Your obsessive pursuit of such affairs might cause you to ignore such traditions."

"And so you will keep him from me? Why in the name of your God did you send for me? You have known me for years! You know me!"

The pain on Coroticus's face could be seen, almost touched. "When I called for you, I did not know what I know now. I reacted without thinking."

"What do you know now?"

"I cannot tell you."

"Why not?" I was beyond frustration. The conversation went in more circles than a wagon wheel.

"Was it in a *confessio*, abbot?" Patrick asked softly.

He nodded.

"He cannot tell you, Malgwyn," Patrick said to me. "He said it in confession to Coroticus. Such confessions cannot be repeated."

I turned and motioned to the soldiers. "Bring Bedevere to me as quickly as you can."

Coroticus's eyes shot to me. Patrick's reaction was somewhat slower. "What are you going to do, Malgwyn?" the old *episcopus* asked.

I stood, my half-arm hurting up into my neck. "Fighting with the church is not something I wish to do. I could let all of this go. But you, Coroticus, were the one that brought me into it. And now that that is done, I will not stop. I will have Bedevere set guards around the abbey precinct and put patrols out to search the region. If I cannot take Gwilym here, I will take him before he returns. Then, I will find out what has happened here and what you are hiding, my lord abbot."

"Malgwyn, I beg you. You do not know what mischief you will bring down on us!" Coroticus too was on his feet.

"Then tell me who or what Gwilym is!"

He dropped his head and turned his down-stretched hands palms up, as if in supplication.

But before I could answer, I heard the odd clink of mail. Bedevere had arrived.

"I came upon your call, Malgwyn." He glanced at Coroticus and Patrick. "How may I serve you?" I realized then that in some ways I had always underestimated Bedevere. In a single glance, he took in the situation and addressed me in a manner intended to aid my task. No pause. No haughty expressions.

"Lord Bedevere, the *monachus* Gwilym has been sent away to a neighboring village." I threw a grimace at the abbot. "I need him, and I need him before he can arrive here and claim sanctuary. Please post guards around the *vallum*. Arrest him before he crosses into the abbey precinct. Send patrols out to search the surrounding villages and countryside."

"And when we catch him?"

"Hold him in the village. Let no one near him."

Bedevere nodded. "As you order." He did not question me;

he did not challenge me. Bedevere nodded sharply and spun around, shouting orders to the soldiers already there.

"Malgwyn," I heard Patrick say. "Forgive my words to you yesterday. For all that you may have been, you are now a different man. I suspect the death of my old friend Elafius will not be a mystery for very much longer. Arthur has chosen well, and my opinion of him is changing too."

Coroticus said nothing, but the expression on his face said everything. He was a most miserable man.

"Be of good heart, Coroticus. I have not had you arrested yet." I tried to sound friendly, but the abbot was not interested. If ever I had seen a man at the point of collapsing, it was Coroticus.

He stood up then and straightened his robes, his fingers adjusting the massive cross to the center. "I will go and see to our evening meal and to the preparations for Elafius's burial."

"As you like," I said. In truth, I felt strongly that once we broke down this wall surrounding the old *monachus* Gwilym we would know how Patrick's friend died.

"Will he be sent to Bannaventa Taburniae? We were born there," Patrick said.

Coroticus shook his head. "Elafius once told me that he wished to be buried here, where he had made his home these many years. We will bury him next to the church. I have already set men to digging his grave and the carpenter to building his coffin."

"May I now view the body?" His words reminded me that we had already objected once.

"Umm, I—" I began, but a wave of the hand from Coroticus stopped me.

"Of course, *episcopus*, whenever you like."

CHAPTER NINE

We all left together, Coroticus walking next to me. Apparently, he had had his men clean and dress Elafius for burial, obscuring my earlier explorations. He seemed more comfortable now that he and I were both keeping secrets from Patrick.

Preparations were further along than Coroticus knew. As we approached the building where Elafius lay, all of the brothers save Gwilym and Coroticus were present. Rhiannon and the women had wisely stayed away. The day had dawned to a clear sky, but gray clouds now blotted out the sun and I could taste rain on the wind.

I saw first the wooden coffin built for the old *monachus*. In our simple village, we mostly lined our graves with stone. Wooden coffins were seen as a rich man's vessel. Death was too common among the villagers, from age, disease, accident, and violence.

Four of the brothers were busied with placing the white-shrouded Elafius in his coffin. They chanted something in Latin as they hoisted their burden to their shoulders. The remaining *monachi* formed a line behind, young Gildas at the front, and followed their departed brother to the grave opened near unto the old church.

We followed along the muddy path, falling in behind the procession. Gildas recited something in Latin, but his voice was low and cracking, and the wind had risen and whispered around the wooden cells.

For some reason, memories of my days here returned to me, and to my surprise, they were surprisingly pleasant. In past times, I had remembered those days as dark and unending, the darkest of my life. But watching the brothers lay their fellow to rest, I suddenly recalled the kindnesses they had accorded me. Aye, even Elafius, annoying as he had been. I recalled the old man finding me one day, in the midst of frustration over learning to do without my right arm. His eyes softened in kindness, he gently patted me on the back and said, "Patience, my son. You lived many years with both of your arms. It will take you time to learn to live with one."

And now, another part of my past was being buried. The gray sky and the somber occasion darkened my mood like nothing in a long time. But as Patrick moved forward, I stayed by his side. The brothers laid Elafius's coffin on the ground, the top not yet affixed. My companion knelt down and studied his old friend's face as the others withdrew a step or two out of respect.

"He seems so old, Malgwyn," Patrick said softly. "But I still see the boy I once knew, hidden behind all those wrinkles. Do I look that old?"

I did not answer. I knew Patrick was suddenly feeling the weight of his years in a way that he never had before. He was feeling the approach of his own death. I watched as his eyes closed and his lips moved in a soundless mumble. I knew not whether he prayed for Elafius's soul or his own, and, in truth, it did not matter.

He began to rise, stumbled, almost falling, but I moved to catch him with my good hand. Patrick looked up at me with a whisper of a smile, patted and then softly squeezed my hand, and rose to his feet. I could feel a tremble along his old frame and so I kept his arm fast in my grip.

"The day is passing us quickly, Malgwyn," he said, leading me away from the burial. Coroticus looked at us questioningly as we brushed by him. I am certain that he thought Patrick would stay, but the *episcopus* had said his good-byes. Watching the coffin lowered into the ground and the sod covering old Elafius would not provide him an end to the story or to his own grief.

Behind us, the chanting began again and Gildas's voice grew stronger. I took the lead then and guided Patrick back to his wooden cell. We sat on the wooden stools we had occupied before, and Patrick stayed silent for a long while.

When I had tired of contemplating how the wisps of smoke from the abbot's kitchen hung in the heavy, moist air, I looked to my colleague. He had aged twenty seasons in as many minutes. His wrinkles, already deep as ravines, deepened yet more. Those brown eyes of his had retreated farther into his skull. His skin seemed stretched tautly over bone, and even in the dull light I could see flakes of dead skin peel away from Patrick's forehead as if they were trying to flee.

" 'Tis almost time for the evening meal, *episcopus*. Why do we not delay our work until tomorrow. By then, Bedevere's men will have found Gwilym and we may question him and, hopefully, reveal the truth of Elafius's death. Until then, you may sup and rest. It has not been your easiest day, I suspect."

He looked up then, with that same soft smile. "You judge well, Malgwyn. Tomorrow, once we conclude our discussion with Gwilym, my aides and I will be off to Castellum Marcus. I believe that once we have talked to the brother, you will have no trouble discovering the truth of this matter." Patrick paused, and I could almost see the new thought entering his mind. "Malgwyn?"

"*Episcopus?*"

"Will you come to Castellum Marcus after the affair with this Gwilym is finished?"

"But why, Patrick?"

"I would have you serve as my advisor as I appear before the commission." His voice held no hint of mischief or laughter. He was all sincerity.

"*Episcopus*, I . . . Why would you want me? I am no *sacerdote*, no *presbyter*. I am not learned in Christly matters. And I abhor that act for which you stand accused. I grant that you were young and much has happened since, but I would seem the worst possible advocate."

"Because you are a man for whom logic is a passion. Your reasoning is not driven by emotion. When my opponents argue their charges against me, you will be able to find the flaws without allowing the alchemy of religion to cloud your judgment."

I drew back as if bitten. "*Episcopus!* You called religion 'alchemy'!" Even I knew that this was next to blasphemy.

Patrick smiled at me and patted my shoulder. "Why, Malgwyn! Someone else might think you believed in the Christ. Some would like to ascribe the powers of the alchemist to *sacerdotes* and *presbyters*, but the Christ is not about their ramblings." He paused again. "You are a good man, and short though our friendship may be, I have come to trust you as I have few men in my life."

I could read the truth of his statement in every line on his face. This was not a man who easily trusted anyone. And after all of those years he had spent among the Scotti, I could readily see why. They were a cruel and vicious people who preyed on others. Much of their wealth came from raiding our coasts, stealing our people and our produce, our tin shipments. Men such as Patrick indeed risked their lives by proposing to convert the Scotti from their pagan ways to those of the Christ.

"What of my work here?"

"I suspect that by morning, Lord Bedevere will have discovered Gwilym. By noon we will have arrived at an answer to the riddle of Elafius's death. Then, I feel certain that Lord Arthur will release you to assist me. It will only be for a short while." Patrick had neatly covered every possibility, though I strongly suspected that we would be searching for Elafius's killer this same time on the morrow.

Despite that, I said the only thing I could. "It would be my honor to serve as the *episcopus*'s counselor in this affair. And should the murderer of Elafius prove that simple to ferret out, I would consider it a great honor to offer my humble services to you."

"And I," the deep voice of Arthur thundered up the lane, "would be honored to give him leave to serve as your counselor in the meeting at Castellum Marcus."

Arthur strode up the path, his crimson robe, which was pinned at his shoulders, flowing behind. Chain mail clad his chest and a dagger marked his belt. His impressive sword dangled at his hip.

"You look prepared for war, my lord. Have we missed some news?"

Arthur sighed. "No, I've been listening to the complaints from local merchants. I find this garb brings more cooperation."

"With what?" Busied as I was with the matter of Elafius, I had lost track of Arthur's work.

"Goods stolen from merchant ships have begun appearing among the lands of the Dumnonii."

"Pirates." I shrugged. "You can never completely stamp them out, and they will find merchants to sell their wares. In truth, 'tis hard to blame the merchants."

"True, but for men dealing with pirate scum they seemed awfully nervous."

"Do any of them owe the pirates aught?"

"They say no."

My eyes narrowed. "That is odd."

"And not so odd, Malgwyn. How goes it with you? Are you ready to resume your duties? After assisting the *episcopus*, I mean," he added hurriedly with a hint of a wink at me. I smiled.

"Bedevere is organizing a search for the *monachus* Gwilym. I believe when we locate him that Elafius's death will become clear." Despite my pleasant, though frustrating, interview with Gwilym earlier, I felt strongly now that he was the culprit. All else he said was simply meant to turn us from the scent. The why of it? Tangled beyond redemption in some mystic religious argument, I supposed. My day with Patrick had taught me how seriously the church took such issues as seemed minor to me.

"Tell me, Lord Arthur, something of how you have your *consilium* organized."

Such pleased Arthur, and so I left them talking to find Bedevere encamped at the abbot's kitchen giving orders and receiving reports as the men hurried about, pausing for an occasional cup of *pulsum*, the vinegar-laced drink soldiers loved.

"What word, Lord Bedevere? Have your men found my wayward *monachus* yet?"

He shook his woolly head. "And 'tis strange, Malgwyn. He is hiding. Only that explains our failure. Granted, word spread quickly of our search, but we moved even more quickly. Were he just visiting villages, we would have found him."

"Will you search through the night?"

He shook his head. "No. We will begin again at first light. A man in hiding has too many sanctuaries in the night. And if he is truly in hiding, he is more dangerous to my men. Better to wait until daylight; less chance of losing a man to accident."

I nodded in agreement. "Are they all returned?"

"No, one three-man patrol sent out toward the Mount of Frogs has not reported."

"Let me know when they do."

"Malgwyn," Bedevere said, half chiding, "you will certainly know if they do not"

"The Mount of Frogs! Malgwyn! It is enchanted!" My newest naysayer was none other than my friend Merlin.

"Merlin, what brings you here?"

"Arthur thought I might be of some assistance to you."

I wrapped my one arm around him and hugged tightly. "I need you as much now as ever, Merlin. I hope your bag of tricks is full."

"I thought he could sleep with us at Coroticus's hall, so he wouldn't be so lonely," Bedevere said, but a thought came to me and I stopped him with a hand.

"No, I will sleep in Elafius's cell; perhaps it will bring me an understanding of this affair."

"Perhaps," Bedevere agreed with a bearded grin. "But perhaps you will just wake up chilled in the morning." *Monachi* were not allowed to have fires in their cells. It was said to be an old tradition, emphasizing the suffering *monachi* endured for their Christ. In reality it was to keep the *monachi* from burning down their huts. They tended to be somewhat forgetful in that regard, and the ground was marked in places with the burned remnants of such a *monachus*.

"Perhaps, but Merlin will need a place to rest, and I would have him do that in your chamber. I need silence, to sort out this matter."

"And I am too loud for you," Merlin muttered. "If you could but hear the ravings of his snores and the blasts of his . . ."

"I have, my friend." Bedevere smiled broadly, a rare occurrence. "And yours as well."

"So this is the famous Merlin of whom I have heard so much." Patrick's voice crackled over the gathering as he joined us, with Arthur beside him.

Merlin tensed for a moment, but when the old *episcopus* clapped a hand on his back, I noted that Merlin relaxed. In moments the two men were laughing.

This boded well for us, I thought. I felt certain that Gwilym would give us the key to Elafius's demise. In my heart I felt bad, because whoever Gwilym was, Coroticus and Rhiannon seemed duty bound to keep it hidden. Whatever fate might befall them for preserving that secret was sad, but I suspected that they knew the hazard of their actions. I felt especially bad about Rhiannon. She was a beautiful woman, one with spirit. I could not deny my feelings for Ygerne, but those growing for Rhiannon were stronger yet. As she was a sister of the community, though, I knew I would never see a chance to grow those feelings yet deeper.

In actuality, the death of Elafius was more than likely a

simple affair. Coroticus's hurried plea and the lies about Gwilym's true identity merely made it seem more ominous. In my experience with men of the religious orders, they tended to puff up small matters, as a flat goat flagon would grow thrice its size when filled.

The more I turned it over in my mind, the more I thought that Patrick's quandary was the most critical. If I had any skills at defense, Patrick was a man worthy to expend them on.

We were in something of an oddly festive mood, considering the burial of Brother Elafius. But Patrick's mission had become less important, it seemed, and since he had confided to me his real reason for coming to our island, I think a great weight had been lifted from him. Perhaps he had dreaded his meeting with Elafius and confessing to his boyhood friend. Perhaps in Elafius's death had lain some relief, but I realized that I was being unkind.

Over my shoulder, I noticed that Bedevere had pulled Arthur to the side with a note of concern on his face. I joined them and immediately observed that Arthur was tugging on the ends of his mustache. He did this only when something nagged at him.

"A problem?" I queried.

"I am not certain. There is something out of sorts but I cannot reckon it. Lauhiir is too anxious to please, and he seems well equipped for a young noble in his first command. The village and abbey seem too prosperous for these times."

I had been so busy with the matter of Elafius and handling Patrick that I had forgotten my own curiosity about these things. "What make you of this?"

Arthur shrugged. "I am not sure. I had hoped that you would be finished with this Elafius affair and could apply that brain of yours to something more important."

"Be at ease, my lord. I suspect that by morning all will be settled. The old *monachus* Gwilym will not avoid Bedevere's patrols tomorrow for long. His companions will weary of the task and, besides, *monachi* are trained to serve the Christ, not to evade pursuers."

"You believe he killed Elafius?"

"I believe he was the only one with reason and no one can say he didn't kill him. I believe that the yew extract was left to implicate Rhiannon. But I doubt her complicity though I also know that two people had a hand in his death." I paused. "Until I can question Gwilym, this is all I know."

"Now, tell me of this commission and why you need to accompany Patrick to Castellum Marcus."

"Arthur, I promised Patrick that I would go to Castellum Marcus with him and counsel him."

Arthur's expression surpassed annoyance. "I need you here! Besides, he has been no friend to the nobles of Britannia. Make your apologies and remain with me."

"But Arthur, you told him I would have your leave to go."

He brushed a leaf from his sleeve as if he were brushing my argument aside. "You know little of religion."

Aye, this was true. But Arthur wanted me to disappoint Patrick. He had no wish to do so himself.

"My lord, he is a man in trouble. Should it matter that he has opposed you from time to time? And remember, Ceredig deserved every word Patrick said against him. The man lined up new believers in the Christ and slit their throats, Arthur!"

The Rigotamos did not like my defiance, but he had never liked it. He suffered it because he knew that, like him, I tried to do the right thing. "Why would he wish you to go with him to

Castellum Marcus? What is happening there that could possibly involve you?"

"He is being called before a special commission, meeting at Castellum Marcus, to answer charges of rape and murder newly levied against him. If his accusers succeed, they will strip his bishopric from him."

"When did this happen? Where? Among the Scotti?"

"No, no. Many, many years ago, before Patrick was taken as a *servi*. A young girl was murdered and violated, and Patrick now stands accused." I was careful in my wording. There was no need to violate Patrick's confidence.

"And he wishes you to investigate a murder that happened before any of us were born?"

"He wishes me to be his counselor only, my lord. Arthur, it has become obvious to me that the church operates much as a band of lords. No one lord should be perceived to be more popular or more famous. Now there are elements in the church who believe that Patrick has reached such a renown. They hope to drag him down, no matter how old the evidence. Please, Arthur, it will take but a few days at most. Whatever is happening here will keep for that long. And when I return, I will be able to concentrate more fully on these strange doings. In truth, I have noted an uncommon prosperity." Then, I remembered the little thief Llynfann, and his errand. "Early this morning, I dispatched Llynfann to find the source of all of this bounty imported by Coroticus and Lauhiir." I looked about but saw no sign of him. "Bedevere, have you seen any hint of the little bandit?"

"No, Malgwyn. But I have not been looking."

Arthur seemed to feel better upon hearing that I had not been blind to the situation. He relaxed, his shoulders sagging a bit. "So, you expect it to be only a few days?"

"A week at the most."

"Then I will gather my forces and return to Castellum Arturius when we have settled with this Gwilym. To remain longer at this time would cause too much curiosity. And if Lauhiir is up to some evil, I would not have him know that I am suspicious. Not yet, at any rate."

"A question, Arthur?" Bedevere spoke up. "So the village at Ynys-witrin is prosperous? So Lauhiir seems wealthier than perhaps he should be?"

It was then that I learned to value Bedevere as much as Kay. While Kay's friendship and loyalty knew no bounds, Bedevere, though quiet, was not afraid to seek out the weaknesses in an argument and force you to face them. His queries were good and valid ones. Where Kay was often led by his heart, Bedevere spoke with his brain.

Arthur's mouth curled into a frown, drawing his mustache down. "False prosperity is no prosperity at all and is but misery waiting to befall those who experience it." Arthur had an ability to see beyond the immediate, to look to the future. Not into it. But to it. Some gave Merlin the ability to foresee the future, but he did not. He never claimed such a thing. Others claimed it for him.

The servants were hurrying platters and jugs from the abbot's kitchen to his hall. Tonight was to be a proper feasting in honor of Arthur and Patrick. No chanting. No reading of sacred texts. From the smells wafting past us, I knew we would be treated to the finest wines and foods, finer even than that provided by Arthur at his table. Amphorae from Syria and Italy, filled to the brim with wine, were carted across the muddy pathway. I saw platters of oysters, the moist, white skin of freshly dressed chickens, and pink pork loins seasoned and ready for the hearth, bowls of young vegetables harvested by the *monachi*, fresh-baked bread from the abbot's ovens.

In two big pits outside the kitchen, heaped with glowing, orange coals, two of the servants dug carefully, to the accompaniment of sparks and rising smoke. Moments later, they gingerly removed one, two, and then three long, ash-gray objects, and my mouth immediately began watering. This was a dish I dearly loved. Salmon, stuffed with plums, bread, and herbs, covered in salt dough and buried beneath an open fire. The dough baked hard and kept all of the juices inside. My Gwyneth, my long-dead wife, had cooked salmon in this manner, and every time I ate it, it reminded me of her, brought her close to me in good memories.

I was grateful to see several *mortaria* carried across, bowls with special knobs in the bottom in which food was ground for those whose teeth were worn down. My problem lay not with my teeth but with my difficulty in cutting my food, so I favored the pastelike food that I could spoon into my mouth.

"Savoring the food already, Malgwyn?" Merlin's cracked voice broke over my shoulder, and I felt the light touch of his age-spotted hand land on my arm. I turned and by his side I saw Patrick, fewer wrinkles in his face now. He seemed younger, happier.

"And what have you and the *episcopus* been discussing?"

Merlin winked. "He has converted me to this Christianity, and I have promised to persuade our Lord Arthur that all nonbelievers should be foresworn from drinking alcohol until they convert."

Even Patrick laughed at this. "If that were true," he added, "I would no longer have a mission."

Coroticus, wearing his abbot's furs and jewelry, appeared

from his hall. I smiled inwardly at his show of wealth. He knew that it would, or should, infuriate Patrick. I reckoned it as the only way Coroticus could show his independence, to show his displeasure with the way we had treated him.

"Welcome to my hall. It is a bit early for our evening meal, but I invite you to enter and enjoy some warmed and spiced wine. I expect Lord Liguessac and the sister Rhiannon to join us. The brothers will eat separately from us tonight so that they may keep to their practices, and so that we may be free to discuss those matters of an earthly nature that concern us."

I suspected that that was Coroticus's way of saying that we would talk about Elafius's murder, and perhaps it might signal the beginning of some negotiation for the surrender of Gwilym. For that, I could not blame him. He was sworn to protect the brethren, and Patrick would denounce him for betraying that as quickly as he would for harboring a murderer.

I smiled, though, to know that Rhiannon would be among us. Part of me was excited by her. Part of me hated that I was. Ygerne was ever present in my mind, but the shade of my brother guarded her and kept me from pressing my suit. It was silly. This I knew. Perhaps if I had not so neglected my brother and his family for so many years, I would not feel so strangely about it. No matter the cause, I did feel odd, and until I could conquer that feeling I could not bring myself to let Ygerne know my heart. Heart. A man's heart is a creature of conflict, and none more so than mine.

We went in then and found seats around Coroticus's long table. His servants hustled about, filling our beakers from bowls of steaming wine. The beakers all matched, and I recognized them as products of Gaul. I knew that they had not been cheap. Another sign of that pesky prosperity that worried Arthur.

As if he had heard, I saw the Rigotamos cock his head to one side and look straight at me, jiggling his beaker in his hand. I nodded, but so slightly that only Arthur would have noticed. He was telling me that tonight, this night, I was back working as his counselor, not in a *coito* with Patrick.

I took up my beaker and enjoyed the scent of the fennel and clove mixed with the steaming, pale red wine. One sip told me that it was only lightly watered, and that the spices enhanced its flavor nicely. As I drank, I saw Rhiannon sweep into the hall, her long robe lofting behind her. She wore a kind of wrap around her head and a silver cross at her neck.

Almost on her heels, Lauhiir hurried in, his face red and puffy and his tunic stained with sweat. He stumbled to a halt before Coroticus and bowed. "My apologies, my lord abbot, for being so late. Pressing business on the Tor delayed me."

Coroticus nodded as did Arthur, and Lauhiir hustled to his seat. My father told me that the old Romans used to lie on couches around their tables. I smiled at the thought. No wonder their empire was falling apart. Even Arthur, for all his devotion to things Roman, would never countenance such luxury, such softness. But that was the soldier in him. For us, the realities of life made a luxury of social niceties. We ate when we had food. Starved when we had none. Whether we did that standing up or sitting down was of little consequence to us. But to eat lying down implied that we were sick or near death. I chuckled out loud at the thought. For what had the Roman empire been but sick and near death? The softer they got, my father had said, the closer to ruin they had come.

Now that all the guests were present, the servants streamed in with baskets and baskets of hard-boiled eggs and oysters still in their blackish-gray shells.

As they worked, I glanced around and looked, really, at Coroticus's hall for the first time. Strangely, I noticed that there was little difference between this, an abbot's hall, and Arthur's hall, that of a king. Banners covered the sturdy timber walls. One held what I took to be a portrait of the Christ set against the Greek letters *chi* and *rho*. Others held figures of the cross. I had seen the same thing on floor mosaics in old Roman buildings. These designs were woven skillfully into a long cloth banner. This bothered me. Skilled weavers, at least this skilled, were not many in our lands, and importing such would not be cheap.

A wall at one end blocked off Coroticus's suite of chambers, where Bedevere and I had stayed the night before. I looked back toward the entrance and found my nose but inches from Rhiannon's. So lost was I in surveying Coroticus's hall, I had not noticed that she had circled the table and slipped into a chair next to me.

"You are not half so grim and ugly when you are not questioning people, Master Malgwyn," she teased me. "What causes you to study the walls?"

"I wondered where the abbot obtained his wall hangings." I turned away, resuming staring at the wall.

Next, I felt her breath, warm and scented with chewed mint leaves, blow on my neck. The hairs rose and a flush spread up my face. I leaned away and turned toward her finally.

"You do not act like a sister of the Christ, my lady." And, in truth, she did not.

She was beautiful. Free of the cosmetics of chalk and berry juice, her skin showed no blemish. Her defiant chin, thrust out toward me, was one of her most appealing attractions. I truly longed for her. And this I could not show.

"Are you and Coroticus intent on enraging Patrick?"

She smiled and nodded across the table to Bedevere. "Why say you this?"

"Your clothing. It is just that kind of thing that makes Patrick angry. His has been a life of simple things, of hunger and deprivation. For him, sacrifice is the way to the Christ. For him, luxuries are the province of the corrupt, fine jewelry"— and I reached and held her ornate cross in my palm—"the properties of the evil."

She looked away, her eyes now focusing on the wall. "I would argue that if one truly loves the Christ, then displaying His symbols, in whatever manner, is praiseworthy. That I appreciate fine workmanship should not matter."

"As you wish," I said. In truth, I cared little about her clothing. "How did a sister come into possession of such an ornate cross? Did you not take a vow of poverty?"

"I did, but it was a gift from the abbot when I took over the sisters' community, a symbol of my new office."

"He seems not to have deprived himself either," I said sourly.

"And why should he? He is the abbot, not one of the *monachi*. His station requires him to attend councils and feasts. You cannot command respect in tattered rags. Besides, he comes from a rich family."

I knew one beggar, his clothes soiled and smelly, whom a king raised high, but I decided not to mention it. Such would seem as bragging, and I had nothing to brag about.

"What bothers me, Rhiannon, is that Coroticus has only recently begun adorning himself with such trinkets. And now he is sharing his bounty with you."

She stared at me then, with the most intent look I had ever

received from anyone. My neck and forehead grew wet, and it was not from the heat of the fire. "I have not bedded Coroticus, and I do not intend to, though he would welcome it most heartily. He is too much the politician for my taste, and one should never find one's pleasure too close to home."

I recoiled, but slightly. I did not expect such candor. "What of your vow of chastity?"

"That is not required, only suggested."

"Strongly suggested." I was thinking of Guinevere and her expulsion from the same community this woman now headed. Obviously, many things had changed with Rhiannon's arrival.

Rhiannon shrugged at my comment. She seemed to look away, but I saw her eyes flit back and forth as she furtively watched me. But Coroticus had risen and stolen my attention.

"My lord Arthur, *episcopus* Patrick, lords and lady." He added that last with a smile at Rhiannon. "It is my pleasure to offer this small bounty for your nourishment."

This "small bounty" was more than Arthur or any lord of the *consilium* could offer. Yet another puzzling sign of prosperity.

As more delicacies like dates, which must have been shipped in casks from Egypt, and meats were served, the talk turned to taxes and the church's obligation. Coroticus argued that the church should be exempt from taxes. Arthur asked, simply, why? And with that came talk of Arthur's church. I sighed. Patrick remained neutral

While this debate, which Lauhiir seemed to observe with great amusement, continued, I watched as one of Arthur's soldiers slipped quietly beside Bedevere and whispered in his ear. He immediately rose, and without begging Arthur's leave, strode to the door. I followed, glad to leave the argument at the table behind.

CHAPTER TEN

At the door I saw Illtud, one of Arthur's leading command-ers. A tall, handsome man, with flowing hair somewhere between red and brown, he had brought two troops of horse at Arthur's call, though the Rigotamos had just asked for one. Ill-tud was the kind of officer a general, or a king, needed. He did not hesitate to apply his own common sense to his orders. And caution was his byword. If Arthur asked for one troop, he would bring two.

Now, his copper hair was darkened by sweat and a look of concern marked his face. "Malgwyn, 'tis good to see you." He nodded to me, but he was clearly distracted and turned his attention to Bedevere immediately. "The last patrol has still not returned. I seek permission to send another ten-man patrol to seek them out."

"More than just this bothers you, Illtud," I interrupted. "What else is there? Why do you worry about a late patrol so?"

"My men are trained to send a rider back to report on their status. If they have bedded down for the night, one of them would have been dispatched back here. But no rider has re-turned. The area they searched had only a couple of villages where the old *monachus* could hide. Two hours and their search should have been completed. They should have been the first patrol back, Malgwyn!"

I saw then Illtud's concern. A hunt for an old *monachus* would have hardly gotten the soldiers' blood up. They would probably have been looking for a reason to give up the search to return to the relative comforts of the abbey, not camping in the forest.

Among Mordred's troops or David's or even Lauhiir's, such a mission would be an excuse to raid the local villages. But Arthur's men were of a different breed and training. Those of his men who committed crimes against the people were treated harshly; whippings, or even execution, if the crimes were serious enough. Arthur believed that if the people saw the army as their protector, their defender, then they would welcome them, support them. He would have to worry little about the people selling information to his enemies.

Bedevere frowned. "Go. Send the patrol, but make it twenty. I want a large enough body to fight off most any threat they might meet. And send a rider to Castellum Artorius. Muster two, no three, more troops and hurry them here. I will advise the Rigotamos of this."

Frustration painted the air with a dark hue. Beyond the door, I saw the faint glow of mist settling in around the hills that marked Ynys-witrin. We were frustrated, the three of us, because we knew that something was amiss, but we could not fathom it. Not then. Not yet.

Illtud disappeared into the blackening night, and Bedevere and I turned back to the feasting hall, the air inside flavored with chicken, pork, garum, and a light veneer of wood smoke.

From the way that Arthur and Coroticus were avoiding each other, I assumed that their discussion on the cruciform church had concluded in its usual fashion. Patrick and Merlin were head to head in some conversation that had them both laughing. It was not often that Merlin encountered someone as old as he. Despite his fatherlike closeness to Arthur, Merlin had never embraced the Christ. Like me, he was not much for any religion. For me it was part reluctance to accept something I could not see and part a belief that I was unworthy, ever unworthy.

I rejoiced to see them have such fun. Merlin had been haunted by digestive problems for a fortnight, but he seemed good on this eve. Patrick had the problems of the world bundled on his back. His life's work was to be judged over the next days against an accident of youth. One of Merlin's strengths was his charm, his unending supply of stories and inventions. Immersed in them, Patrick was able to forget his own troubles for a few hours.

A hand touched my thigh when I resumed my chair. I turned and saw a familiar look in Rhiannon's eyes. Despite everything, I wanted this woman. Were she a witch, she could have no more securely enchanted me.

"What of the search for Gwilym?"

I wanted to tell her of the missing patrol, but I knew that would be an error. "Nothing yet. I'm sure we will have him by morning."

"I still do not believe he killed Elafius," she repeated with conviction.

"I would like to believe you, Rhiannon. He did not seem a murderer to me when I spoke with him. Aye, he is a likable man. But the facts point in his direction."

"At least some of them," she conceded. As if to emphasize her point, she retrieved an intricately carved bone pin from her gown and secured her hair. I thought it ornate for a sister. Those entrancing eyes caught mine and she smiled. "Another gift from the abbot."

I raised my eyebrows. "He is generous."

She lowered her head with a wicked smile. "He is hopeful."

The chuckle burst out in spite of myself. She had a spirit that I could learn to love.

"Are you sleeping here?"

"No," I said. "I will stay in Elafius's cell. Perhaps his walls will speak to me."

At that moment, Patrick rose to speak. A smile still marked his lips. "I wish to thank you, lord abbot, for your hospitality during my visit. My short sojourn here has shown me that the reports of Pelagianism have been overexaggerated. While there may be some among the *monachi* who favor the teachings of Pelagius, I find that the church will be pleased with how the way to salvation is being taught here."

Coroticus smiled and nodded once to acknowledge the compliment. I wished that young Gildas were there to hear the unspoken reprimand. But he had been banished to eating with the other *monachi*, Coroticus's way of reminding him of his station.

"I am equally pleased to tell you that I will be reporting to your *episcopus* that I find Lord Arthur's election as Rigotamos a hopeful sign that order will soon return to our land. And that the persecution of Christians will stop."

Although Lauhiir looked as if he had eaten a bad oyster, the others seemed pleased at Patrick's announcement, even Rhiannon. While I had grown an appreciation for Patrick, I thought it rather pompous for him to make such pronouncements. But then the church seemed to be fertile ground for pomposity.

"And finally, Coroticus has informed me that he has commissioned a proper stone cross to bless Lord Liguessac's fortress on the Tor. This is a good thing and will bring God's favor to his efforts."

Despite his upset stomach, Lauhiir managed a pained smile. I enjoyed his discomfort.

"Our Lord, the Christ, has truly blessed this place. When I depart to confer with Dubricius and Severus at Castellum Marcus—a journey Master Malgwyn will make with me as my counselor—I will have aught but good things to say of this abbey."

"And poor Elafius?" Coroticus queried, a touch of eagerness in his voice. "What of Malgwyn's charge here?"

Patrick smiled at the abbot. "Malgwyn has assured me that that affair will be settled on the morn." I appreciated the sour look Patrick's reply put on the abbot's face, and I attempted to smile in return but I doubt that it was convincing. Then was not the time to talk about missing patrols and missing *monachi*, however.

Moments later, the feast was finished. No late-night drinking bouts for this audience. As we all said our farewells, I felt Rhiannon's breath on my ear. She leaned in close and whispered, "Leave your door unlatched this eve." Then, she was gone.

Arthur motioned for me before I could react. "Bedevere has told me of the patrol. What think you of this?"

"I do not know what to think, my lord. I know only that your men are well trained, and that they would not ignore all that they have been taught unless something dire happened. But that is more an informed guess than a true analysis. We must wait for word from your search party."

"He's right, Arthur. Let Illtud's men do their work. The morn may bring answers. I have sent for three more troop of horse."

Arthur tugged at his beard and nodded in distracted approval. "That is prudent." He turned to me. "Malgwyn, should this not be resolved tomorrow, you may have to disappoint Patrick." He raised a gloved hand to stop my protest. "The situation has changed, Malgwyn. If aught has happened to this missing patrol, then I will need you here to help sort it out."

He was right. For some reason, I reached to my belt and felt comfort at finding my dagger secured there. "I will be in Elafius's cell tonight, Rigotamos. Perhaps some solitude in his chamber will bring me answers as to his death."

At that, we parted ways. I trudged back out the front door and headed down a path marked by lit torches toward the dead *monachus*'s cell.

"Malgwyn!" I heard the cry and looked across the compound. Patrick was seeking me out.

"Yes, *episcopus*."

"We should meet early on the morrow and plan our day."

"Agreed. Sleep well, Patrick."

"And you, my friend."

I continued on and entered Elafius's cell, lighting an oil lamp. It had been straightened some, but nothing had been removed that I could see. The scrolls were stacked neatly on a table now, rather than scattered about the floor. There seemed to be fewer of them though. I ran through them quickly. Those on metallurgy were missing. That was odd. I thought it a bit strange that old Elafius would offer his aid to Lauhiir, but not strange at all that Lauhiir would need help. Mining had fallen by the wayside in the wake of the Roman departure and those with expertise in the different processes of smelting tin, iron, and lead were few.

First Ambrosius and then Arthur had pushed for the re-opening of the mines and especially the export of the tin as a way to bring more money into Britannia. Lauhiir's charge had included revitalizing the tin mining in this region, and Lord Mark had committed to reopening the tin mines near Castellum Marcus. Mark, though, had been reluctant to do so with his son, Tristan, held captive at Castellum Arturius.

I thought of the *denarius*, but as I reached for my pouch I heard the leather hinges on the door creak. A hooded figure slipped in, quickly securing the door behind. Rhiannon.

She slipped easily out of the hooded cloak and laid it on the table, keeping her back to me.

"You have information for me?" I asked, my voice catching in my throat.

"I did not come to trade information, Malgwyn. I came here for you."

I narrowed my eyes and assumed an indifference that I did not feel. "For me, my lady? I am naught but a servant of the Rigotamos."

She moved across the room smoothly, touching the furniture lightly, almost as if she were not even aware that she had. After a moment, she turned and gave me the most direct look a woman had ever bestowed on me, her full lips parted just slightly. "You are a man who fears neither God nor man, king nor peasant. I have never met such as you, and I would have you."

Though I had suspected this, her directness surprised me. "Lady Rhiannon, I have done many things in my life, but bedding a woman pledged to the Christ is not one of them."

"Are you certain? I am told that you have not always been so honorable in your conquests. Nor is it your family's habit to hold such vows inviolable."

Before I knew it, my arm had pinned her to the wall, below her throat. I had no wish to kill her, but this was a lesson she must learn, she had to learn. "You will not speak so of Guinevere. She is a finer woman than any in the land, and I include you!"

But rather than fear in her eyes, I saw laughter and a sparkle in her eye, and I smelled the fresh mint on her breath as a hint of dampness shone on her lip.

And her hands did not push me away, but grasped my tunic and pulled me closer, pulled me tight against her breasts.

And I took her.

The moon was full and pale yellow. I could see it through the cracks in the door. Rhiannon's smooth body, unmarred by child-birth, lay next to me. I started to make a joke about how little this chamber had been used for such activities, but then I real-ized that I had no idea about Elafius's habits.

I felt a strange sadness about Ygerne. My feelings for her had been true. But there would always be the specter of Cune-glas hanging above us, I feared. Rhiannon brought no such burden, but for her leadership among the sisters. Suddenly, I realized that Arthur and I now shared more than just the mem-ory of battles won and lost.

"I must go soon," Rhiannon said softly, her hand resting on my chest. "It would not do for me to be missing from the women's community at the day's first prayer."

I lifted myself to a sitting position. "Then you've picked the wrong night. We have doubled the guard at all entrances to the abbey and across the *vallum* as well as set a roving patrol. You would be better off to stay here and slip out once people are about their daily routine. Otherwise, all will know that you left here in the middle of the night."

She smiled and shook her head. "No. My presence would be missed in our community. Besides, I have ways to get across the *vallum* unseen."

Part of me wanted to ask her about those ways, but another, stronger part was afraid of the answer.

Holding a fur around her, she stood and retrieved her gown. "You are a good man, Malgwyn. I would see you again. I could fall . . ." But her sentence remained unfinished as she turned away.

I rose and caressed her neck. "We have much to learn about each other. Do not say things that you might regret later."

She looked up into my face then and a soft smile grew on hers. "Who said that I would ever have cause to regret any words I chose to speak?"

"Belligerent to the end, my Rhiannon." And I pulled her back against me.

"I like the way you say that, Malgwyn." Then she spun away. "But I have no time to show my appreciation."

A flurry of robes and gowns later and Rhiannon was dressed and ready to leave. She quickly kissed my cheek and slipped through the door without another word.

Twenty-four hours before, I would not have guessed how the day would end. Rhiannon was the first woman I had been with since my brother's death. Indeed, she was the first woman to attract my attention, besides Ygerne. Most women I saw held no interest for me, nor I for them. A man missing an arm or leg or hand was deemed of little value in our world; indeed, some believed them cursed. The women that I had pleasured myself with usually did so for the price of a wineskin or a cheap bauble. I wanted nothing more than the pleasure of the flesh, so I received no more. I never believed a good woman would show any interest in me and so I showed none for them.

Except for Ygerne. But I had been fond of her long before I lost my arm. Now, I wondered why the sister had so easily captured my attention. She was outspoken, independent, and a woman of unusual strength, much like Ygerne. But there was a lust to her that was also unusual.

As I lay back amongst the furs, still damp from our ardor and still laden with our scents, I decided not to question the path my life had taken. When the morning arrived, I would have more on my mind than Rhiannon, and it would be some time before I might have the opportunity to explore that path again.

My life was about to end! That was the first fleeting thought as I felt the hand on my shoulder. But I swung my left leg even as I pulled the dagger from its hiding place amongst the furs. In seconds, I was atop my intruder with my knife at his throat.

"Malgwyn!" It was Bedevere, his voice strained from the tip of my blade.

I spun around and got off his chest, sitting back on my haunches. "Do not assume, Bedevere, that because I am lacking an arm that I also lack the ability to defend myself." My breath came in deep draughts from the fright. "What has happened?"

My old friend sat up and rubbed his throat. "I will not make the same mistake again," he croaked. "There has been news, Malgwyn, of the missing patrol."

I shook my head to clear away the last remnants of sleep. From the taste of the breeze and the look of the sky, I took it to be an hour, perhaps two, before daybreak. "Did they lose their way?"

Bedevere dragged himself over to a wall and leaned back. I could not fathom the look on his face. It was one not of sadness, but almost of resignation. "They are dead."

"What!" I struggled to my feet. "Where? How?"

"Be silent, Malgwyn! That is why I came for you; we do not wish the entire village to know."

I paid heed to his warning and sat back down. "Tell me."

"Illtud's patrol discovered two riderless horses with Arthur's mark on them. They backtracked the horses to a place at the end of an old trail two hours to the south of here, near a stream. Illtud found our men's bodies hidden under some brush.

"Arthur sent me for you. He must stay here to keep this thing silent, but he must know who has done this. That is your task. If it involves this old *monachus*, that is one thing, but if it does not, that calls forth yet a stranger answer and one that may have grave consequences."

"Is the place protected?"

"Illtud himself commands the watchmen."

"Bring forth Merlin, but do not wake Coroticus or Patrick."

"As you wish." Anyone but Bedevere would ask why I sent for an old man such as Merlin, but no one knew the forest like Merlin did. No one could read the signs left by man or animal as clearly as my old friend. He had spent too many years as a child, surviving in the forest. "I have a horse prepared for you." He reached down and picked up my tunic, his nose wrinkling. "Malgwyn, have you started wearing women's scented water?"

"I am not at liberty to say, master of the horse. If you ask again, I have the Rigotamos's permission to remove your head."

Bedevere smiled. "I doubt that, but each of us has a right to his little secrets."

"We've wasted enough time."

"That we have, Master Malgwyn. Let's away."

Once we arrived, it took me less than an hour to discover who had murdered Arthur's men. And most of that time was spent in riding to the secluded glen where Illtud and his men guarded the bodies of their comrades. The site lay just off a well-traveled road, across the bridge over the River Brue, and between Ynys-witrin and Lindinis, once a prosperous Roman town. The path was worn deeply, ending near a stream where four large fires had been built. The grass had been worn away all around the stream.

I could tell at a glance that tin ore was being panned from the stream, and from the look of the big fires, it was being smelted as well. A rickety shed stood to one side and a heavy wooden table was before it. I looked first at it and saw broken bits of metal, familiar bits of metal, decorating the top.

"Malgwyn! Here!" Illtud directed me behind the shed. There were three soldiers in a bloody pile.

I shook my head. Regretfully, I was more used to this kind of death than that of Eleonore's or Elafius's. Carefully studying their relative positions, I got three of Illtud's men to help separate the bodies so I could better view their wounds.

They had dismounted before meeting their murderers. Only one had been struck from the front. The other two had taken broadsword strokes across their backs from two right-handed attackers. A look of shock was frozen on the face of the man who had seen his assailants. I was saddened by the mustachioed face of the dead man. I did not know his name, but he had been helpful and respectful in times past.

Leaning down, I hefted the arms and legs. The stiffening had come and gone, so these men had been killed not long after they had started their search. Something in the severity of the wounds told me that their attackers had been both surprised and frightened by Arthur's men. Frightened, yet very decisive about what course of action to take.

Men who are uncertain often make lighter cuts first as if they were pulling the blows. Not in this case. They had followed through almost viciously. When I learned their identities, I felt that I would understand their urgency. I ordered the bodies covered and went back to the shed. I was becoming convinced that Lauhiir's tin-smelting operation was at the heart of Elafius's death and the death of these three men.

"They dismounted here, Malgwyn." I heard a crackly but familiar voice across the clearing. Merlin had arrived.

"How do you know? There are enough horses here to mount a campaign against Horsa and Hengist."

"I had them keep their horses to the perimeter, Malgwyn," Bedevere assured me. "I remembered how you discovered where Eleonore was murdered."

"Sorry, Bedevere. My humors are out of sorts."

"And whose would not be, Malgwyn? All of this mystery. Murder," Merlin muttered. "It misted last night and the ground was already damp. No mud, but the ground was soft."

I saw what he did. Hoofprints, the front ones cutting in deeper when the horses came almost uniformly to a halt, lined up at the edge of the clearing. The soldiers' *caligae* with their Roman-style hobnails had left their distinctive marks. Other boot prints were present but their soles held no hobnails.

Following the steps, I could see the soldiers cross the clearing, stopping at the table. Something happened there. The feet without nails had, one pair anyway, spun around and begun to run toward the rear of the shed. I followed, and at the back edge, just in the shadows, was a pool of blood, black and hardening. Two of the soldiers were killed here.

The third, following closely behind them, turned and headed back to the horses. He may have gotten his sword out, for I saw two more great sprays of blood, misting the ground as an arrow pointing to one spot. This would seem to match the soldier struck between the shoulders from behind. His attacker did not wait until he turned about.

In the sandy soil, I could see where he had lain, and I discerned two separate sets of boots on either side. They dragged him back to where he lay now, behind the shed piled upon the others.

"Whoever they were," I said in a half-whisper, "our men knew them or knew of them."

"Why say you that?" Bedevere's voice, half in my ear, scared me.

"They dismounted, Bedevere. Their footprints show that they followed someone to the rear of the building, no sign of running. Only then was there any clue of a struggle. They followed someone that they had no reason to distrust and died for their misjudgment."

"How? How do you do this, Malgwyn?" Illtud asked, shaking his woolly head in disbelief.

I found a stump and sat down. "It is only a question of

looking beyond the dead to see how they got there. There is no magic to it. Much of it is just common sense."

"I can add something to the mix, Malgwyn," Merlin said, holding a piece of thick cloth in his hand. "I found it in the crook of a branch. It must have torn off in their haste to escape."

Bedevere rushed up and snatched it from the old man. "Malgwyn! This is . . ."

I rose. "Yes, it's a piece of a tunic from one of Lauhiir's men." Lauhiir arrayed his men in stunning white tunics with a green cross. This fragment showed a part of one of the cross's points.

Holding the cloth in my one hand, I stood and surveyed the area before me, the tin mining, the smelting, the large work-table. I went into the shed with Merlin and Bedevere on my heels. In one corner, clearly marked in the dirt, were the outlines of six oblong boxes. Their edges had cut deeply into the dirt, as if other, equally heavy boxes had been laid atop.

"Malgwyn, though I am not your equal in sorting these things out, I believe I can help with this," offered Merlin.

"Please."

"You have tin mining and smelting, fragments of both tin and silver and bronze, and a place where big, heavy crates were stacked," he began.

"And," I said, picking up his line of thought, "you have men willing to kill to cover up their activities. And this." I pulled the silver *denarius* that I had found in Elafius's cell from my pouch. Reaching down and taking a ragged piece of rock from the ground, I scraped the coin's surface. Its bright silver proved only a thin skin, beneath which lay a dull gray.

"They have been forging coins!" Bedevere proclaimed. "Lauhiir has been forging coins."

"That makes many things clear," I said. From the day of his

189

appointment to command the Tor, I had thought that it was like putting the thief in charge of the treasure room. But his family was prominent and had supported Ambrosius strongly. Our land was so fragmented, so split by families and factions, that such loyalties could not be forgotten. Politics weighed heavily in every decision the Rigotamos made, even when common sense argued against it.

"So, this is the source of that prosperity that bothers Arthur so much," Bedevere said into the silence.

"It must be so," I said. Suddenly it all became clear. Lauhiir had been purchasing his luxuries with his forged coins. The coins circulated in the village and eventually a goodly number found their way into the church's hands, hence Coroticus's ability to so lavishly provide for his table. It was a false prosperity and Arthur had been right to worry. No doubt, Lauhiir explained his sudden wealth of coins as profit from the sale of tin. Tin was valuable, but not as valuable as silver, and that is what the receiver of the coins thought he was getting.

This solved the question of Elafius's murder. In helping Lauhiir's efforts at tin mining and smelting, the old *monachus* must have discovered the forging. He would have felt honor bound to report it to Coroticus, and so Lauhiir had had the old man killed to keep him quiet.

But now it had turned into something much more evil. For in this lame attempt to conceal a crime that could be forgiven, Lauhiir's men had committed the unforgivable. They had killed three of the Rigotamos's soldiers. The punishment for that was death. And while the actual doers of this deed must be punished, so must their commander, Lauhiir.

I heard shouting and looked up. Bedevere was shouting orders to Illtud, to arrest Lauhiir, I knew. Other men he was dispatching to bring their dead comrades back to the abbey. My strength was all but gone, and I rose slowly from my seat.

As soldiers mounted and rode around us in a bustle of activity, Merlin walked up next to me and hooked his wrinkled hand into the crook of my one good arm.

"Malgwyn?"

"Aye."

"Did you see how deep were the marks those crates left?"

"Aye." I spoke softly.

"They held far more coins than are needed for a bit of food and a few trinkets. And this would not have been his only or even his biggest hoard. That would be on the Tor. Something else is happening here. That many coins call for a larger purpose."

I nodded. He was right. And unless Lauhiir was quickly captured, sorting out that purpose might be beyond my abilities. Patrick. He would speak honestly and from experience about the ways of nobles. I trusted Arthur, but in this I needed an objective mind, someone who did not hold nobles in awe. Yes, Patrick. I would seek his counsel.

But I never got the chance to put his counsel in play. For, not two hours later, when I arrived at the cell appointed to Patrick, no voice bade me enter, and when I pulled the rough-hewn wooden door back, I was met not by the greetings or the grumblings of the aged *episcopus*, but by his very dead corpse sprawled on the floor.

CHAPTER ELEVEN

I had noticed, over the years, that death diminished a man, stole his essence, left him small and pale. Not Patrick. Patrick looked as solemn and dignified in death as he had in life. And as fierce. Even in death, he retained his size and dignity; even as his life's blood soaked the ground darkly, he was formidable.

He lay on his stomach, his head turned toward the door, his eyes open. They stared at nothing, of course, but I sensed no reproach in them, only an acceptance. The old man had seen his death approaching and did not flinch in its face.

I knelt on the hard-packed earthen floor, the buzz of the crowd outside the door hardly penetrating my confusion and my frustration. That his death was not connected to that of Elafius was simply too bizarre a notion to even countenance. But, back in the glen, it had seemed clear that Lauhiir was responsible for Elafius's death. And I could see no reason for Lauhiir wanting or needing Patrick dead. But two childhood friends, both servants of the Christ, dead within two days of each other at the same place? How could they not be connected?

I rose and turned back to the door; I sent runners, a few of the brothers, to fetch Bedevere and Ider from their errands. Others I sent for Patrick's attendants.

I should have foreseen this; my skin felt tight and my head seemed to burst with guilt. While I worried about goods bought and sold, about corrupt lords, something else, so much simpler, had been going on. Patrick, no matter my own feelings, believed strongly in the Christ. And not just in the divinity of the Christ, but in those beliefs accepted and espoused by the church in Rome. Yet he came to Ynys-witrin not so much to defend the church, but to apologize to an old friend for a horrible error in his youth, an error that was even now threatening his future.

I twisted my head and looked past the dark forms crowding the door and to the hills surrounding. They seemed like a cage to me now, a cage in which had been trapped men, and women, who believed passionately in opposing theories, and I was trapped within a cage as well, a cage of arrogance. This puzzle seemed too much for my poor, addled brain. I had missed something, something I could not fathom, and now another man, a great man, was dead.

"Malgwyn?"

Arthur's voice quietly called me. I didn't turn, just continued staring at Patrick's silent form.

"Bring me a skin of wine, Arthur."

"No."

"I know you mean only good things, my lord. But this man's death lies at my door. I was blind. I am finished. No more playing with people's lives, pretending I am more than I am. Bring me wine and leave me alone."

I heard the rustle of his tunic and felt it brush me as he knelt beside me, and then his hand fell lightly on my shoulder.

"No, Malgwyn. You could not have foreseen this death unless you were a wizard or a prophet. Guinevere and I were wrong the night before, wrong to lead your suspicions away from Rhiannon, wrong to try to divert your focus. It was not you who was wrong. I was wrong."

And that gave me pause more than anything else. For a lord, aye, the Rigotamos himself, to admit that he had been wrong about anything was rare. But Arthur was unlike any Rigotamos there had been, and, I was reasonably certain, unlike any that was yet to come.

He grabbed my elbow and pulled me to my feet. "Outside," he commanded with a jerk of his head, the brown hair flowing freely about his shoulders. I rose as he turned to the door and the crowd parted before him. Bedevere, expressionless as always, stood near the door. "Let no one enter," I told him. He nodded. Ider, at his arm, wore a look of sheer confusion and abject depression. Poor Ider! His young life had left him ill equipped for so many shocks, so soon.

Once away from the crowd, Arthur moved close. "This may not be about my crown, as Eleonore's affair was, but it is at least as important," he said in a low voice. "Think, old friend! Patrick carried influence greater than any other *episcopus* from our lands, greater than even Dubricius. If we do not resolve this matter, the church fathers in Rome will send others to do so.

"Malgwyn, you know I love the Christ and that I worship Him. But you know too that Roman favor is often purchased with a purse, not devotion. One of the ways that I hold my power is to keep new sources of power from arising. If Patrick's death is not resolved, and someone like Germanus is sent here, my enemies may take the opportunity to marry themselves to Rome and hence gain new power. Coroticus and I are not friends, but we know and understand each other. I do not wish to see him replaced. It could harm what peace we now have. Now, forget this talk of drink and bring your focus to bear on this new problem. For I tell you most honestly that I am confused beyond all understanding."

With that, I shook my head to clear it and gazed again at the green hills surrounding Ynys-witrin, a pall of morning mist draping around them. Off to my right, I could see the windswept summit of Wirral Hill, with its lone thorn tree pointing like a finger toward the heavens, planted by Joseph of Arimathea the brothers had taught me; at that moment, I felt as alone as that thorn tree and as weary as those pilgrims of long ago.

Arthur was right. Focus. I had to focus. This was not the killing of the young boy, aye, within this very place. Nor was it the killing of Eleonore within the unruly, messy lanes of Arthur's castle. No, whatever the source of these murders, it ranged from the distant Tor, through the village, and across the abbey and beyond.

I breathed deeply of earth-tainted air and turned back to the hut where Patrick lay. The brothers and others who were gathered round quieted their gossiping and, as they had for Arthur, made way for me.

"Bedevere, send two of your soldiers and Ider to scour the abbey and the village. Ask if anyone saw aught of Patrick last eve. I'll find you when I have finished here."

With my shock behind me, I sent one brother for candles. While the flood of daylight exposed the area just inside the door, the corners of the room remained draped in darkness. Within moments, enough light splayed in dancing fingers from the circle of candles to see inside the shelter.

Poor Patrick! Somehow I felt he was victim to his own beliefs, to his own faith. His had not been an easy life, nor a completely simple one. I knew without his telling me that Patrick's youthful error had contributed greatly to his seeking a life of service to the Christ. I chuckled a morbid sort of chuckle. Were killing someone all it took to send a man down the path of God, I would have worn the cobblestones thin and brittle as cold bread, and I would undoubtedly be the most devout man in all of the world. Too many men had counted my face the last they saw.

To the work at hand. I turned my attention away from the story that was Patrick's life to the body that was Patrick's house on earth. He had been stabbed from behind and allowed to fall to the floor.

It had happened sometime just hours before. Without even moving his body, I could see that where his cheek touched the floor it was dark. And lifting his arm, I saw that it was yet stiff. Casting about, I could see that little was disturbed. Not that Patrick had aught but a pallet on which to sleep. He did not. And his companions had been sheltered in a hut near unto his own. Patrick was not wearing the long robes of his bishopric, but the shorter tunic favored by men for sleeping, tied with a cloth belt at the waist.

A thought struck me and I lifted him by the arm not without great effort. Beneath his privates, the ground was damp in a tiny circle, matching the dark circle on his tunic. I smelled the unmistakable odor of urine, but just a bit, not what a man normally releases when his soul departs his body. Much, much less. Things became a bit clearer.

Rising, I held an oil lamp and studied the hard-packed floor.

Despite the shadows, I thought I could discern small scrapings from behind the door. Now, I understood.

Whoever killed Patrick came to his cell to find the old *episcopus* gone to void himself. He hid behind the door, and when Patrick entered, he moved forward, stabbed him, and laid him on the ground. A man loses all control at the moment of death, but Patrick had little to soil himself with. The killer had then left without touching a thing.

What all of this told me was that whoever killed Patrick was not looking for something among his belongings. This was the act of an assassin. His goal had been to kill Patrick. He had hidden in the shadows and awaited his prey. As I squatted on my heels at Patrick's side, I considered the why of it.

Random killing was no stranger to our lands. But even in those deaths, there was yet a reason—theft, rape, even mere cruelty, but a reason nonetheless. A man of Patrick's stature and disposition made enemies. The old *tyrannus* Ceredig would have especial reason for killing Patrick. The *episcopus* had written an open letter to his soldiers urging them to leave the old devil's service. They did not heed his advice, but that would not deter Ceredig from seeking revenge.

Ceredig's lands lay far away from Ynys-witrin though, and he was an old and ill man now, living off the riches he had stolen from the people. No, Patrick's killer lay close by. I reached deep within my brain, trying to pry loose those things I knew about the old priest. Rhiannon might have reason to kill him, if she were guilty of Elafius's death, or even if she thought that Patrick might lay the old *monachus*'s death at her feet. But she had been with me.

My dear friend Coroticus was hiding something, but

I could not fathom what would cause him to take Patrick's life. Unless Coroticus *was* bedding Rhiannon and she had used her charms to lead him to this. While I was no scholar of religious things, I knew from my days at the abbey that priests and bishops were discouraged from involvement with women. Some *episcopus* named Augustine had declared that when men entered the priesthood they should forsake such earthly pleasures.

Even given all of this, Arthur was still right. Should I be unsuccessful in finding Patrick's killer, the church in Rome would send priests of Germanus's stripe stomping loudly throughout our lands, confiscating the abbey, stripping Coroticus of his position. To kill Patrick in light of that was illogical. All the same, he could not be assumed innocent. Men involved with women were nothing if not illogical.

Setting those thoughts aside for the moment, I continued scanning the small hut. I noticed then a bundle of scrolls lying atop the single table. Unrolling one, I read the title "On the Ruination of the Community of Brethren at Ynys-witrin." Snorting, I turned to the last page and saw the signature of the young Gildas. So this was the epistle that had brought Patrick here. I took a moment to scan it.

Among the more sensational claims by the pretentious little *monachus*, Gildas asserted that upon his arrival at Ynys-witrin he had found unfettered Pelagianism, men of God indulging in pleasures of the flesh (I assumed this was a reference to Coroticus and Rhiannon), and, most interesting of all, an "unholy influence exerted by Arthur, the Rigotamos, and certain of his minions." I could only think that he was referring to Lauhiir in this, but I could not say for certain.

He ended with a plea for Patrick to hurry at all due speed to Ynys-witrin, moaning that had he, Gildas, not arrived when he did the entire island of Brittania might have been lost to Satan. Well, that is not exactly what he said, but the intent was the same.

The thought struck me that perhaps Gildas could have committed these crimes. I did not tarry over the thought long however. The little *monachus* was certainly odious, and he was physically able to plunge a knife in Patrick's back, but he struck me as the kind of man who persuaded others to do his work for him. Not at all like his brothers. Huaill, at least, had been man enough to face Arthur in combat, not shrinking or shirking from the mortal match. Their father, Caw, had been one of the holdouts from the *consilium*, refusing to ally himself and his people with that coalition. Affairs had not broken into open warfare until after Caw's death. Even Celyn had had the courage to confront Arthur face-to-face at his election. Such was not Gildas's way.

Rolling Gildas's missive back up, I turned my attention to another scroll. It too was a letter to Patrick, but this one was from Dubricius at Castellum Marcus, Lord Mark's headquarters. He was asking Patrick to inquire among the Scotti about pirate raids up and down the coastline. It was his feeling that the Scotti were at fault, but he asked Patrick to endeavor to find out.

Not a particularly easy job when one was trying to convert those same Scotti to Christianity. But in my experience, our bishop was not a man who understood subtleties.

I knew of these incursions by pirates on our western coast. But we had suffered such attacks to the south for years, and they had always proven to be the work of Saxons. The Scotti and Picts had not resorted to piracy since Vortigern's days. Indeed, it was the advent of those awful raids that convinced Vortigern to bring the Saxons to our island. But in recent years, the barbarians had found more profitable ways to pillage and the Saxons had adopted piracy to further their own goals.

I had no reason to suppose that these raids sprang from a different source and could only wonder that the bishop did. They were simply harassment, stealing a few items, killing a few villagers, burning a few huts. Arthur and I had discussed this very subject not a full moon past. I had ventured that they were an effort by the Saxons to drive our coastal villages further inland, leaving room for their own settlements. Arthur had agreed.

The other scrolls were various items of correspondence, none of which seemed connected. I lowered myself into the one rickety chair, just sticks of wood bound together with leather strips.

"Malgwyn?" I looked up to see Coroticus standing in the doorway.

"Yes? What is it?" My tone was sharp, testy, to match my mood. Whoever killed Patrick had left less behind him than a simple cutthroat would. And it hid the motive most effectively.

"Bedevere must speak with you. May he enter?" Something in Coroticus's voice caused me to study him closely. He was unhappy, more than unhappy. He seemed ill. It was as if he had lived three lives since I had last seen him.

"Are you well?"

The abbot swallowed deeply, the lines marking his face growing ever deeper. "Yes, Malgwyn. But first Elafius and now Patrick! Lauhiir has disappeared too! I do not understand these things." Again I felt strongly that he was withholding information from me. But this was not the time to press him.

"Neither do I," I said, attempting to sound sympathetic

when in reality frustration was closer to my true feelings. Bedevere appeared over his shoulder and I motioned him in.

"Malgwyn, I must speak with you." He glanced at Coroticus, who immediately saw his meaning.

"I will leave you to your labors," he said gracefully and slipped out.

"Yes, old friend?" I prodded Bedevere, whose eyes were locked to Patrick's corpse.

He started at the sound of my voice and turned reluctantly from the unfortunate old bishop. "Two of Lauhiir's men say they were in this area last night and saw the old priest, Gwilym, entering Patrick's cell."

"How? We had all approaches guarded. He could not enter!"

Bedevere raised a hand. "We have just taken Gwilym prisoner, within the abbey. He is claiming sanctuary."

"Where?"

"In his cell."

"When did Lauhiir's man see him at Patrick's cell?"

"An hour after the midnight."

"Did he see nothing else?"

"No, at least he said nothing. Ider is with him now at the abbot's hall. I knew you would wish to question him further, so I held him." Having spoken, Bedevere looked away from me, a hint of a blush marking his cheeks.

Gwilym! Within the abbey? Within the *vallum*? How in the name of the gods had he managed that? Armed patrols scouring the countryside, and armed guards and patrols protecting the abbey itself! Arthur just might order some horrible punishments for this failure. No wonder Bedevere was embarrassed. Were any other man commanding the troops, I fear Arthur might have done something rash, but Bedevere was too close to him, their friendship born of too many moons together for Arthur to do more than bluster and grow angry.

I tried to focus on what Bedevere had reported. Gwilym had been seen after the midnight. That would seem a bit early, but not too much so, for the condition of Patrick's corpse. I found it interesting that Lauhiir's men had been about the abbey precinct that late. But they could have been visiting one of the women in the village and returned via the abbey.

"What of the night Elafius died?"

Bedevere shrugged. "We did not ask; he did not say. Is there more yet to do here?"

I shook my head. The darkness that had clouded my path some time before returned to haunt me. At least I had someone to question, someone who might have reason to kill Patrick. But I did not feel his guilt strongly. That he was a vigorous old man was certain, but he did not strike me as a murderer. Like Bedevere, I shrugged. Many people could be driven to kill given the right reason.

I cast one last look at the remarkable old bishop and then followed Bedevere from the hut.

CHAPTER TWELVE

As we sloshed through the mud to the abbot's hall, I saw one of the newly arrived troops of horse entering the abbey grounds from the village. Illtud was at its head; he must have gone out to the river bridge and led them in. In theory, with Lauhiir now a fugitive, Arthur could have commandeered Lauhiir's men, but the men allying themselves to the greasy little lord were too unpredictable. Better to have men you knew and trusted at your side.

Soldiers from the earlier troop stood close by the hall. "Is Arthur inside?"

"No. He is meeting with a *decurion* in the village," Bedevere answered. "I sent most of the troop with him as an escort. He did not argue. He is worried."

I nodded. He should be. Lauhiir's men, by killing Arthur's men, either with Lauhiir's approval or not, had essentially declared open warfare with the Rigotamos. It was an odd sort of war, because in Lauhiir's absence his men seemed confused. So was I. And with that, we stepped inside. At the end of the long room, I noted Coroticus, Gwilym, Ider, and two soldiers in Lauhiir's service. They swayed uneasily, leaning first on one leg then the other. Coroticus too looked uneasy, but old Gwilym seemed as implacable as ever. My young friend Ider was his usual, hand-wringing self.

"Gwilym, these soldiers say they saw you outside Patrick's cell last night after the midnight. Is this true?"

"I suppose so. You could also say that I saw them outside Patrick's cell after the midnight."

There would be nothing easy about this. "Did you visit Patrick?"

"I would have but he was already dead."

"You raised no alarm?"

Gwilym turned those piercing eyes upon me, and they struck me with the force of a battle-axe. "I am not stupid, Master Malgwyn. I knew how it would look."

"That I would immediately think you did this thing?"

"Yes."

"And I suppose you had nothing to do with it?" My irritation was as loud as a cock's crow in the morning.

"You may suppose that, but I am telling you that it is fact. I did not kill Patrick or Elafius. Will you take the word of a pair of drunken soldiers over that of a man of God?"

I looked at Lauhiir's men. Their soldier's tunics looked no more ragged than I would expect, and their eyes were less bleary than many I had seen. And Gwilym had been less than forthcoming, far less. He would not like my answer, but it was the only one that made sense.

"Yes, I do. We have been seeking you since yesterday. Extra guards were posted at the entrance to the abbey and around the *vallum*. How did you make entry here without being seen?"

"That is of no consequence now, Malgwyn," Coroticus

chimed in quickly. "He is here now and is afforded the sanctuary of this holy place."

I frowned at the abbot. "Let us understand one another, Coroticus. If this *monachus* killed Patrick, he had best be prepared to spend the rest of his life within these confines. For I will move to Ynys-witrin and watch this place as a hawk stalks its prey. And if he sets one foot beyond the *vallum*, I will arrest him and see that he is executed for his crime."

"He is not outside of the abbey precinct, and thus he is under my protection and that of the church. Therefore, Malgwyn, you have no authority."

I smiled at him. "Actually, my lord abbot, I do. You gave it to me to investigate the death of Elafius. And while I would not betray the abbot's right of granting sanctuary by trying or punishing Gwilym, I will have him watched over. He has a bad habit of disappearing at the most opportune of times. Lord Bedevere, please have Brother Gwilym confined to his cell under guard."

I thought Coroticus was going to be ill, though he had looked that way almost since our arrival. He could have stripped me of the authority that he himself had bestowed, but he knew that would make him appear the lesser man. So, he made no protest.

Lauhiir's two soldiers moved forward. "We'll take him, master."

Something in their eyes warned me against it. "No. The Rigotamos's men will handle it."

The great wooden doors of the hall slammed open, and Arthur, followed by a three-man escort, strode quickly into the room. This did not bode well at all. He ignored Gwilym. And he glanced at Lauhiir's men with disgust. "Either exchange those tunics for those of my service or begone before I have the lot of you beheaded. Malgwyn, Coroticus! We must speak in private, NOW!"

I motioned to Bedevere and he grasped the old *monachus* by the arm, gently to be sure. Coroticus led us to his inner chamber, leaving Lauhiir's men as if rooted to the spot in their shock at Arthur's tirade.

Once beyond the hearing of the others, Arthur spun upon us, his long brown hair whipping about his face. "We have trouble."

I chuckled. "What more trouble could we have? We have a dead *monachus* and a dead bishop, three of your own soldiers dead, and the lord responsible missing."

For once, Arthur's dark eyes brooked no criticism. "A rider has sped word from Rome. An envoy is on his way from Rome to attend this meeting at Castellum Marcus about Patrick's mission to the Scotti. Apparently, there are those, highly placed in Rome, who seek his removal. It seems, Malgwyn, that they are more serious than you thought."

Coroticus turned even more pale and unsteady. I gave him my one arm to hold. "There are those who believe he has become too powerful in Hibernia; they believe that there were more riches to be gathered there than the devout Patrick would agree on."

"And?" Arthur could cut through all the dressing that we often clothed our words in. "What else?"

Coroticus's eyes flicked back and forth, and he licked his lips wetly. "I—"

At that I dropped Coroticus's elbow, allowing it to almost drop to the floor, and he stumbled. "Patrick killed someone in his youth, at Bannaventa. Only one other person knew of it, and that person told someone in the church. For what reason, I do not know and neither did Patrick."

"How come you to know this?" Arthur asked.

"Patrick told me yesterday."

"Why would he tell you? You are no *presbyter*, no *sacerdote*." Coroticus was confused, confused and flustered.

"That is of no consequence." I paused and turned to Arthur. "We could have Kay question his credentials at the eastern border?"

Arthur settled into a rickety chair and held his bearded chin in his hands. "Aye, we can do that. But it will buy us little time. Romans object to delay." Such was ironic, considering that Arthur held great pride in his Roman heritage. He stayed silent for a while. "Our agents in Gaul tell of his arrival in Brittany with an assistant named Johannes Paulus, a young *sacerdote* of our lands."

"And the envoy?"

"A newly made bishop from Rome, named Francesco, known for his learning and passion. They will be here within days, perhaps sooner if my spies misjudge. The spread of Pelagianism is as a foul pestilence to Rome and Patrick's letter sparked swift action. Now, when this Francesco arrives and finds that Patrick's been murdered it will be havoc." He turned to me, his eyes pleading. "Malgwyn, this affair must be settled quickly, more quickly than before. Though I prize many Roman ways, I know enough of the situation in the empire that they will move swiftly and heavy-handedly. We have achieved our independence, fragile though it might be. I do not relish Roman troops quartered among us once more. They could easily splinter the *consilium*."

I could be nothing else than honest with Arthur. He had saved me twice, from the battlefield and from my own self-pity. "Gwilym may be the killer, but I see no immediate reason. Pelagianism is not a killing matter. For debate? Yes. For murder? No. That his murder is connected with that of Elafius I see no other alternative. But there is something different, almost passionless, in Patrick's demise. And when I discover the reason behind that element, I will understand it all."

Arthur ran his stubby fingers through his beard. "I agree, but what shall I do with this Francesco, this envoy from Rome?"

And that gave me pause, until I remembered a certain female of my acquaintance. "Fetch Guinevere."

The Rigotamos looked at me as if I were crazy. His eyes flashed at me, and I thought for a second he would draw his sword.

"Fetch Guinevere," I repeated, unmoved by his anger.

Those thick eyebrows of his knitted closely together and his frown was one of epic proportions. He jerked his head at one of his troopers, standing just beyond the door. The soldier nodded and disappeared. Torches had already been lit around the chamber. Though our days were growing longer, the prospect of dusk was yet upon us. I could see little that I had accomplished on this day—indeed, my tasks had multiplied—but that would not keep it from coming to an end.

I thought for a moment. "Patrick's death may be traced to his youth, when he killed a girl. A horrible event that has given him great trouble in years past."

"How could that be part of this affair?" Bedevere asked. 'Twas a logical question. A murder years and miles away seemed a poor candidate to hold the key to our current maze.

208

"Patrick's enemies were becoming concerned at his growing prestige and were dredging up the old tales to discredit him and strip him of his bishopric. Two men who played critical roles in those long-ago events died but hours apart. I need little more than that to suggest that there are things from many years ago that someone wishes hidden. The deaths of Elafius and Patrick lie not in the here and now, not in the aspirations and ambition of a young lord, but in the long-past days of their youths. Quite frankly, my lord, I have no other path to follow. It seems the only place to find a connection."

I paused. "The Rigotamos can handle Lauhiir and this new *episcopus*. I must travel farther afield." With that I began to strip off my crimson tunic.

"What's this?" Arthur asked.

"Divesting myself of this tunic," I said. "Returning to the garb of Mad Malgwyn for a time. I have places to go and people to question who would be too cautious if confronted by a king's counselor. Mad Malgwyn is more likely to attract their confidence."

"And you hope to find what?"

I shook my head. "Allow me a few secrets, my lord. Should my excursion prove successful, I will have at least some of my questions answered."

"The coast?"

"Bannaventa."

"Patrick's home?"

"Patrick's home." I nodded. "It may be that Patrick's death was determined long ago in his old home. Francesco could not know that he is dead. The old man's murder has another cause."

"And of Elafius?" Ider asked.

"I cannot fathom that. It seems unrelated, but it must be connected. Perhaps when I resolve Patrick's death, I will understand why Elafius was killed."

Arthur rose to his full height, his broad shoulders strong and thick. "Do not be gone long, my friend. I shall need you, I fear."

"I'll return as quickly as I can. But Bedevere will serve you much better than I. Now, bring me Guinevere."

An hour later, as I prepared for my journey, a knock came to the door. My cousin, dressed in a plain gown, her hair held back with beautiful bone pins, slipped inside and kissed my cheek. "You sent for me, Malgwyn?"

"Cousin! I need your help. Do you still keep company with the women in the community?"

She cocked an eye and looked at me suspiciously. "What evil are you intending?"

"Guinevere!" I said with mock surprise. "I need a woman."

"Malgwyn!"

"Not for me. I need an attractive woman who has a way with men, one who is not afraid of her own shadow and can wrap a man around her finger."

She pursed her lips and looked at me intently. "Who must she seduce?"

"A newly named bishop of Rome, one Francesco . . ."

Dressed as "Mad Malgwyn," I attracted little notice as I slipped quietly from the abbey on foot and headed down the trail to Bannaventa, a journey of twenty miles toward the coast. It was there that Patrick had been taken as a *servi* by Scotti raiders. And if, as I believed, the answer to his and Elafius's deaths was tied to their long-past youth, that is where that answer would be.

The rotten grass and muddy earth left a fetid smell in the air along the path. In my short time among the Rigotamos's counselors, I had forgotten the smell of the paupers' sweat and soil. My nose revealed my distaste. An ancient beggar laughed at me. "Best get used to it, friend. You'll smell just like it soon enough."

The journey to Bannaventa took some six hours. In dry weather, on good roads, a man fresh and strong could cover four or five miles in an hour. But the roads were muddy and crowded; I often felt as if I were swimming against the current in a mighty river. Hundreds of people had flooded the roads leading to Ynys-witrin.

"Why come to Ynys-witrin, old man?"

One traveler responded to my query. "Are you daft? The great *episcopus* Patrick is there, and he is granting blessings and healing the lame."

This man was dressed well, with a linen *camisia* showing beneath his tunic. "Good sir," I began. "Please do not take my words as insult, but you are not lame, and you seem to already be blessed with the finer things of life. What need have you of Patrick's blessings?"

The fellow smiled at me, encouraged by my tone. "We come to seek his blessings for our welfare. Armed soldiers have begun raiding villages to the west and north of here."

"Soldiers of Lord Liguessac? Scotti? Pirates?"

He looked around suspiciously and then shoved me to the side of the road. Leaning in, he sniffed of me and eyed me in disbelief. "Who are you? You look like a beggar, but you smell of rose water. And you seem uncommonly familiar with the human hazards of these lands."

This was a clever man. "Be at thy ease, master. I serve the Rigotamos, though my garb would say otherwise. Speak to me."

His plump, ruddy face relaxed. "We do not know whose soldiers they are, but they are not common pirates or even the Scotti. They are disciplined. Please take this word to the Rigotamos."

I patted his arm. "I will. For now," I said, "there is a greater hazard to the west. But I will not forget this."

He quickly rejoined the river of humanity pushing the road to the flooding stage. I frowned. More complications, I did not need. But I stowed the complaint into a pouch in the corner of my mind and plunged back into my journey as dark, gray clouds seemed to boil up from the horizon. Great winds were pushing them, I knew, and such boded ill for the day ahead.

All along the western road to Bannaventa, I encountered groups of travelers, some alone, some in families with ox-drawn carts. Such a flood of people I had only seen in advance of the Saxon armies pushing into our lands. They were fleeing as if they were a retreating army, dragging the possessions they could carry in bundles and bags, or strapped onto carts with leather ties.

A shift came in the flow after I passed a certain point in my journey. Rather than heading east, toward Ynys-witrin, the current began heading west, toward Bannaventa. The danger, I perceived, lay to the north. I had no time to scout that region, but perhaps on my return I would. Arthur's patrols would certainly become aware of this soon.

The gray clouds turned to deep purple, and thunder rumbled from them as the sky lit up. As I rounded a turn in the lane, drops of rain fell from the sky, but I realized that I had finally reached the edge of Bannaventa. An old round stone house sat wedged into a bend of the road. The first two or three courses were stone, surmounted by wattle and daub. A child, a little boy, peered from the door. As I made to approach him, he disappeared inside and a great, burly man replaced him. "Your business here?"

"I seek the family of Patrick, the *episcopus* in the land of the Scotti. Can you direct me to them?"

His eyes narrowed a bit. "Who seeks them?"

"I am called Malgwyn, a friend of the bishop. I promised him I would call on his people if I chanced in this direction."

He relaxed then, and I noticed his hand slip away from the dagger at his belt. "You came for naught then. They are all gone. Only the old villa is left, but it stands in ruins now. Strange that he would not know this."

"He has long been abroad. None of his people are left?"

"Dead mostly. Or moved on."

I thought for a moment. "I need an old man with a long memory then. Someone who has spent his life in these lands."

"You have great needs for a man paying a friendly visit," he pointed out, and rightly so.

I reached into my pouch and pulled a silver *denarius* out. Tossing it to him, I drew my own dagger as he moved to catch the coin. "That's yours to pocket if you'll help me."

His eyes grew wide at the sight of the dagger and wider still at the *denarius*. He pursed his lips. "I know of no man, but of a woman. Aye, she had some connection to old Calpornius, a *servi*, perhaps."

"Perhaps?" The way he so quickly avoided my glance told me he knew more than he revealed.

"Some call her a witch, but . . ." His voice trailed off.

"You believe it or not?"

"She is but an odd old woman," he said, looking at me finally.

"Just tell me where to find her and I'll be on my way." Quickly, as the thunder ushered in the rain in sheets, he directed me to the old woman's house.

Half an hour later, I stood before a creaky, wind-snatched wattle-and-daub house built against the wall of an old Roman villa. An old ragged cloth covered the doorway, fluttering now in the wind. I did not bother to announce myself, because of the rain, and I ducked my head to enter the house. 'Twas good that I did, for the song of a dagger split the air where my head had been and drove its point into the wooden beam framing the doorway.

Crouching, I ducked left and then right in the darkened room.

"Who are you? What do you want here?" The voice was aged beyond any I had heard, crackling and hissing like a fire doused with water.

The room was as black as night, and I marveled that she had come so close to pinning my throat to her door with the dagger.

"I am a friend. I mean you no harm."

"Since when did any friend enter an old woman's house without permission? What's your name?"

"I am Malgwyn of the River Cam."

She sniffed from the darkness of her corner. "You are Malgwyn ap Cuneglas, the one-armed scribe of Arthur, the Rigotamos."

Searching the blackened corner, I could just dimly make

out her figure, seated with her legs crossed beneath her and a fur piled about her.

"Do I know you, woman? Or are you a witch?"

"Neither." She laughed, though it was more of a cackle. "I caught a whiff of rose water when you entered. Only a noble or his servant would use such. When you ducked the dagger, I heard only the sound of one set of fingers balancing you. A two-armed man would have used both. Who in the western lands has not heard the songs being sung of 'Smiling Malgwyn,' who could kill Saxons with his grin and who can look at a man and ferret out the evil deeds in his heart?"

I felt my face go red. "You have the advantage, woman. You can see me but you sit in darkness."

Another laugh and the sound of a flint, a spark and a flame brightened the room.

I had never seen a woman, or anyone, so old. Her wrinkles were deeper than the River Brue. And with a shock, I realized that her milky blue eyes were as dead as my lost arm. She was blind.

A bit later, I had gathered more firewood for her and was heating a measure of mead. I settled in opposite her and poured a beaker for us both.

"Why have you traveled so far, Malgwyn, to talk to an old blind woman?" Myndora, for that was her name, asked.

"I seek information from the past. A man up the road said that you had been a servant to the family of Patrick, he who is now *episcopus* to the Scotti."

"A servant? No, I was no servant, but I knew them all well. Calpornius, Patrick, even old Potitus, the *decurion*."

Finally, I thought. Answers. "Did you know Patrick's friends, Tremayne and Elafius?"

She grinned again and sipped her mead from a battered beaker. I saw she had no teeth but two upper ones and those were worn to the nub. "Know them? Yes, I knew them well. Until Patrick was taken by the pirates, that is. That spoiled everything for us. That was a bad year. Little Addiena was ravaged and killed. Patrick taken. Nothing was the same after that."

"Aye." I nodded. "I know of Addiena's death."

She pulled back. "Your voice and your deeds make you too young to know aught of this. How come you to know of Addiena?"

"Patrick told me."

Myndora looked away then with those sightless eyes. "And did he tell you that he killed her?"

Then it was my turn to be shocked. "How came you to know this? Patrick said he only told one other soul!"

Myndora nodded and grinned. "Aye, Tremayne. My brother.

" 'Tis so long ago now," she began. I sipped my own warmed mead and listened as I had to Patrick. Some stories are worth waiting for. I felt, rather than knew, that this was one.

I was in love with Patrick, though he never knew it. He was strong and tall and handsome. Patrick was confident, not like Elafius; he could not shut up.

Tremayne cautioned me about Patrick, who was older than me. He said that though he loved Patrick as a brother, there was yet something dark and sad about him. Tremayne was very protective of me and would as lief I not play with them.

And then all in our village were shocked and crazed by the killing of Addiena. I remember the men searching the forest and the coast.

I remember poor Elafius so stricken by grief that he would not leave her body except to choke down a little food.

But once, during one of those times, Tremayne slipped me into the hut where she lay, and he pulled the wrap from her throat to show me where Patrick's hands had bruised her. "You see, do you not? That could be you! I saw him choke her until her eyes bulged and they began to turn red with blood!" I refused to believe it. I shook Tremayne's hands off and flew like the wind into the fields and the forests. Tremayne found me there, hiding behind a huge yew tree.

I protested again, and that is when Tremayne told me. "I watched him do it, Myndora! I watched from afar. And later, Patrick confessed it to me, and swore me to secrecy."

"But you must tell!" I scolded him. "No," he answered. "I do love Patrick and I know it was an accident. I break my promise only to show you that there is truly something dark and cruel in him."

I stopped her then. Many things she said created questions in my mind. "These are the words he spoke to you? Are you certain?"

"I will never forget those words, if I live another lifetime."

"If Patrick told no one but Tremayne, then how did the church find out about Patrick's crime, for they are calling him to account even now?"

"Oh, that." She chuckled and hid her toothless smile behind a hand. "Years later when my brother was battling the church, he blurted it out in haste to Germanus's pet *sacerdote*, Severus, to prove that the church is not infallible in its judgment of men or theology. Severus was taken captive in the east before he could look into the matter further."

"But why would Tremayne argue with Severus?"

"Oh, well, he was not called Tremayne by then. Like many

who enter the service of the Christ, he took a new name. Then, he was called Agricola."

I felt the breath leave my chest and my knees grow weak. "Patrick's boyhood friend was the Pelagian Agricola?"

"Certainly. And do you think that Patrick was the only true believer of the Christ from Bannaventa?"

"But Agricola fled after Germanus's visit. Everyone knows this."

"My brother left, it is true, but he did not do so to honor that blowhard Germanus. He went to Gaul to fight yet another day. Once there, he took another name and served the Christ for many years there."

"Then he is dead." A statement, not a question. A sudden sadness came over me as I realized that all three boyhood friends, who had all dedicated their lives to the Christ, were gone.

"No! No!" Myndora protested. "My brother is not dead. He is in these lands now. He came to see me not a full moon past."

"Agricola? Here?" My heart beat faster as I suddenly realized that at least one of the answers I sought had been before me all of the time.

"Of course," said Myndora happily. "Only now his name is Gwilym and he is a *monachus* at Ynys-witrin."

"Gwilym," I repeated, more in a mumble than not. And I took a huge gulp of the now cool mead.

"Yes, and he brought his daughter along, a lively, head-strong girl named Rhiannon."

And then I drained my beaker and nearly collapsed.

CHAPTER THIRTEEN

Gwilym was Agricola! And not only that but he was Patrick's friend Tremayne! And Rhiannon was his daughter! My poor old head would never be the same. Yet it made sense. It was not uncommon for men to change their names when joining the church. And Agricola could hardly use his own name when returning to his homeland.

So much was clear now. So many puzzling things fell into place. Gwilym hid from Patrick because he knew that Patrick would recognize him as both Tremayne and Agricola. Poor old Elafius did well just to remember his own name. A part of me smiled. Gwilym must have enjoyed baiting his forgetful old playmate.

I wondered if Coroticus knew who he was sheltering, or had he taken Gwilym in to better his chances of bedding Rhiannon? Something told me that he did know at least part of it. That Gwilym knew Patrick may not have been a secret the abbot kept, but I would have bet a pot of *solidi* that he knew he harbored the great Pelagian Agricola.

Poor Coroticus! The murky stew of complications he had

cooked up might cost him his post after all. Outside the storm had risen to great heights, battering the old walls of the house and ripping at the cloth door. And then ripping it away with a horrendous screech.

I huddled against the old woman to protect her from the storm. She grabbed my shoulders with surprising strength, releasing them only long enough for me to pound some vagrant intruding on our space with a stick of firewood.

All through the night, her thin arms clutched my chest, only the shallow movement of her chest letting me know she lived. I kept the fire blazing but we spoke no more words. No words were needed, at any rate. She seemed to be afraid that she would destroy this fragile bond we had established.

"Whose villa is this that you have built onto?" I ventured during one lull in the storm.

"Is that of concern?"

"Curiosity more than anything. I like to know whose hospitality I'm usurping."

"Abandoned hospitality, my one-armed scribe. This was Patrick's villa, or rather his father's, Calpornianus. But surely your friend Patrick will consent."

"Would," I mumbled.

"What was that!" Myndora's hearing was as clear as a newborn's.

I sank down then, amongst a pile of furs and stared at the floor.

"What have you not told me, Malgwyn?"

I turned away from her as wind whipped through the door.

"What?" She sounded less now like the old woman and more like the young girl she had once been. "Speak now!"

Still, reluctantly, I slowly turned my head and faced her.

"Patrick's heart no longer beats among us. He was killed not two nights past, Myndora."

Though her eyes could no longer see, they filled with tears. "You could have told me that my father was dead and I would shed no greater tears. How did he die?"

And so amid the cry of the wind, the bashing of the branches, and drumbeat of the rain, I held Myndora as she cried and told her some of Patrick's demise, but only some. She did not need to know how he had been taken from us.

"Did Gwilym and Patrick see each other before he died?"

"No, Myndora. Tremayne's duties took him to other villages and he did not know of Patrick's arrival."

"Elafius did not tell him that Patrick was due to arrive?"

"It was a sudden visit; even we were not aware when we left Castellum Arturius. Word did not reach Arthur until we arrived at Ynys-witrin." Beyond the flapping door, I could smell sea air, salt air. I held the cloth tightly and watched the lane. Nothing. No travelers. No merchants. No one. Something was wrong. Where was the stream of travelers I had seen the day before? If they were not here, that could only mean that they saw some danger in this place as well.

"Myndora, hear you nothing?"

"I've heard little since you arrived."

"Is there a tower in the villa?"

"A tower?"

"A watchtower. A tall cornice, anything, any place from which I can see the countryside about."

"Potitus built a chapel down near the stream. It held a tower at the apse, with a cross atop it."

"Do you know if it is still there?" The stupidity of my question hit me.

"Of course."

And I asked another stupid question. "How do you know?"

"I hear every sound in this place. The wind from the great channel makes a certain pitch when it passes around the cross. That's how I know it's still there."

I looked at her with something approaching love and respect. That she had survived for this long, blind, and that her hearing was so remarkable was beyond understanding. Quickly, I pulled a white sheet, bold and mangy. The walls of the villa were dirty gray, and the sheet would nearly match them.

"Wait here."

"And where else should I be waiting?"

I left her grumbling, cackling voice behind and slipped between the villa buildings, the old bathhouse, the kitchen block, until I could see the chapel with its tower surmounted by a cross close by.

I stacked three large stones in an uneasy pile, which started me on my journey. With just one whole arm, the going was truly touchy, but my legs counted for much. Soon I was atop it, my one arm wrapped around the cross, and I hung on for life itself to my post atop the windy, stormy cross. It felt like my skin was freezing to the post. Just a few kilometers away I could see the cold channel, the sea between the land of the Scotti, "Hibernia" the Romans called it, and our own. I saw easily how a band of Scotti could have landed and stolen up here to take Patrick in his sleep.

It took but a few moments to adjust myself to this blowing gale, the rain striking my face like little pebbles. I was forced to continually wipe my eyes with my forearm, unable to release the base of the cross. In a moment, the rain eased and I could see the coastline and beyond. But what I saw was more than surprising, more than remarkable.

Forty longboats, jammed with soldiers, Scotti by the look of them, were but minutes from making their landing. Scotti! They had never launched such a mighty invasion of our shores. Why, there were three hundred men if there were one, with more boats carrying storage jars, weapons!

I watched as they maneuvered their craft into a small cove. They beached them and immediately began unloading. Once finished, they pushed the boat back out to sea quickly and just as quickly moved to the next in line. One man was obviously the leader. Tall and broad chested, he wore a thick beard, thicker than my own, of red hair. His cloak, of a woven gold and white design, was hooked by two brooches, one over each shoulder. The tunic, banded in gold, reached near to his feet. If there were a king among them, it was he.

Knowing that I had to find out more, I began my slippery descent down the cross, onto the canted roof, the hobnails on my leather caligae *giving* no purchase.

I slipped twice but managed to maintain my balance and kept from plunging headfirst into muck and mud below. Seconds later, with my hand showing bloody splinters, I leaped the remaining feet to the ground, slightly twisting my ankle in the process.

Wasting no time, I half hobbled, half ran to Myndora's hut.

"What is it?" she asked before I could even announce myself.

"Scotti! Hundreds of them! You must let me carry you to hiding. Come, we'll gather what we can and—"

"And nothing! You think I have not avoided capture by the Scotti before? You go! It is you who are in most danger."

I paused, torn between my duty to Arthur and my concern for Myndora.

"Malgwyn." And I felt her hand touch mine. "I am touched by your worrying after an old woman, but listen to me. Bannaventa is lost to you already. You must find Arthur, and he must stop the Scotti before they cross the river of sorrows.

"You have learned all you can here about Patrick and Addiena. Anyone else who could tell you more is long dead or at Ynys-witrin. The Scotti must be your concern now. So, go! We will meet again."

Though I thought it unlikely, a certainty in her words swelled them in my mind, gave them substance and therefore truth.

I brushed her cheek with my hand and disappeared out the door, hoping that we would meet once more, someday.

Now I was more confused than ever. Whatever was driving people from the north of Ynys-witrin was not the Scotti. I saw no signs of an earlier landing party. Aye, the group I had seen had begun to enlarge the clearing where they had beached.

But three hundred men! Such was a small army in those days. Not enough to defeat Arthur's forces, but that assumed Arthur had time to prepare. And that left me with two problems. First, they had chosen a clever place. The closest watchpost was at the Mount of Frogs, some miles to the north. It was manned by Teilo's men. He was a minor lord in that region; I knew little about him. The cove was small and well hidden, and they had landed in the early evening hours, in heavy weather when the sea could play tricks on your eyes.

Second, Arthur needed to know as much as possible about this new threat. As I already knew, the army I had seen, while posing a threat, was not enough to defeat Arthur outright. But what if there were a second party of the same size? That seemed unlikely. The Scotti were many, but it would require a large confederation of their kings to field a six-hundred-man army. And even then they would not be assured of victory. But they could devastate much of the western half of our island simply by taking provisions. So, what was their aim? A foothold? An expansion of their territory? Patrick had said nothing about a threat from the Scotti, and he would have done so had he heard a single word.

Patrick! The issue of Patrick's killing had fled from my mind as swiftly as a rabbit flees from a hunter's approach. And now I had no time to ponder it. I felt a fleeting moment of sadness that the death of a man like Patrick could so easily be put aside. The time to mourn him would come, I knew, I hoped. But what his chosen people were up to must now take precedence.

Though my purchase was slippery and my lungs burned with the struggle, I raced across the levels and made the steep climb up to the *meneds*, the hills, the moorlands that skirted the great flats to the south. Most of the year, the flood waters joined with the Axe and the Brue to create a great new sea that left Ynys-witrin an island. At this season the waters had receded to the riverbanks, and the newly arrived Scotti would, I guessed, stay in the shadows of the *meneds* to shield themselves from our soldiers at watch on the Mount of Frogs.

Once atop the *meneds*, I braced myself against a tree and recovered my breath. It was fully dark now, the last vague hint of sun swallowed up by the clouds roiling on the western horizon. Where the hills touched the levels, it looked for all the world like a crack in the earth, black and brooding. If I closed my eyes, I could almost smell the hint of sulfur said to lie deep within. Somewhere down there, I thought, Gwynn ap Nudd, the fairy king, ruled. One wrong step and I could easily tumble in. But the gods protected me, kept my one good arm held fast to the tree. My cheek brushed against the bark, and I thought of poor Elafius; it was a yew tree. The last few days had not been lucky ones for the church or for sons of Bannaventa.

No matter how hard they tried, an army of men was bound to make some noise, and I did not have too long to wait before I made out the creaks and groans of a large party on the move. And they were either so stupid or so arrogant that they carried a number of small torches.

My plan was simple. If I could but trail them to their destination, I might know their purpose. That they moved inland so quickly told me much. These were traveling parties, not colonizing groups. Traveling parties implied that they were going somewhere. But where? The presence of a Scotti raiding party was not unusual, troublesome, but not unusual. Again, it was the size of it that worried me. It was ten times the number normally seen in a single group.

Taking a deep breath, I crouched and began my journey along the ridge above them. My path was more treacherous than theirs as I had to navigate the heights above them without benefit of a torch. The ground was slippery and uneven; great yawning holes and sheer drop-offs marked the edge of the *meneds*.

The Scotti seemed to have brought no horses, no chariots. Indeed, they seemed not to have brought anything they could not carry on their backs. Simple, round shields, spears. Their commander, the one that I had spied wearing the white tunic, was setting them a swift pace. That could mean any number of things, but nothing clear.

I started to become hungry and the hunger passed into weakness, and still they continued, always hugging the base of the hills as the terrain allowed. The clouds soon parted, and the moon spread its light across the levels and touched the dampened grass and trees with a shimmer like promised gold, that color that lies somewhere between white and yellow.

My mind told me that they were hurrying to a rendezvous. My stomach told me that I was beginning not to care. The only farms near me, where I might steal some cheese or bread, were too far back from the edge of the *meneds* to keep an eye on my quarry, or they were on the high spots in the levels, which would cause me to have to cross the Scotti's route. While I might not have seen any horses, they would be fools to be moving across enemy ground without scouts ahead and on their flank to warn of any threat.

My legs were beginning to tremble though, and as if by magic the flickering of the Scotti torches spelled the slowing of their march. I checked the now clear sky and saw that we had been some ten hours on this treacherous journey. They would rest now, for a short while. I propped myself up on one hand and bent over, my empty stomach nearly heaving from hunger and exertion.

From my vantage point, I could see that we had crossed almost to the edge of the *meneds*, where I could look into the distance and see the flickering fire of the Tor at Ynys-witrin and the smaller, yet still discernible, fires of the abbey. I turned and looked back through the forest. Distance was hard to judge, but I thought I could see the glow of a light between the trunks of the massive trees.

I looked back quickly to the still-halted torches of the Scotti. With any luck, I could dash to the farmstead, raid a storage pit, and be back before they started again. At worst, I might be an hour behind, but so clear was the night and so bright their torches, I would have no trouble catching up.

Pivoting on my heels, I dashed off toward the distant light. It was only after I was already a hundred paces along my journey that I realized that the Scotti could have stopped to douse their torches and continue on in the moonlight. But I was committed by then, and it was only a few moments before I emerged into a large clearing.

It took but seconds to realize where I was—the barrows on the top of the *meneds*, dug by the old people to bury their dead. Old tales told of a golden coffin buried in one, but we honored these burial places because of their purpose, not old tales. Aye, we buried our own near them in hopes that those old ones would protect them in the afterlife. I did not know about all of that, but I knew that it gave me comfort that my old dad and mother and brother Cuneglas lay together with our ancestors.

Ahead I saw an old roundhouse with a pair of sheds set about ten yards away. A lamp burned within, and I could detect a wisp of smoke from a hole in the roof. Just as I determined to get closer, a woman emerged from the house and walked, heavily, toward one of the sheds. She stopped short of the shed though, and leaned down into its moonshadows toward a bump in the ground. I watched as she kicked a small rock aside, lifted a wooden cover, took something out, let the cover drop, and replaced the rock with a swift movement of her foot.

A little smile stretched my face as I realized I had found my target. And my grumbling stomach and weakening knees told me that it was not a second too soon.

As soon as she was back in the roundhouse, I bolted from my hideaway and dashed across the open ground in a half-crouch.

Man has many failings. Allowing his physical needs to block his common sense is but one of them. When the two Scotti warriors stepped out of the house, wiping their daggers on their tunics and tucking them back into their belts, I knew that my hunger had been the death of me.

So shocked was I at their appearance that I literally stopped in my tracks, frozen to the spot.

I could not move.

They saw me immediately, and my surprise was all the time they needed.

I reacted, but the delay and my tired old legs cost me precious time.

I was knocked to the ground by one who straddled my chest with his dagger at my throat while my hand clawed at my belt for my own knife. But he caught me in the attempt, stripped the dagger from my belt and flung it away. His companion, well trained, scanned the area for others with me.

My captor's face was close enough to mine that I could smell his rancid breath, laden with onion and cheese. His dagger-laden fist drew back for the fatal blow, and I was just preparing to kick him or roll him off, anything to avoid that blow, when something odd happened.

He stopped.

His other hand had slipped down my half arm to find the empty sleeve and his eyes grew wide. As quickly as he was on me, he lost his balance and fell sideways and scrambled away as if in fear.

The other Scotti, satisfied that I was alone, spun around, saw his companion sprawled some feet from me, and started toward me with his own dagger. But his friend spouted something in their hellish language, and I knew so little of it that I could not understand exactly what he said. I did catch the word "arm." But that was all.

I stood, slowly, eyes fixed on the two Scotti. They continued jabbering at each other. I glanced quickly around. No others that I could see. I began to measure the distance to the forest, calculating if I had even half a chance of making it into the darkness before they cut me down.

Then they did something strange. My first attacker was now on his feet. They replaced their daggers in their belts and held their hands up, palms out. Taking their move as an apology, I nodded curtly and went to retrieve my dagger, but they cut me off, still with frightened looks on their faces, still without weapons in hand.

I turned then to leave, but again they blocked my path. It seemed I would not be allowed to rearm myself or to leave on my own, but neither would I be killed. At least not here and now.

They herded me (and I use that for lack of a better word) back toward the roundhouse, a typical wattle-and-daub structure, the likes of which dotted our landscape. A lamp still burned within, but I suspected that the occupants lay with their throats slit after providing food for the Scotti.

My new guardians indicated that I was to wait outside while one of them ducked through the door. I could hear a scrambling and scuffling inside and then a small bundle flew out the door and slid across the mud.

Llynfann, my little thief! Bound hand and foot.

Chapter Fourteen

"Master Malgwyn!"

One of the Scotti hustled over and cut the cords binding my little friend's legs and then hauled him to his feet.

I looked him over as well as I could in the moonlight. He was muddy and obviously exhausted, but I saw little sign of ill treatment, save some bruises and a trickle of blood flowing from a cut lip.

"What happened to you? What is all of—"

But Llynfann clumsily bowed and knelt. With head dropped he spoke as clearly as he could. "Treat me as a recalcitrant servant. Show no tenderness. I am alive only because I convinced them that I am your *servus*."

Before the words were hardly out of his mouth, I slapped him with my one good hand, hard, knocking him to the ground. The Scotti laughed at Llynfann as he struggled upright, giving me a quick wink.

"They know not our language or Latin. We can speak safely as long as we act as master and *servi*. I stayed alive by telling them that I was *servi* to a great wizard, one who had lost an arm to a mighty dragon. And that to kill me would bring your wrath down upon them."

"And they believed you?"

"Not completely," he admitted. "They caught me watching them as they unloaded goods at Bannaventa for Lauhiir's men. These Scotti are not smart. They did not understand why I was watching them. Lauhiir's men had already left before they found me.

"I made up the story about you, and they were confused and superstitious enough to hold me. The leader, a dim-witted man himself, sent me with these two to 'the gathering' to be dealt with."

"The gathering? What could that be?"

"I know not. But I know that the delivery I saw was of spears and shields and enough dried meat and fish to feed an army."

I nodded, making certain to scowl as well. "I saw a band of three hundred making shore at Bannaventa. They are even now at the edge of the levels, skirting the base of the *meneds*, heading south by southeast." A thought struck me. "Did the guards at the Mount of Frogs not see these goods changing hands? You must have been right beneath them." From the Mount of Frogs, you could see up and down the coast easily.

Llynfann turned his head from me. "I watched as Lauhiir's men bribed them with coins."

I laughed to myself. Such was exactly what I would expect. "Llynfann, my little friend, the coins are forgeries, fakes, made by Lauhiir. And that swine's men killed three of Arthur's men to hide it."

The little thief's head snapped up with alarm. He knew immediately what that meant for the lord of the Tor. I heard our captors getting restless and mumbling something in their foul language.

"They are talking about killing us or taking us with them. The one who attacked you is frightened. He is afraid that he has mortally offended you and that you will strike him dead. The other is less certain and believes that they have wasted enough time. He also thinks that you look more like a drunk than a wizard." He paused as the jabbering grew louder. Finally, he visibly relaxed. "They have decided that to kill us would be tempting the gods, and they still do not understand why I was watching them."

"So we are to be taken to this 'gathering'?"

"Aye." Llynfann glanced quickly about. "You could try to rush them, but unless you can get my hands untied and we could both attack them, they would have done for us both in a flash."

He was right. They had all the weapons, plus four arms to our three. I cursed my missing limb, but I did not feel the anger I normally would. Where would I go if they released us? To warn Arthur of course. At least this way, I was assured of safe passage to their destination. We might not find escape when we got there, but at least we would have some idea of what these remarkable events meant, more information for Arthur. Although I was beginning to get an idea, and it frightened me.

Our path was circuitous and treacherous. The Scotti had left my arm free, and that helped me stay on my feet as they set a torrid pace. Our trail led us along the *meneds*. An hour later and we were drawing close to a place I knew in passing and had heard of many times. The "river of sorrows" flowed through

233

caves there, below a steep cliff. My father told me that the caves were haunted by the shades of Roman soldiers, murdered there by Druid priests in the old days. Druids had no love for Romans. Smugglers were said to hide their treasure there, and a witch, legend had it, cursed all who entered.

When I was at the abbey, healing from my wounds, the *monachi* encouraged me to take long rides. They claimed that healing the mind had much to do with healing the body. On many of those rides, I had passed the cave's entrance a few times, tucked though it was at the head of a small hollow, but the stories were enough to hold me at bay. Besides, I was not fond of dark, damp places when the open sky was available.

The closer we drew, the more Scotti we saw, and, to my amazement, soldiers wearing the tunics of Teilo and Dochu, a pair of lesser lords from across the channel near unto Caermarthen. Neither had the prestige or territory to merit a seat on the *consilium*. But more amazing yet were the soldiers of Lord David, manning guard posts as we descended the cliffs over the cave. The entire area was lit by torches, and I wondered at the brazenness of their actions. Then my memory of this hollow in the daylight blossomed. The hills surrounding were close; it was a very secluded place. What the hills did not block, the trees would. The torches could not be seen unless you were almost on top of the entrance.

A campfire was set next to the river flowing out of the cave. I thought for a moment that our guards were going to take us to the large group of soldiers gathered around the fire, but they directed us instead toward a smaller opening in the rock face of the cliff.

Once inside we were shoved into a side chamber, carved out of the rock. The two Scotti disappeared and were replaced by two of Lord David's men. Llynfann smiled at me. "A better class of guard, Malgwyn." They left my arm free and I felt the damp walls with my hand. I could not think of a more secure prison. One exit and solid rock all around.

"Calm yourself, Malgwyn," Llynfann exhorted me. "We are yet breathing, and so long as we still breathe, there is hope. I have escaped stronger jails than this."

I chuckled at his bragging. Part of me wanted to tell him that he was young and hope was a gift of the young. But it took only a single glance at my companion—the lines already growing on his face, the hint of gray in his beard, and most especially the tired glint in his eye—to know that the little thief had lived ten men's lives already.

"I would that neither of us be in this mess, Llynfann. But that we are still alive is cause for wonderment. I do not doubt that your stories of wizards would fool the Scotti. They are pagans and unsophisticated. But our lords will not be so easily confounded. Aye, David knows me by sight, all too well. If he is here, as I am sure he is, we are doomed."

"None of that! We are not dead and do not pretend that we are!"

I saw no use in arguing with him. He was one of those beings fated to always take the most positive view. I was too practical for that. I saw little chance of ever alerting Arthur to this threat, but I stayed awake the rest of the night, while Llynfann slept the sleep of the trusting. Though I could hardly believe it, the cave did not grow colder, not really, but it stayed just as damp. With nothing else to do, I applied my brain and observed.

I looked out the rock-carved door to our prison, and at an angle I could see the cluster of men around the main campfire.

They seemed to pace aimlessly back and forth, except for one small group who were arguing, it seemed, arms waving and gesticulating wildly.

At odd intervals, messengers galloped up, the horses sliding in the mud as their riders hopped down. Without exception, each of these arrivals caused yet more argument. The more I watched, the more I understood what was transpiring.

It took no great genius to see that Teilo, Dochu, and David were allying with the Scotti. That Lauhiir's men had bribed Arthur's troops at the Mount of Frogs was proof to me that he was involved in this rebellion as well.

David, Teilo, Dochu, and Lauhiir. Together they could not field an army capable of moving against Arthur, but throw the Scotti into the mix and make it a quick strike to kidnap or kill Arthur at Ynys-witrin? That was more than possible. That was nearly a certainty. By the time that Kay, Gawain, Gaheris, and the other lords could react, David would have staked his claim as Rigotamos. If nothing else, he could establish a northern confederacy operating outside the *consilium*'s control.

That was the very thing that Arthur was trying so hard to prevent. If we were divided, the Saxons could slice through us like a sharp dagger through pig. But all David and his friends dreamed of was their own power, their own purses, their own greed. Already these lords held too much power in their incapable hands. None of them could see beyond their own noses. True Britons understood the need for solidarity; even poor misguided Vortigern had understood this before he became besotted with the Saxons.

But what was causing the consternation at the campfire? I saw nothing of the Scotti leader I had watched at Bannaventa. Something was not working with their plans and the flow of riders was not bringing the information they needed. For with each rider, their frustration was more and more obvious.

Then, with a start, I recognized the two Scotti who had captured us, being pushed into the circle of light. They were but foot soldiers and deserved little respect, or so thought our lords, I suspected.

One Scotti, the one that had wanted to kill us, I thought, was on his knees, begging, it seemed. At one juncture he pointed toward us. A tall, imposing figure, still merely silhouetted against the campfire, yelled out. Two figures rushed in our direction. As they drew closer, I saw that they wore the tunic of David.

I had never seen David's two soldiers before. They had not been with his escort at Arthur's castle for the election. One, a tall man with his hair braided, ordered the guard at the door away. The other, shorter and stouter, bulled his way in and grabbed the sleeping Llynfann by his hair.

I dove forward to stop him, but his companion with the braided hair was suddenly on me with his dagger at my throat.

Still, I pushed forward until the dagger tore my skin, but I heard Llynfann's voice call out gaily to me.

"No, Malgwyn! These lads just want to talk to me a bit! I'll be back."

And then my little friend was gone. I rushed to the door again, but the two guards still barred my way. My eyes searched the darkness but wherever they had taken him was out of my field of view.

Time passed. I tried to question my guards, but they completely ignored me. I worried about Llynfann. He would not be in this mess had I not commandeered him and sent him on my mission. At the time, I suspected that Lauhiir and Coroticus were trading with pirates, illegal, but hardly an affair to die over. I had no idea then that it was a conspiracy, aye, one aimed at the heart of our island.

As for the reason I had traveled west, well, I thought I understood the murders now. Myndora had provided many answers, aye, even answers she herself did not realize she possessed. The gods had truly wrapped this puzzle in the thickest clay.

Dawn came and went. No sign of Llynfann, but the Scotti leader, he of the white and gold tunic and hair as red as sunset, strode into camp with an escort. They all carried heavy spears and shields, draped around on their backs. As their leader joined the others at the campfire, the men of the escort found an empty spot and squatted.

I watched closely as the tallest of our lords, a man I now recognized as David, spoke to the Scotti. His hands outstretched, palms upturned, I knew at once that he was pleading with the Scotti leader. Maybe whatever problem faced them would have the conspirators at each other's throats.

Turning back into the cave's chamber, I took up a bowl of pig meat that they had graciously given me. Sitting on the floor, I wedged it into my lap and began shoveling the food into my mouth. Still no sign of Llynfann. I suspected that the little thief was spinning another tale of wizardry and dragons. But I knew something he did not. Once David got a look at me, no story Llynfann told could save us.

It took but a few minutes to finish the meat. All it did was dull the pain in my stomach. I flung the bowl against the rock wall where it shattered.

"You should be more grateful, Malgwyn."

I turned to see Lord David standing in the entrance to the chamber. I did not stand. "And why is that, my lord?"

"I almost had you killed before I realized that one of Arthur's principal counselors was among us."

"And why did you not? Not four moons ago, you were quite ready to see me lose my head."

"I have a problem, you see. And I am wondering if you can solve it." David circled me. The way he hunched his shoulders and scrubbed his hands would forever remind me of a vulture. "Is that not what you are famed for?"

"Whatever skills I have in that regard have caused you troubles in the past. Why should I use them to help you?"

"Because I am going to spare your life if you do."

I knew that he lied. My life was over. But the longer I led him along, the longer there was hope. "Go ahead. Tell me your problems."

"As I am sure you have guessed by now, Teilo, Dochu, and myself have allied with Lauhiir to overthrow Arthur."

"My lord! You shock me!"

David shook his head in mock exasperation. "Do not interrupt me, Malgwyn. Now, our plan hinged on two things—first, Lauhiir's ability to lure Arthur to Ynys-witrin at the right time was the key element."

"Which he did. Arthur's habit of traveling without a large escort has already spread across the land."

"Exactly. Without a full escort, he could easily be killed or taken prisoner. Second, the Scotti, as you have already seen, have joined with us as well. Their task was to raid to the south and southeast of here as a diversion. That would draw troops from Arthur's castle and from Mordred's forces as well."

"Mordred is not privy to this?"

Lord David smoothed his mustache as he snickered. "Mordred has his own ambitions, and seeing me crowned as the next

Rigotamos is not among them. You misunderstand me, Malgwyn. I mean only the best for our lands. Arthur's way is too weak. We need strength. That is what I shall give the people."

"So you would risk a civil war to correct a mistake you think the *consilium* made by naming Arthur?"

"Malgwyn, Malgwyn! Look around you. We are in a perpetual state of civil war. This is not a country, not yet. And if you have not noticed the rotting villas, the Romans are gone. The *consilium* is but a dream, an illusion created so that the people can feel safe, so that they have someone to complain to. I propose to give them more than that, a true king who can rule from strength, not compromise!"

"Our people have already had that. From Vortigern, who ignored the *consilium*, ignored the people, and ended up feasting off his own lusts. Something has obviously gone wrong in your little scheme, David. What is it?"

He squatted before me. "Lauhiir is missing, and while I could do without his pitiful force, he has something else I do need."

And then I understood so much. "Let me guess. Lauhiir has the coins to pay off the Scotti. They are merely mercenaries, paid to wreak havoc on our people."

"Yes! What do you know of this?"

"Enough that you should be begging me for your life."

His eyes narrowed. "What?"

"Have you no spies in Ynys-witrin? Do you not know what has taken place there?"

"I know that the bishop Patrick is there. That was something we had not foreseen, but of little consequence. But Lauhiir provided us with our ears in that place. And—"

"And you have not heard from him for almost two days." I said it flatly, as fact.

"I have underestimated you, Malgwyn. Obviously, you have information that I need. Speak and you shall have a chance to save your life."

"How kind of you, Lord David." At that moment, I would not have given a dry crust of bread for my chances of living.

I knew that he was really just toying with me, trying to infuriate me enough to get me to reveal what he needed to know, what he assumed I knew. But I wanted to see the look in David's face when he realized how far afield his plans had gone. Perhaps he should have included Mordred in his scheme. Mordred was a far better planner.

"Lauhiir's forgery operation has been revealed. When that happened, his men killed three of Arthur's. Lauhiir is now a fugitive. His men have been offered the choice of joining Arthur's forces or being executed. I will leave it to you to guess which they chose."

"Hmph! How do I know that you tell the truth?"

"Have you seen more than a handful of Lauhiir's men in recent hours? Have those you have seen been from the troop charged with bribing the watchmen at the Mount of Frogs?"

Lord David licked his lips nervously and looked away.

"Did you know that Patrick, the bishop of the Scotti, is dead? Or that Arthur now has ten troop of horse at Ynyswitrin?" It was actually only about six troop, but a dead man has a right to a last jest.

David's eyes widened. "Ten?"

In truth, ten troop of horse was not that formidable a force. In numbers. But Arthur's horse were superbly trained and the equal of twice or three times their number. What it meant in practical terms was that instead of a single troop which could be dispatched quickly, the conspirators were looking at a pitched battle in which victory was no certainty. And traitors sought certainty.

Much as was Arthur's habit, David chewed the end of his mustache. "What caused Arthur to bring more horse to Ynys-witrin?"

"Lauhiir's treachery."

"What does Arthur know of this?"

And now I was the one chewing my lip. The truth? Or did I know the truth? More than a day had passed since I last saw Arthur and Bedevere. I knew nothing of what had transpired except that Lauhiir had not run to his fellows. I thought quickly of what I would have done in Lauhiir's place. The answer came just as quickly. Dodging Arthur's patrols was risky at best. The one place he could be sure of preserving his life was to claim sanctuary at Ynys-witrin.

The truth was enough to dash Lord David's hopes. I did not need to lie. "I do not know what Lauhiir may have told him. But when I left, he was suspicious of all of the coins flowing through the village. He had no idea of what forces had gathered against him. But Patrick's death and Lauhiir's fumbling have made him wary. Do not doubt that Lauhiir will give you up to save his own worthless hide.

"So, what does Arthur know? I suspect by now that he knows it all."

Surprisingly, I did not see defeat written upon Lord David's face. Rather, a calculating expression settled there, pulling his mouth at the corners and raising his bushy eyebrows.

He stood swiftly and moved to the entrance.

"What of your promise to spare my life?"

"I have no time to settle accounts with you now. That will have to wait. But rest assured, I will return."

"Then what of my *servus*?"

David, about to leave, turned back with a smile that I did not like. "Malgwyn, you have no *servi*. If you mean the bandit, well, he was not as helpful as you." He jerked his head at one of the guards who disappeared for a moment.

Before I understood what was happening, a round object bounced on the dirt floor before me. As it rolled to a halt, I stared into the open yet blank eyes of Llynfann, my little thief.

"He died well," David said, almost regretfully. "Much better than I would have allowed for a thief." And then he was gone, leaving me with the head of poor Llynfann, who was now bereft of hope.

I do not know how long I sat and stared at Llynfann's head and the ragged and bloody stump of his neck. Something about it transfixed me. Oh, I had sent men to their deaths before when I served as one of Arthur's captains. But that was different. Those men knew that following my orders could mean death. My little thief saw it as but a lark, something to earn another coin or two for his purse, something to brag to Gareth and the other *latrunculi* about.

Finally, as the sun disappeared and only the campfire and a single torch outside my chamber offered any light, I looked away, back toward the door cut from rock. Only one guard stood there now. I was sorely tempted to kill him, take his sword, and rush headlong into the pack of nobles around the fire, killing as many as I could before they took me down. If Arthur's god smiled on me, I might further disrupt their plans, perhaps even enough to stop them. After all, I would not be missed.

I stopped myself after only two steps from the door.

Mariam! Mariam, my daughter! She would miss me. I would have abandoned her again. And this time no one would be there to explain why I had left her. But I could not just sit here and wait to die either. Arthur would not be helped and Llynfann would not be avenged. Elafius would have died for nothing, and, perhaps, Patrick too. And I would leave Mariam and, yes, Ygerne, alone.

This required more thought. I edged close to the door and studied the land outside. I knew that the River Axe, the "river of sorrows," flowed out of the cave, split in two, and thence one branch south and one to the west. Stepping to my right, I looked deeper into the cave.

Just beyond my little chamber, the torches disappeared, though I saw an odd amber glow of light twenty or thirty feet down the shaft. I noticed too that my guard was not one of Lord David's now, but one of Teilo's, a lazy-looking oaf with a big belly and puffy lips. He looked hungry, but then he probably always looked hungry.

It might work.

Maybe.

I picked up Llynfann's head, balanced it in my one hand, and then, with a silent plea to the shade of my little friend for forgiveness, I threw it, clipping the side of the guard's head and bouncing off the tunnel wall opposite.

"Do you expect me to eat that?" I shouted.

He bolted around and, seeing Llynfann's head, fell back a step or two in fright.

"Well? I am hungry, you lout! Did they not tell you that I was a wizard? That I lost this"—and I waved my half-arm at him—"to a dragon? Either find me food or I will smite you with the flame of the dragon I slew!"

With my long hair flying wildly about, my half-empty sleeve, and the crazed look in my eye, I found it amazing that he did not die of fright. He did fall back against the tunnel wall, bringing a shower of small rock down around him.

"Food, you fool!"

He licked his lips, looked at me, looked at the campfire where I could see a pig roasting, and then back to me. He summoned up some courage, waved his spear at me, and said, "Do not move."

With that, he was gone, lumbering off to the campfire, snatching quick glances back toward me as he went to fetch food.

I wasted no time. Ducking out of the chamber, rather than bolting out of the tunnel, I turned left and went deeper, away from the world and into the realms of the witch.

CHAPTER FIFTEEN

I decided fifteen feet into the cave that I would not choose to live in one. It was not cold, but it was disagreeably cool. The farther in I went, the narrower the tunnel became. I glanced back behind me, but I heard no shouts of discovery. My guard may have decided to enjoy some food himself, I hoped.

Just ahead, I could see the glow, now a curious mix of amber with a bluish tint, that I had spied from my chamber. It seemed to be coming from ahead of me, from a curved opening into another chamber partially blocked with mud and rock. Dropping to my knees, I scrambled into the crevice of the opening, using my one hand to dig enough debris out that I could fit into the opening. Pathetic though the attempt, I used my half-arm to drag and push back the sludge.

In the distance, I could hear a pair of voices drawing closer, but in the strange echoes of the cave, I could not really judge how far away they were. So, I dug faster.

Progress was slow. The rocks were heavy and slippery, the mud sticky. But before I expected it, the voices were on top of me and I saw torchlight suddenly bouncing off the ceiling.

Without warning, the air was full of some kind of flying creature!

They were all around me, all over me! Hundreds of them! Making some sort of screeching sound.

I flailed about with my arm and knocked two or three to the ground. In the dim light streaming through the opening, I saw that it was some sort of ratlike creature with wings. They had faces of pure evil with devilish teeth. Bats. They were common—especially in our forests where they lived in hollow trees and frightened passersby.

From the entrance of the tunnel I could hear shouts of alarm go up. They knew I was missing now.

The screeching stopped almost as quickly as it started, and the flying creatures disappeared. I slipped my legs through the opening, praying that they would find purchase on the other side.

They did not.

With my face plastered against mud and rock, and my one poor hand barely holding on as my feet and legs swung below me, I saw the dancing torchlight moving down the tunnel, toward me.

I let go.

For a moment, it was like falling into a bluish-orange cloud and I thought how pretty it was, until I slammed into the ground and the blow stole all of my breath.

I waited in the dark for a few moments as my eyes adjusted to the eerie glow. As I caught my breath, I realized that I had landed in sand, something I thought strange in a cave.

Slowly, the chamber I had fallen into took on shape and proportion. Above me, some fifteen feet, the hole through which I had fallen looked like a window. Beside me, the River Axe flowed beneath a ceiling as high as that of any hall where I had ever feasted. I lay on a sandbank next to the river, far back into the cave from where it exited. Unless my pursuers chanced to look in the hole above, they would never find me here.

As the thought struck me, I heard the screech of the flying rats from above. The scuffling of *caligae* on rock drifted down as curses rang out. I had to chuckle.

Until I turned over and came face-to-face with a skull.

I scrambled back against the wall of the cave, as far as I could get from the grinning skull, its forehead shining from grains of sand catching the vague light.

He was buried up to his chest in sand. I could not tell if the sand had once covered him completely and washed away, or if it were just now layering over him. Suddenly, legends of Druids and sacrificed Romans seemed more real.

No more sounds drifted down from the small hole I had come through. They would be looking outside now, believing that I had somehow slipped past the guards and was making my way south, which I intended to do. Just not where they were looking so earnestly.

But what was David up to? And, in truth, had Arthur caught Lauhiir? What might he have told them of this conspiracy? I ground my teeth. Now was not the time to be asking such questions. Now I had to be about the task of getting back to Ynyswitrin, back to Arthur. I held a number of debts that needed to be repaid.

The River Axe, the "river of sorrows," flowed gently, and clear, so clear that I could see nearly to the bottom. But I knew that was a trick of the eye. It was far, far deeper.

I slipped into the water, cold as it was, took a deep breath, and began to pull myself slowly along the bank, edging closer and closer to the mouth of the cave and the torchlight. Then suddenly I was in the light and I felt naked.

But no one was even looking my way. From what little I could see, a handful of Teilo's soldiers were scouring the steep bank across the hollow from me. But the rest, Teilo and Dochu among them, were eating and drinking by the fire. David was not to be seen, causing me to wonder again at what scheme he was up to.

My plan was to hug the bank as closely as I could, keep my head below bank level and slip past the soldiers arrayed around the campfire. Once I was out of immediate danger, I could climb onto dry land and work my way south. I knew that my path might very well take me across David's battle lines, but I knew too that no battle had yet begun. Too many soldiers still lazed about. No urgency stirred the air. They were waiting for something, but now that David knew of Lauhiir's troubles I could not imagine what.

I kept on, moving ever so slowly, doing my best to draw no attention my way. My legs were numbed by the cold water. Were it not for my hand edging me along, I would have been in terrible trouble.

Just as I drew abreast of the campfire, some thirty feet distant, I heard the sound of *caligae* stomping loudly across the ground. I froze. To move was to beg discovery.

Above me, I could hear the soldier's heavy breathing. Seconds later I felt a warm liquid strike my head, and I smelled the putrid odor of mead-laden piss. I could not move. I could do nothing until he finished.

For a moment I thought he had drunk an entire jug, and it took every ounce of strength I could muster to keep my teeth from chattering. Finally, his flood ended, and I continued my frigid journey.

It took nearly half an hour longer to get clear of the knot of soldiers gathered around the cave. I pulled myself from the stream, though it took all my remaining strength. The chill of the stream had left my lower body with no feeling. I knew sensation would return, but it would take a little time.

Nearby was another yew tree, another reminder of Elafius. As a little life returned to my legs, I pulled and pushed myself into the shelter of the tree.

With my back against the tree, I used my one hand to knead some feeling into my legs. Pain began shooting through them and I knew that they were recovering. My stomach grumbled, and I cursed myself once again. Had I not been so interested in feeding my belly up on the *meneds*, I would be back in Ynyswitrin and Arthur would be prepared for this threat.

A sadness struck me, sudden and sharp. Llynfann would still be dead. His fate was sealed when I sent him off to trace the flow of goods. I slammed my fist into the ground. The little fellow had simply looked at it all as a game. Life for people like him was usually short and violent in our lands. Life for everyone was short and violent. I knew few older folk, mostly *monachi* or old women. So many died so young, like my Gwyneth and her sister Eleonore, and Cuneglas.

A deep sigh escaped my lungs as I realized that unless I moved, and quickly, I would die sooner rather than later myself. I cast about, looking to judge where, exactly, I had landed.

The river had fallen away a good bit from where it flowed out of the cave, from where the soldiers were gathered. I could see the glow of the campfire in the distance, but as I had guessed, the narrowness of the gorge hid it well.

A path ran alongside the river, and I could see through the bushes and shrubs that there were two guards posted down below me a spear's throw away. More important, a horse snorted and stomped its hooves. My best chance of reaching safety was to steal the horse and ride like demons were after me, all the way down to Ynys-witrin.

The tingle in my feet told me that they had warmed enough to carry me. I cast about, looking for something to use as a weapon, but I saw nothing. I certainly could not defeat them with my charm. Indeed, in my state, I had no charm with which to assault them.

Flopping onto my belly, I crawled slowly to another tree, closer to the soldiers and with a better view. They were David's men, but not among his best. Their tunics were dirty and their sandals untied. They held their spears loosely and seemed more suited to holding skins of wine than weapons. It puzzled me for a moment, and then I realized that this would be far behind the point of action, exactly where I would put soldiers of questionable ability.

This river path seemed seldom traveled. I knew that another lane lay on the other side of the gorge, a wider, better maintained one, no more than two hundred yards from where I lay. I could hear the sound of hooves pounding on packed earth in that direction. Soldiers were moving finally. Back toward the main campfire, I could hear shouts being raised.

Looking back to the two soldiers by the river, I saw that their attention had been drawn to the burst of activity. They watched for a few moments and then, almost in unison, slouched back against a tree, figuring, I guessed, that with the soldiers finally moving, there would be less work for them. Had David seen them, their heads would be feeding the fish in the River Axe.

Even from this distance, I could see their eyes open and close lazily until they did not open again. I waited a few more minutes.

When I was sure that they had drifted off, I stood up. On the other side of the tree, I found a broken limb big enough to make a club. The club was my last resort.

The horse was tied off to a tree about ten yards away from the guards where there was plenty of grass for it to graze. It shuffled around but seemed unconcerned by my presence as I walked up to the sleeping guards.

My mood was not one of forgiveness. I stood before one of the slovenly guards for a few seconds. For all I knew, these were the ones who had done for poor Llynfann. If they were, they killed a better man than they had ever been.

I reached down, yanked one soldier's dagger from his belt, and plunged it in his heart. His eyes flew open and his mouth formed a perfect circle, but he never made a sound.

Withdrawing the dagger and tucking it into my belt, I trod softly around the tree. His companion was snoring still. I smiled and took up the club. With one swing, I bashed in his head with a soft thud, spattering the tree with blood. To be certain, I dropped the club and slit his throat with the dagger. I did not really think about it; I just did it.

A sudden calm had come over me. I could not feel the chill in my legs. I replaced the dagger in my belt and took up both spears from the soldiers.

With a tenderness even I did not understand, I approached the horse and let her sniff my half-arm. Whatever she sensed, it calmed her. Taking my time, I strapped the spears to her saddle, a leather contraption in those days with a thick pad running round it and cinched with leather straps underneath the horse's belly and around in front of her breast. The spears were close enough to reach and loose enough to come free with but a tug, the way we mounted them in war.

That done, I went back to the soldiers, judged their general height and weight, and clumsily took the tunic from the one whose head I had bashed. The head blow killed him, so there had been no spray from his slit throat.

Moments later, I looked as one of David's soldiers, though probably more disheveled than his best, except for my half-arm. It might not be noticed immediately, but if I were subjected to any real scrutiny, it would give me away. I was not the only man in Britannia missing an arm, but such a man would be seen as bad luck as a soldier.

With a smile, an idea formed. Snatching up one of the shields, I quickly mounted the horse. Once there, I lashed the shield to my half-arm. It was not a perfect disguise, but it would do. Grasping the reins in my one good hand, I turned the horse's head, kicked her in her flanks, and headed her off toward the abbey and Arthur.

An hour later, I was still traveling slowly, following the course of the river. The sight of a soldier on a horse, riding at full gait, would attract too much attention. A few soldiers, those of Teilo and Dochu, had chanced my way, but a wave of my shield satisfied them and they kept moving. In my heart, I knew that luck had ridden on my shoulder to get even this far. Soon, if not already, the two dead soldiers would be found and word would spread that a tunic was missing. If luck, or the gods, were still with me, I would be at Arthur's side by then.

Off to my right, in the far distance, I could see the strong, yellow glow of torches, the gathering place I figured for the Scotti and their traitorous colleagues. I knew the area slightly, knew that a series of low hills would block the gathering from almost any watchman in the south.

As I reached the curve in the River Axe where it sweeps off to the west, I saw two hills to the south of me. My wanderings had carried me often enough in their vicinity that I could recognize them easily. I knew that if I rode due south, between them, that I could cross the marshy levels to the northwestern corner of Ynys-witrin's range of hills.

Ahead of me, I recognized a ford across the River Axe. Turning the horse's head, I prepared to cross and begin my run to safety. Just as I reached it, a knot of horsemen rode up, three nobles and others of their escorts. They were lesser nobles, two of Teilo's banner and one of Dochu's. I ducked my head and moved to ride on when I heard a shout.

"You! Soldier!"

I thought about riding on, but I knew he was shouting at me and to ignore it was simply to draw attention to myself.

Turning my horse to face them, I raised my hand in salute. "Aye, my lord."

It was a boy lord wearing Dochu's banner on his tunic. "Attend us. We are riding to a council of war on the little tor ahead. We may have need of you as a messenger."

A council of war was the last place I wanted to be, but they were riding in the right direction, and I reasoned that once there, perhaps I could slip away. Councils of war brought many men together. 'Twas easier to lose oneself in a crowd.

I fell in behind them as their horses splashed across the ford. The other soldiers were haphazardly dressed, a sign that their lords were short of funds. David's men were, at least, arrayed uniformly. The old Roman gold mines lay within David's lands. I wondered, for half a second, why he did not use this gold, if he had it, to bribe the Scotti. But then I realized that David was cagey, and he would not hazard his own purse on so risky an enterprise. No, he would leave that burden to others.

We rode at a brisk pace. I learned nothing from the escorts save for the name of a woman who served good *cervesas* as well as other necessities. But the trip took only about twenty minutes, and we soldiers were left at the base of a wooded hill, holding the reins of the nobles as they climbed the steep incline.

Among the other escorts, I saw a half-dozen of David's and my heart leaped into my throat. I was sure to be caught out. Keeping my head low, I hung to the outer edge of the clump of soldiers, hoping that I could skirt them and drift off quietly. A path had been cut through the trees on the slope, but they grew fairly thick around the base. If I could but get around them, they would block me from view.

Acknowledging the greetings of other soldiers with a grunt and half-salute, I kept my horse at a slow gait, wandering, almost aimlessly it must have seemed, to the trees on our right, a cluster of chestnut and maple.

Then I saw him, carefully descending the newly cut path, the white blazes of fresh wood dotting the hill like iron studs on a belt.

David.

Worse yet, he saw me.

Our eyes locked.

Recognition flared.

A swift kick to the horse's flanks and I was off, as I heard David shouting instructions behind me.

I had rounded the trees and headed down the southern trail when I heard the horse's hooves behind me, pounding the ground like one of our old tribal drums.

Even as I heard the whistle of a spear in flight, I did not dare look around, not even when its sharp edge clipped my ear and I could feel the warm blood run down my neck. I simply kicked the horse all the harder, urging it faster.

As if it could hear me, the horse laid its ears back and lengthened its stride.

Then, with at least one of my pursuers without his spear, I chanced to glance behind me. Four horsemen pursued me, all four David's men. The others must have wondered why David's men chased another of their lord's soldiers, for I certainly looked like such.

Over all of the shouting, I heard a familiar voice rise. Another glance back, and I caught a glimpse of David, his fist raised in a gloved clench, shouting curses at me. I would have smiled but for the quartet of men chasing me.

I was out in the levels by then, those flat, marshy lands surrounding Ynys-witrin. In the distance, in the bright moonlight, I could see the rising hills that made an island of the Tor. Another ten minutes' hard ride and I would be safe.

Or I would have been until my poor horse stepped into a badger hole.

For a second, I flew through the air, the shield lashed to my half-arm flailing wildly about. I broke my fall into the soft ground with the shield. It sent me tumbling, wrenching my knee, but I had no time for pain.

As quickly as I could, I got to my feet and staggered back toward my horse. Poor fellow, his leg was broken badly, so badly the bone showed whitely through his hide. Swiftly, without hesitation, I loosed the spears tied to his saddle and thrust one deeply into his throat. He had borne me too well to suffer. As the blood gushed forth, I stepped back and wished him well on his trip to the next life.

In the distance, I heard the hoofbeats of my pursuers drawing closer. The Tor and Ynys-witrin were still too far away to run for it, not when chased by four horsemen. A fast look about revealed no easy escapes, no high river bluffs from which to jump. Just four traitors to face.

Some low shrubs and hedges marked the ground, and I ducked down low. I had only one advantage, surprise. With any luck, the odds would be cut from four to one to two to one. With luck.

And then they were on me.

Or rather over me.

By the time they had caught up with me, they were riding so fast that they overshot my hiding place. Aye, they would have swept on into the early morning light, just beginning to show its face beyond the Tor, but my poor horse gave me away.

As it was, the first two soldiers missed the horse's carcass completely. It was the third whose eye caught it.

And it was the third whose eye caught my first spear.

I rose swiftly, hiding only two or three feet from where he stopped. It was no skillful deed to sink my spear point into his eye socket, thrusting into his brain, twisting for good measure and then jerking it loose.

Only it did not come cleanly loose and only succeeded in yanking the soldier from his perch and wrenching the spear from my one-handed grasp. I snatched up the other spear and whirled around to face my fourth pursuer.

His horse, racing up on the scene, reared up in fright,

toppling its rider to the ground. I was on him before he could scramble to his feet, driving the spear into his unprotected neck, sending a gout of blood spurting into the air. I snatched the dagger from his belt, tucked it in my own, and then spun to face his fellows.

They were on me.

The first was a seasoned soldier who bore down on me without hesitation. I tried to block his sword with my spear, but he was a man of uncommon strength, and the blow broke the shaft below the point.

Having dodged him, I could not dodge the second. His sword split the air by my head and cleaved a slice off the side of my head.

Pain exploded as I fell to the ground and my stomach revolted against me as I threw up the bad bile collected there. The world was spinning as I struggled to regain my feet. Blood was flooding down the side of my face, obscuring my vision and stealing yet more of my strength.

In a scarlet-colored haze, I thought I saw one of the soldiers dismount to finish the kill. I had made it to my knees by then, willing myself to rise. I paused to catch my breath as he closed in.

Then, with every bit of strength I had left, just as he came near enough to smell him, I drove my dagger into his stomach and twisted.

I fell away then, saying a prayer for Mariam and Ygerne. An odd satisfaction came over me as I reckoned that I had accounted for three of them. Not bad for a one-armed man.

But then blackness closed in and stole the prayer from my lips.

CHAPTER SIXTEEN

At first, I heard nothing but voices, dim, confused, as if spoken from a barrel or through a heavy cloth. My eyes tried to open yet they felt glued shut. A voice broke through the fog finally.

"He's trying to open his eyes! Clean his eyes!"

Then I felt a wet piece of cloth, warm and comforting, wiping across my eyes. My eyelids came open and I saw Merlin's face nearly against my own.

"Good. He is awake." Merlin withdrew his face, much to my relief, and turned away from me. The pain in my head pounded like a dozen Saxons beating it with rocks.

I felt a hand under my head and a beaker held to my lips. A lukewarm liquid passed my lips, burning my throat. "What is that, poison?"

"Extract of willow bark, Malgwyn, as you know all too well," Merlin chastised me. "I believe that sword sliced off some of your good sense."

"A sword, Merlin?" I heard Arthur's voice. "I thought Malgwyn had taken the orders and this was some new tonsure."

With a start, I remembered all that had passed. I jerked to a sitting position. "Arthur! Lord David, Teilo, Dochu, the Scotti." It all came rushing out. Arthur patted me on the shoulder.

"I know, Malgwyn. I know. David has already sent a messenger in."

"Demanding your surrender?"

The whole room, Merlin, Bedevere, Illtud, and Arthur, burst into laughter. "Malgwyn, that sword must have indeed upset your brain. David is on our side."

Despite Arthur's jest and the pounding in my skull, my brain was working just fine. But I would have to approach this carefully. "What did his messenger say?"

"That Lauhiir, Teilo, and Dochu were conspiring to attack me here, take me captive or kill me. That David was playing along with their game to better serve me, but when their attack came, he would turn his forces on them."

David's treachery knew no bounds. When he saw that his plans were falling apart, he simply arranged to change sides. Except that I had been slated for death. "How come me here?"

"One of my patrols came upon you in the levels, not far from here," Illtud answered. "My soldiers saw a man race away on a horse. We found you with three of Lord David's men slain, lying about you."

"Malgwyn," Arthur began sternly, "I trust you have a good reason for killing them. If I am to hold Lauhiir accountable for killing my men, I cannot excuse you for killing David's."

Bedevere handed me a beaker of mead and I drank deeply. The pain in my head was receding a bit. "Rigotamos, have I ever lied to you?"

Arthur cocked his head to the side. "No, Malgwyn, you have not."

"Then listen carefully. David is not your ally. He changed

260

sides when he learned that his plans had fallen apart. This he told me himself."

"But Malgwyn—"

"Arthur!" Merlin stopped him with his most schoolmasterly voice. "Listen to him."

So, between drinks of watered wine, I told Arthur my tale, from the journey to Bannaventa to following the Scotti, to my capture, imprisonment, the death of Llynfann, and my escape.

Arthur had long ago taken up a chair next to where I lay. He tugged on his beard and stayed silent for several minutes. "You make much sense. Illtud's patrols spied the gathering of soldiers some hours ago, before David's messenger arrived. But what you tell of Lauhiir bribing the Scotti to raid our southern lands is news indeed. If all you say is true, we may have a serious fight on our hands, Malgwyn."

"Do not take David's vows of allegiance at face value, my lord. Watch carefully. He may merely hold his men in reserve until he sees how we fare against the others. Watch your flanks. Send scouts to oversee David's forces. Be prepared for a strike even as you prepare for his assistance." I was on truly safe ground here. It was just such advice that first brought me to Arthur's notice. "And, if there has been killing, my lord, David began it. Llynfann was operating under my instructions, therefore he was in your service."

Arthur nodded. "Understood and agreed."

"How stand your forces here?"

"We have moved up all but a hundred from the castle. But that may not be enough to handle the threat that Teilo and Dochu present, especially if the Scotti are convinced to join in battle here. Lauhiir's men have scattered. Some have come to my banner; others may have joined the rebels. I have sent messengers to Gawain in the north and Mark in the south to gather their men and set patrols out immediately. Kay is too far away to help us here."

"Has Lauhiir been found? I suspect he will confirm much of what I have said. Anything, I imagine, to save his own neck."

I watched as every head in the room turned to avoid my eyes. "What?"

Bedevere spoke first. "He has sought sanctuary with Coroticus. As long as he remains within the abbey precinct, we cannot touch him."

"How did he cross the *vallum*? How did he get past your guards?"

No one answered at first. Finally, Merlin, with a scowl, ventured an answer. "We do not know. He just appeared near the burying ground. Our men took him immediately, but Coroticus hurried up and granted him sanctuary."

Regardless of how my head hurt, despite the weakness that gave tremors to my legs, I rose from my pallet. The time had come to put an end to this affair. Aye, this affair and that of Elafius and Patrick as well. I was tired of this puzzle, and I was beginning to believe that I understood how to unravel it.

"Bring me Lauhiir, Gwilym, Coroticus, and Rhiannon. I have had enough of their lies and half-truths. It is time for answers. When that is finished, I have an idea of how to handle the battle ahead."

With Merlin and Bedevere helping me, we moved into Coroticus's main hall. Merlin gave me more of the willow bark extract. As I waited for the group to gather, I steeled myself for the task ahead. Questions were to be asked and answered. Lies and secrets were to be revealed. But my plan lay along two paths—one of justice, and one of truth. Now was just the prelude, the beginning. The true ending would come later.

Several minutes later, the hall had been transformed into a tribunal, with myself as chief inquisitor. I had the quartet seated in front of me in a row. Arthur, Bedevere, and Merlin were arrayed behind me. At my direction, two soldiers guarded the doors, as much to keep people out as in. Ider and Gildas, I knew, were pacing outside. I had no trouble with Ider's presence, but Gildas was not welcome.

"Let us understand some things first," I began. "I will not spare anyone. It is time for all to be known."

Lauhiir favored me with a greasy, smug smile, believing that his sanctuary excused him of all misdeeds.

"Lord Liguessac!"

He fairly leaped from his seat. "What?"

"Did you kill Elafius because he threatened to reveal your forging operation? Despite being an annoying old man, he was a good man and would have objected to your plan."

"What forging? What do you mean?"

At that Arthur rose and in two steps had fronted Lauhiir and jerked him about. "Enough, you mongrel! Everyone here knows that you were using the tin mining to aid in your forging of Roman coins. Else you would not be seeking sanctuary with Coroticus. And thanks to Malgwyn, we know that you conspired with Teilo and Dochu and the Scotti to overthrow me."

I wondered that he did not mention David, and I saw a subtle hint of a question in Lauhiir's eyes as well.

"Rigotamos," I said calmly. "It does not matter if Lord Liguessac admits to such. We all know it is true. Elafius discovered in some manner that you were forging coins." Reaching into my pouch, I extracted the silver *denarius* I had found on Elafius's floor. "He had this with him when he died. I suspect you missed this one when you searched his cell for the others."

Lauhiir shifted uncomfortably. "You have proven nothing."

"Who else stood to profit from Elafius's death? Only you. Had he revealed your secret to anyone, it would have meant your death for treason."

"If that is so, how did I get in and out of the abbey precinct without being seen? Answer that, Master Malgwyn!"

Glancing behind me, I saw that Arthur and Bedevere were both leaning forward. We had all wondered how Gwilym and Lauhiir had gotten past our cordon around the abbey *vallum*.

I smiled at Lauhiir. "I remember something Lady Rhiannon said to me once, about there being 'ways.' Did you have the tunnel dug, Coroticus?" I said, spinning to face the abbot. "Or was it already here?"

"They, Malgwyn, they were already here. Though I will admit to having them widened."

"What tunnels, Malgwyn? What are you talking about?" Arthur was confused, as well he might be. I had pondered the question deeply. I knew the efficiency of Arthur's men. I knew that the chances of not just one, but two men avoiding detection while slipping into the abbey precinct were slim at best. But the fact was that both Lauhiir and Gwilym had appeared within the abbey defenses unseen. And a man like Coroticus would not resist the opportunity to either create an escape avenue or to use one already there.

"Where are they?"

Coroticus sighed. "The one that Lauhiir and Gwilym used runs from the chapel well, under the women's community, and comes out near the spring below Lauhiir's fort."

"And the others?"

"The others are none of your business, Malgwyn. I am still abbot here and beholden only to the Christ and his church."

I heard Arthur grumble behind me, but the abbot was technically right. Although the abbey operated under the sufferance of the local lord and the Rigotamos, it operated under the nominal control of the bishop, in this case, Dubricius.

"Which now brings us to the question of Patrick's death. I confess that I was utterly and totally confused as to how this fit in with the murder of poor Elafius. Until, that is, I realized that the two were not connected. Elafius was killed to protect the conspiracy against Arthur. Patrick was killed to keep another secret."

Coroticus stood. "This is nonsense, Malgwyn! You must be drunk!"

"Sit down and be silent, abbot. Or I will disregard your office. I may be one-armed, but I can still throttle you," I said in a calm, even tone.

Coroticus sat.

"I was convinced that Patrick's and Elafius's deaths stemmed from the same cause, until I went to Bannaventa." As I expected, two pairs of eyebrows rose. "No, we did not advertise that I was going. I garbed myself as 'Mad Malgwyn,' and I went in search of answers, answers to an old mystery."

"What old mystery? Rigotamos, why do you allow him such liberties?"

"Need I remind you, abbot, that it was you who called

Malgwyn to this task. And your protestations simply make you look guilty in this affair." Arthur's voice was stern, brooking no retort.

"Patrick told me that he had been called to account for a deed he had done as a youth, a deed he had told only to his best friend, a youngster named Tremayne. That would be you, Gwilym."

The old *monachus* had remained quiet throughout. Now, he looked only sad. "You have visited my sister, Myndora."

"Aye, I have. She told me of your friendship with Patrick, of the death of Addiena."

"He killed Patrick because of some childhood disagreement?" Poor Lauhiir. He really understood so little.

"No. He killed Patrick because he knew that Patrick would recognize him, would recognize him and reveal that Gwilym here has also been known as Agricola, the Pelagian."

Arthur rose in surprise. Bedevere quickly followed. Rhiannon began to rise, but Gwilym took her arm and guided her back to her seat.

"Patrick's death was necessary, sad but necessary," Gwilym said. "He would have stopped me in my quest to continue Pelagius's mission. I did what I had to do to protect my task. It was, he was, a divine sacrifice, dedicated to the glory of God."

"No!" Rhiannon cried, clutching Gwilym's arm. But he pushed her away.

"No, my girl! I have nothing to fear. I am under the abbot's protection."

I smiled at that. "It is only natural, Gwilym, for a daughter to wish to protect her father."

At that, my old friend Coroticus turned pale and nearly passed out. He had not known.

"So, that is it?" Merlin queried. "Lauhiir killed Elafius and Gwilym killed Patrick?"

"Yes," I lied. "And both are protected by the ancient laws of sanctuary."

Arthur grimaced. "Lord Liguessac, this is not finished. You cannot remain here forever. And you now have more to answer for than just the killing of three of my men. Malgwyn has shown you to be a murderer in your own right as well as a traitor." He turned to Coroticus. "You, dear abbot, are risking the survival of your abbey by protecting these people. Of this, we have much more to discuss. Much more. Right now, I have a rebellion to put down. Bedevere!"

"Yes, Rigotamos!"

"Set guards on the old *monachus* and Liguessac. They may be protected by the laws of sanctuary, but that does not mean we cannot keep our eyes on them."

"Immediately, my lord."

"Rigotamos?" I did not know how Arthur would respond to my request, but I was determined in my course.

"Yes, Malgwyn."

"I want a troop of horse to command."

Arthur, Bedevere, Merlin, Rhiannon, they all looked at me as if I were crazy. "Malgwyn, half your head is bloodied. You are not steady on your feet."

"Arthur, give me a troop to command or I will join the battle as a simple soldier. This you cannot stop." At that moment, a heat rose in me, blocking out all knowledge of pain. I had felt it before, but never this strong. Blood. I wanted to soak myself in the blood of my enemies, and fatigue and the great wound to my head would not stop me. An energy coursed through me that could only be sated by my sword sunk to the hilt in the rebels' bellies. This time, only death would steal me from the battle.

To my surprise, Bedevere stepped forward. "Rigotamos, we need him. We are far short of experienced commanders. We have none of the other lords nor Kay."

"He is right, Arthur," Merlin added.

"It seems that I am outvoted, Malgwyn. May God have mercy on us and lead us to victory."

As we left the hall, Merlin walked up beside me and whispered, "You left a great deal out, Malgwyn. It was not very satisfactory, nor particularly logical."

I draped my good arm about his ancient shoulders and squeezed. "No, my friend, it was not. But the time will come. Trust me."

I leaned forward in my saddle and studied the ground as a beautiful sun burned off the early morning mist. I did not understand why the rebels had dithered and wasted a full day, but I was grateful for it. The delay had allowed me to mend a bit more and compose a message for my daughter, Mariam, and Ygerne, my brother's widow and now Mariam's mother.

Our strategy was bold, and depended as much on Teilo's and Dochu's inexperience as on any faith in Lord David. Bedevere commanded our left flank, Arthur the center, and I the right. Illtud commanded our reserve, slated to enter battle only if David betrayed us at a critical moment or if the tide of battle turned against us in some other way.

Our scouts told us that all was confusion in the rebel camp. The Scotti were still there; apparently the rebels had found some other form of payment. Their presence made our victory a chancy thing, but that there was confusion was good. I remembered, too well, the Scotti lord of the white and gold tunic. He struck me as a man of confidence, a man to respect in battle, and no fool. He would not spend his men on a failed cause.

We moved in force down from the hills of Ynys-witrin and across the marshy levels. All of us, that is, except Illtud, who led his force far to the right. That provided him with the clearest and quickest avenue to enter the fray. Arthur and Bedevere were to make the primary assault, hitting the center and the left. When the rebel leaders began to pull troops from the right to reinforce, I would strike their weakened flank and ride up into their rear.

I was proud as I watched our army take the line. Arthur, as was his way, rode forward, chestnut hair flowing behind him, unhindered by a helmet. Pausing for a moment, he pulled his sword, thrust it in the air, and declared in a voice that rang across the land, "For God and Brittania!"

And then nothing could be heard but the screams of our woad-painted warriors and the thunderous pounding of horses' hooves as they charged the rebels at the base of the hills to the north.

Minutes later, as our plan unfolded, I too thrust my sword into the air. But my cry was a little different, and the words caught in my throat just a bit as I screamed, "For God, Brittania, and Llynfann!"

And we charged.

CHAPTER SEVENTEEN

Later, Arthur claimed that it was my assault on the right that sealed our victory. Whoever earned the triumph, the cost had been great. At the last, Teilo and Dochu had retreated onto the small hills just before the *meneds*. We surrounded them and they fought fiercely. The hills were littered with bodies as were the levels themselves. The blood mixed with the marshy ground, staining it a dark gray. The battle had been savage, and severed limbs and broken bodies were thick enough to walk upon without touching earth.

I had personally accounted for Teilo, riding recklessly into his escort, my shield little more than splinters, and scoring a lucky blow with my sword, leaving his head hanging by a strip of skin. Arthur himself finished the job, ordering that Dochu's and Teilo's heads be posted on stakes as a warning to other would-be rebels.

Riding down from the hills and back across the levels, I saw three oxcarts, manned by the *monachi*, searching amongst the bodies for the wounded. My men and Bedevere's were stacking the dead. Some of Arthur's were gathering wood for the funeral pyres. The Rigotamos had commanded that all of the men be honored, not just our own. "They are Britons after all," he said, "even if their lords did mislead them." His decree, of course, did not include Dochu or Teilo. Their carcasses would be left for the dogs and pigs to feast on.

The Scotti commander had led his men away from the battle when I charged the flank. I suspected that he was halfway back to *Hibernia*. And David? He did not commit his troops until after we had broken the rebels' backs. Then, he dispatched small detachments to chase down a few escaping soldiers. It was enough to placate Arthur but left the rest of us unconvinced.

The moaning of the wounded and the creaking of the wooden carts and the sloshing of the wheels in the mud broke me free of my thoughts. I looked down from my horse at three *monachi* as they stopped to gather a poor boy whose leg lay gashed open.

One of the *monachi* looked up at me; Gwilym, breaking sanctuary to help with the wounded. His eyes held no fear, only a stubborn challenge. But it was a challenge I had not the strength to take up. Not then. And the *monachi*, and our warriors, needed him too. Merlin had organized a camp for the wounded, but, sadly, most of them would die, many from loss of blood, the rest from putrefaction in their wounds. I rode past Gwilym.

Arthur, Bedevere, and Illtud were together near the center of the battlefield as I trotted my horse into their midst.

"Malgwyn! Your deeds will be sung in my hall!" Arthur was exhilarated. He was always like this after a battle, lively, bursting with words.

I laughed. No doubt my companions would tell the bards of how I looked at that moment. Blood was dried in my hair and beard, my shield still tied to my half-arm, dangling in three pieces. And where blood was not, mud held sway. My sword showed the scars of a battle hard fought, both those from clashing swords and the blackish red of rent flesh. I needed to wipe my blade clean; blood would pit the metal.

"With your permission, Rigotamos, I would return to the abbey to clean this muck from my body."

Before Arthur could answer, a voice behind me spoke, and it made my muscles tense as hard as rocks. David.

"Well, Malgwyn, you have acquitted yourself well this day. I thought never to see you in battle garb again."

With both my sword and the reins in my one hand, I spun my horse around to face him. "I suspect, my lord, you never thought to see me again at all."

"Now, Malgwyn, why would say you that?" The smirk on his face made mine grow hot.

Arthur and Bedevere froze. They had seen me like this before, usually just as someone was about to die. But, with great effort, I controlled the urge to hack the smile from his face.

"That, Lord David, is a conversation for another day. But be assured that that day will come."

With that, I turned my back on him, a mortal insult, and rode toward Ynys-witrin and the abbey.

The spare row of huts along the village street in Ynys-witrin looked empty and forlorn. At Merlin's makeshift infirmary, the cries of the wounded drowned out all else. Rhiannon and the other women were helping as best they could. Coroticus, Ider, and young Gildas were circulating among them, trying to give them comfort in what for many was their final hour. I passed on by.

My horse carried me up the slope to the *vallum* ditch and bank. Our soldiers still guarded the entrance, and they saluted

me as I entered, giving me that stare with which the uniniti-
ated honor battle veterans.

Weary as I was, it took more than a little effort for me to dismount. When I opened the cowhide-covered door to Elafius's
cell, I almost immediately collapsed on the pallet and fell into a
deep sleep.

A day passed, and more. I ventured forth only to find food,
and old Deiniol at the abbot's kitchen kept me well supplied. I
said little, and the *monachi* seemed to sense my need for solitude.
No one said anything about my using the dead *monachus's* cell. I
would have been surprised if they had.

On the second day after the battle, Arthur and Bedevere
left with three quarters of the soldiers. They asked me to go
with them, to return to Arthur's castle, but I declined as did
Merlin. "I am needed here, Arthur," my old, wrinkled friend
told our king. They thought I missed the telling glance that
Merlin threw my way, but I did not. Illtud stayed behind as well
with a sizable force, occupying Lauhiir's old fort. Small rebel
bands were still being spotted to the north.

I took the day to walk to the top of the Tor, where Patrick's
two assistants had established a hermitage in the old bishop's
name. They had agreed with Arthur to keep the watch fire
burning and to pass on any alarms. One was named Arnulph. I
cannot remember the other.

From where I sat on the Tor, I could see across the levels
to the *meneds* in the distance. I could see the muddy, gray area
where we had fought the rebels, and I watched as the smoke
from the warriors' funeral pyres made columns reaching to the
sky. The constant wind carried that sweetish, sickly odor of
burning human flesh. I sat there for a long while, thinking about
Mariam, Ygerne, Arthur, Merlin. I thought of little Llynfann

who did die well, of old Myndora in her ruined villa and her brother, the enigmatic Tremayne, and his daughter, Rhiannon. But most of all, I thought of Elafius and Patrick, two childhood friends whose lives had taken such odd turns all those years before.

Just past the midday, I looked up to see young Ider trudging up the slope. He carried a bit of bread. Sitting down uninvited next to me, he hesitantly offered the bread and I took it with a smile.

"I suppose you want to know things, my friend."

He pursed his lips and spoke falteringly. "Malgwyn, I do not understand all that has transpired."

"Yet you say you want to follow in my footsteps, as a seeker of these things."

The young *monachus* shook his head. "I believed so. I did. But how anyone could find truth and justice in this affair, I cannot see. I know of your assignment of guilt before the battle. It was not logical. It was not true."

I took my one hand and placed it squarely on his shoulder. "Sometimes, my friend, truth and justice are not obtainable, at least not in combination. Sometimes you must settle for one or the other."

Ider, his skin growing rough from the constant winds, was caught between boyhood and manhood, and could not see down the path before him. And he would not, until he had traveled the path a bit further. Such a journey was not one I could guide him along.

He sat with me there, without speaking, as the sun painted its way across the sky.

And when finally the sun began its descent beyond the shores of Hibernia, I stopped thinking, rose, and turned to young Ider. "You have been a good companion, my friend. Now, I must see to the end of this affair." He started to rise. "No, Ider, I must complete this journey on my own."

His cherub cheeks fell. "Ider, you are a good and honest man. If events should place you in my position in an affair like this, remember that justice and truth often do not swim in the same stream."

With that, I walked back down the Tor. Satisfaction was not an emotion that I had ever truly felt when I had untied knots like these. This one was to be no different. Indeed, I felt only a great sadness. With a sigh, I sent one of the *servi* to alert Merlin. The time had come to put this affair behind me.

I found Coroticus in his private chamber adjacent to his feasting hall. He was sitting before a small wooden table, reading a scroll by the light of an old oil lamp. As I entered, he turned and squinted at me in the dim light. I had forgotten how handsome he was, though his hair was now marked with great swatches of gray, and wrinkles grew from the corners of his eyes.

"Malgwyn! How are you feeling?"

"Unsettled."

Coroticus nodded. "The last several days would unsettle anyone. We have been pleased to allow you time to rest and recover from your exertions."

"And I am grateful for your hospitality."

"You are always welcome here, Malgwyn. You know that."

I sighed. "Perhaps not after tonight."

"I do not understand." But he did. I could see it in his eyes.

"Lauhiir did not kill Elafius any more than Gwilym killed Patrick."

"But they admitted to it."

"No," I answered, sitting heavily on the abbot's bed. "Lauhiir did not admit to it, actually. Gwilym accepted responsibility because he was afraid that Rhiannon had killed Patrick to protect him. I knew that she had not, but I would not embarrass her in front of her own father."

Coroticus nodded.

"Lauhiir could not have killed Elafius. He would never have told me that Elafius was helping him with his tin smelting, and he would never have left the silver *denarius* there for me to find.

"Elafius came to you with the counterfeit *denarius*. Perhaps he even told you that he intended to bring it to Arthur's attention when he arrived. I doubt that he understood that you were Lauhiir's partner in this, and I equally doubt that he understood that a rebellion was afoot. But you panicked. Elafius had to be removed before Arthur arrived.

"Indeed, I suspect that the *denarius* was what you were searching for in his cell. The yew extract, I believe, was intended to make his death look natural, but his brittle old neck snapped. One of the other *monachi* was bound to discover the broken neck when they prepared him for burial. So you left the yew needles and berries. At the worst, I would find my way to Rhiannon, since it is well known that poison is a woman's weapon. You did not know, then, that she was Gwilym's daughter, did you? And you never expected me to cut his body open to see how much of the extract he had ingested."

His eyes narrowed but he did not speak.

"What little Elafius knew was too much. So, you were in a corner. Patrick was on his way. You were helping an errant lord foment rebellion and you were harboring Agricola, the last of the great Pelagians. Of course, Elafius was unaware of the last, though he certainly knew that Gwilym was a Pelagian. I doubt, by the way, that Lauhiir even knows what Pelagianism is. You had a choice: be revealed to an icon of the church or kill Elafius. Elafius lost."

"If that is true," Coroticus began, his voice sounding a bit strained, "then why did I call you here to investigate?"

"That puzzled me as well. But I was already on my way here with Arthur. You knew that I would involve myself in this. By sending Ider to fetch me, you effectively directed my inquiry away from you. Which brings us to Patrick."

"Gwilym admitted to killing Patrick."

"Only because he was afraid Rhiannon killed him. She knew the danger that Patrick posed to both of them. She had access to the tunnels to slip in and out without being seen. What Gwilym did not know was that when Patrick was murdered, Rhiannon was bedding me.

"When I continued to show interest in Gwilym, and more especially when Patrick and I formed a *coitus*, you knew that your plans were in real trouble. Especially when Gwilym told you that he and Patrick had been boyhood friends. Patrick was not forgetful like old Elafius; he was of a sound mind. He would have recognized not only his old friend Tremayne, but the Pelagian he became, Agricola. Your position here would have stood forfeit. And Gwilym would have been exposed. Only you had reason to kill both men. Tell me, my lord abbot, did you consider Patrick's death a divine sacrifice as Gwilym does?"

For the first time in all the years I had known the abbot, I saw a truly brutal look on his face. "No, Malgwyn. I considered it divine retribution. Gwilym told me how Patrick had ravished the young girl. Rumors of some great sin of Patrick's had floated across the land for years. But to finally hear it, well, I lost no sleep by killing that fraud.

"So, you have figured it all out so neatly. What will you do now? Summon me before Lord Arthur? Go to Castellum Marcus and denounce me to Dubricius?"

I stood. "In a perfect world, you would be put to the sword. Do not insult me by claiming that you committed these deeds for any high, noble cause. You murdered Elafius and Patrick to protect your own precious hide. But we do not live in a perfect world. No, Coroticus. Arthur said not a fortnight ago that we needed you here, overseeing the abbey, not someone new, someone unknown.

"So here is what you will do. You will withdraw your opposition to Arthur's church. You will pay your taxes. You will use your contacts and your spies to alert us to any future threat against Arthur. You will not assist anyone desiring to overthrow Arthur. And, you will not tell anyone of our agreement. If I find that you have violated any of this, I will not denounce you. I will kill you. Do we understand each other?"

I think the flat tone of my statement shocked Coroticus more than anything else. He nodded slowly, seeming relieved that I was not going to expose him.

"What of Lauhiir?"

"I will not interfere with your grant of sanctuary to Lauhiir. But know that Arthur will keep guards here from now until the end of time to catch him if he ventures beyond the *vallum* ditch and bank. In other words, my old friend, you are stuck with him."

Coroticus grunted. "A small price to pay, I suppose."

"Far too small, abbot."

"And Gwilym?"

"Do as you please with him. I am sure he will want to leave. Let him." I turned to depart, but a thought struck me and I faced him once again. "If it should occur to you to arrange for my death, be assured that I am not a weak old *monachus* nor will I give you a chance to stab me in the back."

My next visit took me to the cell of Gwilym. I found him there with Rhiannon. Pausing in the doorway, I considered the ancient *monachus*. I truly did like him, as much for his willingness to offer his own life for that of his daughter as anything else. It was an emotion familiar to me.

Rhiannon was as beautiful as ever. I wanted to believe that she had given herself to me willingly, but at the back of my mind another truth ate at me. I did not believe that she had not slept with the abbot. He was a virile man in his prime, and she had reason to keep him happy.

"What shall I call you—Tremayne, Agricola, Gwilym?"

"Whatever pleases you. Should I call you 'Smiling Malgwyn' or 'Mad Malgwyn' or 'Malgwyn the Wise'?"

I smiled at the last. "I have been anything but wise in this affair."

"You faced many obstacles."

"I faced many lies."

Gwilym smiled then. "Yes, many lies."

"I know that you did not kill Patrick. I know that you had no hand in Elafius's death. You confessed to Patrick's murder because you feared Rhiannon had done it. She did not."

Even in the cool evening air, a fine sheen of sweat had erupted on his forehead. Now, he visibly relaxed, the contours of his ancient but rigid muscles disappearing beneath his robe.

He reached over and patted Rhiannon's knee. "My daughter is a passionate and devoted woman, Malgwyn. I did not want to believe it, but I could not take that chance. My life is near its end. Better that I be thought guilty than that she forfeit her life protecting me."

"Is that not what being a father is about?"

Rhiannon flashed me a look of gratitude for saying no more than that.

Gwilym hung his head. "I would never have harmed either one. They were, once, my dearest friends. Poor Elafius! He never suspected that I was, in truth, Tremayne."

"Did it amuse you to argue with Elafius?"

"Yes, I will admit to that. His memory was always horrible, even when we were children. So Lauhiir killed him over this forging business?"

I nodded, perpetuating the lie. "Rhiannon, would you please leave your father and me alone?"

She looked quickly to Gwilym, and he just as quickly nodded his assent. With a fleeting glance at me, she disappeared through the door.

Pulling a chair closer to Gwilym, I sat down heavily. "I want to talk about Addiena."

He shook his old white head slowly. " 'Twas a sad thing, Malgwyn. The power of lust has turned many good men evil."

"Yes, it has. I have heard the story twice now, from Patrick and from Myndora. But a few things still bother me."

"Please, ask."

"Patrick told me that he confided to you hours after the attack."

"That is true."

"I see. And when the signs of the Scotti raiding party were

found, you kept his confidence and let the awful deed lie at their feet?"

"Patrick was a good man. He had a moment of weakness, something all men are subject to. Addiena was already dead. Patrick was obviously repentant for his sin. I saw no reason to ruin the rest of his life."

"Yet years later, you told Severus that Patrick had killed and ravished the girl?"

Gwilym hung his head. "I was still young and incautious. I wanted to impress upon Severus that the church was not without error. In a fit of youthful passion, I disclosed Patrick's story. As it was, it did not further my cause. The church, to this day, condemns Pelagius and his beliefs."

"Yes, that is true. But you bring me to my real question. Why did you lie to Patrick and Severus? Indeed, why have you lied your entire life?"

His head flew up. "Lied? Lied about what?"

"You murdered Addiena."

Gwilym exploded to his feet, sending his wooden stool flying across the cell. "How dare you!"

I leaped to my feet and grabbed him by his robe, driving him against the wall, causing the wood to shudder. "It is over, Gwilym!" He was lighter than I thought, and I nearly lifted him from the ground with my one hand. "It is over!" I repeated, my nose just inches from his.

His eyes searched mine for some doubt, some uncertainty, but he found none.

He went limp in my hand and I lowered him slowly to the floor. "How . . . did . . . you know?"

"Myndora told me, though she did not realize it."

"My sister? How? She knew nothing, only what I told her."

I released him and he slumped against the wall, all of the fight gone from his eyes, replaced with a fearsome sadness, the likes of which I had never seen. "You told her too much."

He looked up at me with a question in those eyes.

"According to Patrick, he told you about the assault on Addiena later, after her body had been found."

"That is true. He did."

"But when you told Myndora, when you warned her, you told her you had seen it happen."

He wanted to deny it. He had not thought of that conversation for a lifetime. I could see his eyes flitting back and forth in their sockets as they searched for an answer.

"I . . . I . . ." But he could dredge up no words to counter mine.

"It was more than that though, Gwilym. Let me tell you what I think happened. You were all going to meet that day. But Elafius was late, and he sent Addiena ahead. Patrick was already there when she arrived.

"He was a young boy with all of the desires that mark young boys. Addiena was there. No one else was around. He tried to force himself on her. I suspect, though I have no way of proving it, that he did nothing more than cause her to faint from sudden fright. I believe he has convinced himself over the years that he actually did ravish her.

"And then he ran, frightened beyond all words. But you were there, Gwilym, watching from afar. And you ran up to Addiena, saw her lying there, her gown askew, and you could not resist any more than Patrick could. But she awakened as you attempted to mount her, and you choked the life out of her."

"No! No! Patrick did! You could not possibly know anything about that. It happened before you were born!"

"But I do know how you described Addiena's death to Myndora. You talked about her eyes bulging and turning red with blood as she fought for air, her lips turning blue! Only someone who had been there could know those details! I have studied the bodies of men and women choked to death. I have seen the little points of red in their eyes. But you have to be close, virtually on top of them, to see it. You ravished her and you choked her to death to hide your deed. And then you let Patrick believe he had done it."

Gwilym looked up at me then, his eyes red with tears, tears that overflowed the wrinkles in his face. "How could she remember those things so completely?"

"How could she not, Gwilym? One of her friends had just been murdered, and you were telling her that the boy she loved did it. She will never forget that as long as she lives!"

"I did not mean to kill her. But when she awakened and saw me, I panicked. I knew I could never explain it!"

"Such is the excuse of most murderers, Gwilym. 'I did not mean to' could be etched in stone. But, in your case, I truly believe that you did not intend to kill her. What I do blame you for is not telling Patrick the truth all those years ago. Patrick was a good and honorable man, who has dedicated his life to the Christ. He was your friend. He deserved better!"

Nodding, he wiped the tears from his face with an age-spotted hand. "What will you do with me now?"

Sighing, I placed a hand on his shoulder. "Now, Patrick is dead. There will be no council at Castellum Marcus to judge him. Addiena is dead and few are now alive who even remember her. I see nothing to be gained by revealing your part in this affair. You are free to leave here as you wish. I would suggest Gaul. It is a pleasant enough place, and Rhiannon will be able to fulfill her role in the divine sacrifice without incurring the wrath of the church."

"But I am Agricola, the champion of Pelagius. You do not wish to secure the favor of the church by exposing me?"

"I am Malgwyn, and I could care less about the battles within the church over philosophy. But do not place your trust in Coroticus. He might be tempted. In fact, I think he will be tempted. One further question. Why did you go to Patrick's cell that night?"

The old priest bowed his head. "To beg his forgiveness for betraying his confidence. To plead with him not to betray me to Dubricius and Severus. I was happy here."

I sighed. But he had had no intention of relieving Patrick of the burden he had wrongly carried all these years. Man is a predictable creature. "If it is of any comfort, I believe he would have forgiven you. The Patrick that I came to know in his last days was a man of forgiveness."

Gwilym stood. "I would thank you, but I sense that such would not be appropriate or welcome. You are an uncommon man with an uncommon clarity of vision. Arthur rises in my esteem by keeping such as you close to him."

I turned without speaking and left his cell, only to find Rhiannon waiting for me.

She looked vulnerable and more beautiful than any time I had seen her. Even in her religious robes, designed to hide her figure, she was more than alluring. I think, most of all, I liked her eyes. They seemed always to hold a challenge, always anticipating an argument. They were alive.

"Rhiannon, I will take my leave now. I have yet another journey to make before I return home."

"You have no accusations to make against me?"

I was tired of this affair, so tired. "What would you have me say, Rhiannon? That I know you helped Coroticus kill Elafius? That I wonder if your visit to my cell that night was to distract me, to divert attention away from you while Patrick was being killed? Fine, those are the things that burden my mind. But while I can prove that two people had a hand in killing Elafius, I have no way of proving that you were one of them and, now, no interest in doing so. It is over. Let the dead rest."

The lines in her face tightened with disappointment. "I gave myself to you because I wanted you. What difference does the other make?"

Her words held no comfort for me. Indeed, my heart was already feeling empty and unsure, and now that she had spoken, I felt even worse. But like a farmer's fork, my pain had more than one prong. We had joined that night with no hesitation, no awkwardness, and I had allowed those feelings, those urges, to steal my resolve. It was not what she said that hurt me; it was what she did not say. She denied nothing that I said.

"Go to your father now. He needs you. Our paths were not meant to join but for a moment."

And then I turned and walked away from her, never turning, never looking back, for fear I would lose my way. I passed through the old burying ground and saw that they had buried Patrick next to his friend Elafius. As he requested, there would be no stone to mark his grave.

Merlin waited for me at the entrance to the abbey, perched on top of his horse and holding the reins of mine in his hand. It was odd to begin a journey at night, but so much of this matter had happened in the dark.

As we rode out of the village, I turned my horse to the west.

CHAPTER EIGHTEEN

A week later, as we crossed the River Cam to see Arthur's castle rising above us, its massive ramparts and defensive ditches ringing its slope, I felt a sudden sense of relief. A troop of Arthur's cavalry rode by on the opposite bank and gave me the salute. I returned it and slipped down from my saddle as Merlin urged his horse across the ford. Slapping my horse on her hindquarters, I walked beside the oxen as they pulled the cart into the water.

"What river is this?" a voice asked from within the cart, a woman's voice.

"The River Cam, Myndora."

"Then we must be nearly there."

I just shook my head. Her eyes might be dead, but her mind was as sharp as ever. While I had sat in the cave, uncertain if I would see another sunrise, I had determined to bring her here, where there were people who would care for her. Though she grumbled a bit, convincing her proved to be no problem. She had little, so Merlin and I took but a few minutes to pack her things and get her into the oxcart.

Merlin became fascinated with her incredible sense of

hearing, and he occupied her time—aye, he nearly drove her to distraction—with his incessant questions. But they soon established a friendship of sorts, and I was glad.

Once we had crossed the ford, I remounted and we skirted the base of the fort. We encountered several more of Arthur's men, and each saluted me. I was a little confused. Since the assassination plot against Ambrosius Aurelianus, I had regained some of the respect I had lost during my self-pitying, drunken life. But this was different.

I shrugged and continued leading my little party along the road to the main gate in the southwest. As we negotiated the snakelike road, designed to make assaults more difficult, I heard a great roar of voices. We made the last curve and there, just inside the massive gateway, stood Arthur and Bedevere, with two troop of horse lining the road leading to the market square.

Reining my horse in, I dismounted, surprised and confused at this display. Knowing not what else to do, I walked slowly up to him and took a knee. "My lord Rigotamos. I am at your service." To have done otherwise before so large a gathering would have been an insult.

Arthur strode forward and took my good arm, helping me to rise. "This is not my doing, Malgwyn, but theirs."

I looked and realized that the mounted soldiers were those I had led against the rebels.

"They wished to honor you on your return, for your bravery and your skill in battle. I could not refuse them."

I looked from soldier to soldier. Half were straining to keep a solemn face; the others had given up the task as hopeless. Their horses were impatient at standing still, and they pawed the ground, snorting, their riders' weapons jingling.

"But how did you know I would arrive now?"

Arthur shook his great, shaggy head and grinned. "Malgwyn, our scouts spotted you last night. We have known of your arrival to the minute." He stopped and looked to the cart, walking up beside it. "I see you have returned with Merlin, but who is this beautiful lady?"

"This, my lord," I answered, "is Myndora, many years ago a friend to both Elafius and Patrick. She helped me sort out the threat against your crown."

Arthur walked up to the cart and reached in to take Myndora's hand in his. Though her eyes were sightless, I could tell she was embarrassed by all of this attention. For his part, Arthur ignored her infirmity. He could be as charming as a devil. "Lady Myndora. I welcome you to Castellum Arturius." He turned back to me. "Malgwyn, we will need to find a suitable residence for so distinguished a lady."

Arthur had something in mind. I could tell. "I had thought that she could take my hut, here near the gate."

"No, no, no," he said, shaking that head again. "I am granting her Accolon's old house. And I am sending Nimue from my household to serve her."

Myndora was stunned, but she found it within her to lower her head in respect to Arthur. "Rigotamos," she finally choked out. "I do not know how I can thank you."

"You already have, Lady Myndora."

He smiled and winked at Merlin, who bowed in return. With a flick of his finger, two soldiers bounded forth and led the cart through the gate and into the castle.

"Now, Merlin, what do you and Bedevere think we should do with our wayward scribe?"

"Well, Rigotamos, I have given this a great deal of thought," Merlin began. "Since the lands of the rebel lords, Dochu and

Teilo, stand forfeit, I believe that those lands and the title of lord be granted to Malgwyn. After all, it was only through his dedication to you and bravery in battle that the rebellion was thwarted."

Arthur turned and looked to the soldiers lining the road into the castle. "What say you, men? Should I nominate Malgwyn to the *consilium* as lord?"

Voices shouted, spears rattled together. My eyes, though I willed it not to be so, spilled over with tears, and my words caught in my throat painfully. I cried not for the honor of being proffered as a new lord, but for the honor done me by Arthur and the men I had led in battle. That was worth a thousand titles.

Merlin, seeing my state, turned to Arthur. "Rigotamos, Malgwyn should be given time to consider your offer. 'Tis a great decision to make."

To his credit, Arthur missed nothing and paused not. "Of course he should have time. Come, Malgwyn, a feast is preparing to honor our victory and our soldiers!"

As I passed through the gates, I looked up and saw little Mariam, my daughter, running like the wind toward me. I snatched her up with my one arm and held her tight and she wrapped her arms around my neck, and the tears came again.

A festival was held over the next few days, filled with feasting and drinking and our traditional dances, all to celebrate Arthur's victory over the rebels. Merchants crowded the lanes of the castle with their brooches and pots and food. I took part but showed little interest. My mind was yet unsettled. Even the return of my dear friend Kay from the eastern lands failed to brighten my days.

One evening, after the feasting, I climbed the great wooden wall that surmounted our innermost ditch and bank. A parapet circled the castle for our guards to mount their patrols. My legs carried me to a point in the north wall, near unto our own watchtower, from where I could see the signal fire burning on the great Tor at Ynys-witrin. In the distance, I could hear a screech owl crying into the night. The stars seemed so close I could touch them.

"You are unhappy?"

The voice startled me. It was Bedevere. We had grown closer during our adventure at the abbey, and though he was still a solemn and taciturn man, even with me, he was now more open, more approachable.

"I am bothered by recent events."

"How so?"

"I think of Patrick and Elafius, even Gwilym. I think of how little moments in time can control the rest of our lives. Sometimes, the wrong decision, no matter how small, can rob you of a happy life."

"Granted. Have you made such a small decision?"

My eyes locked with his. "I am afraid that I have been making such a decision, that I have let the shades of the dead steal a chance at a good life."

Bedevere smiled, an unusual expression for him. "I have seldom met a man who is so certain about events outside himself yet so confused when events affect him personally. But the Christ and God his father protect you, Malgwyn. Let the shades of the dead go to their rest. They would not begrudge you that good life you desire."

"I pray you are right, Bedevere." I started to turn away, then hesitated.

"Something else troubles you?"

"Remember when I was 'Smiling Malgwyn,' when I killed Saxons with pleasure and abandon?"

"Of course."

"When I was escaping from the rebels and as I made my way back to Ynys-witrin, I found myself returning to that way. I killed with near joy, certainly without regret. I thought I had left those days behind. But Bedevere, I found myself smiling again! And I did not like it, but I could not stop, not until I was cut down once again. That memory has brought demons to my dreams and shadows to my days."

His face of stone softened, the hard lines melting like butter on hot bread. "Malgwyn, you are an odd man. You have killed, yes. But who has not in these times? You have acted with honor. You killed to revenge the deaths of those you care about, to protect your Rigotamos, and to save your own neck. Show me the wrong in that. Show me the evil in it.

"Now"—and the face of granite returned, almost—"cease worrying about things past. You can do nothing about them. They are like a meal already eaten. It either settles well in your belly or revolts, makes you sick. But once eaten, you have no control over that outcome. Go! The here and now you can mend; the future you can change!"

I knew that he was right. With a determined look on my face, I clutched his shoulder, squeezed it, and went off to the nearest ladder and descended to the ground.

Ignoring the occasional shouts of revelers, I marched through the town lanes, past the house I shared with Merlin, around the market square, and on to a house on one of the back lanes. Rounding one corner, I almost ran into Tristan, the unfortunate noble confined to the castle for his role in

Eleonore's death. He saw me coming and scampered out of the way.

I did not bother to knock. Flinging the door back, I scanned the room, lit by a pair of oil lamps. Mariam and Owain had just carried in a load of wood and were stacking it by the hearth.

Ygerne emerged from a back room, partitioned off by a finely scraped hide hanging from the ceiling. She was tired from a day of caring for and feeding her children. A smudge of ash marked her forehead. But her long red hair glowed just as brightly as I remembered it, and her figure pushed at her gown in all the places that stirred me.

I walked to her, deliberately and determinedly. She saw me and began to smile, but her eyes quickly grew a question. I had become a constant visitor over the last months, but she had never seen me act like this.

"Malgwyn? What—"

And with a quick shake of my head, I wrapped my arm around her, pulled her body against me, and kissed her with all the ardor and passion in my heart.

After what seemed like the most pleasant moments of my life, Ygerne gently pushed me back, propped both hands on her hips and said, "What took you so long?"

Down below me, I felt something grab my legs. I looked and it was Mariam, who wrapped her arms around both of us and hugged with all of her might. She looked up and smiled at us, and then buried her face in my breeches.

Later, after the children had gone to sleep, and Ygerne and I had tasted that fruit I had thought forbidden but found sweet as a ripened apple, the two of us wandered back through the lanes of the town. She walked not on my good side, but on the side with my half-arm, which she wrapped her own hand around. It did not make me uncomfortable though, as I thought it might; rather, it felt natural and welcome.

Our wanderings led us back to the parapet, facing north. We leaned on the wall, and I pointed out the fire on the Tor at Ynys-witrin. A warm breeze blew out of the south and against our backs. Ygerne moved closer to me.

"Your journey was difficult." She knew me too well.

"I do not know that I have ever had a more dangerous or twisted path," I said honestly. "And I bear another mark of my stupidity."

Ygerne touched the wound on the side of my head, healing but still pink and tender. "And you bring home yet another badge of honor. And not unlike that which killed your brother."

I had forced myself not to think of that; I did not want to think of that. "Why such a blow killed one of us and not the other is a question beyond my ken. If I tried to sort it out I am afraid I would lose my mind."

"Then put it far from your thoughts." She stopped and turned back toward the point of light that was Ynys-witrin. In the distance, across the land somewhere, a screech owl cried in the night. "What did you see out there that made you change your mind?"

"He saw how easily life can slip away."

Arthur.

We turned and saw the Rigotamos and Guinevere walking along the parapet to join us. "My lord." I nodded at him. "Cousin."

"This is a welcome sight, Malgwyn," Guinevere said. "I thought you would never come to your senses."

I smiled at her. "It was a long and truly bloody road. Too many good men died. Too many scoundrels yet live. And for what, power, wealth?"

"Look out there, Malgwyn," Arthur said. In the moonlight, the hills and flatlands stood in stark relief to the star-crowded sky. Occasionally, here and there, the dim lights of farms twinkled on the landscape. "That is what they died for. Aye, even our little thief Llynfann. Even Patrick and Elafius."

"Too many died," I repeated, softly.

"Tomorrow, Malgwyn, those folk, living on their farms, will arise and milk the cows, feed the hogs. They will cook their meals and tend their crops. And they will do all of that without fear of plundering Saxons or treacherous rebels. Who is to say what price is too high for that? You? Me? No. Only God in his heaven can make that judgment."

A thought struck me at the mention of God, something I had completely forgotten. I turned to Guinevere. "Cousin, what happened to the emissary, this Francesco from Rome? Did he arrive? By the time I returned to Ynys-witrin from Bannaventa, I had nothing on my mind but the rebellion."

Arthur looked away, trying to suppress a smile. Ygerne looked at us, confused. "Well, Malgwyn," Guinevere began, "I paired him with a Pictish woman named Sinead. She had little enthusiasm for a life of service to the Christ, but she found great enthusiasm for the emissary. Aye, so great that I am not sure they have even yet ventured from his chamber."

And we all laughed then, and it felt good. We stood for a while, the four of us, staring across the land and breathing the clean air of Britannia.

GLOSSARY AND GAZETTEER

Aquae Sulis — This was the Roman name for what is now Bath, England.

braccae — Breeches worn by both Saxons and the Brythonic tribes. The only extant examples come from peat bogs in Europe. There was a certain disdain by Romans toward the Gallic tribes for wearing pants.

Breton — A native or inhabitant of Brittany, or the Celtic language of the Breton people.

castellum — Castle, but not in the High Middle Ages sense, with thick stone walls, towers, and damsels in distress. Usually a defensive position with stacked rock and timber defensive rings.

Castellum Artorius — For the purposes of this novel, Cadbury Castle at South Cadbury, Somerset, is the location for Arthur's castle. Excavations during the 1960s identified it as having been significantly rebuilt and reinforced during the late fifth century by a warlord of Arthurian stature, although no explicit evidence linking the site to Arthur himself was discovered.

Castellum Marcus — Castellum Marcus in southeast Cornwall is believed to have been the site of King Mark's headquarters. Nearby was found the famous Tristan stone, a gravestone believed to commemorate the historical Tristan, making it the one contemporary piece of evidence for the historicity of a character in the Arthurian canon.

cervesa — The Latin name for the beer made by the local tribes during the Roman occupation. According to tablets unearthed at Vindolanda near Hadrian's Wall, Roman soldiers were not shy about drinking *cervesa*.

consilium — A council. Gildas refers to a *consilium* ruling pre-Saxon Britannia that ended in Vortigern hiring Saxon mercenaries to help put down the raids of the Picts and Scots. It is safe to assume that any warlord that exerted influence over large areas in central and western England would have done so at the behest and the agreement of such a council of lesser kings.

Dumnonia (Dumnonii) — A tribe residing in the area of Cornwall and throughout the west lands. Mark is thought to have been a king of the Dumnonii during the general period of Arthur's life. Christopher Snyder suggests in *The Britons* that people in the post-Roman period referred to themselves by tribal designations.

Durotrigia (Durotrigii) — A tribe residing in the area surrounding Glastonbury down through the South Cadbury area to the southern coast.

Gildas—A monk who wrote one of the few histories of post-Roman Britain. He unquestionably had strong connections to southwest England, and some late sources connect him to Arthur. According to one story, Gildas was the brother of Huaill, who was allegedly killed by Arthur.

iudex pedaneus—A Roman official assigned to investigate crimes and offenses. It is known that such titles were still used in post-Roman Britannia.

latrunculii—A term applied to groups of bandits that ran rampant during the fifth century, not to be confused with a Roman board game of the same era.

Londinium—As would be expected, this is the Roman name for what is now London.

meneds—The *meneds* is the ancient name for the Mendip hills of northwest England.

mortaria—A type of bowl with knots or beads in the bottom to make it easier to grind vegetables to a pulp.

peplos—A type of gown worn by women, having a Roman cut.

presbyter—A Latin term applied to priests or other church officers. Remember that this was a time before parish priests.

sacerdote—A term used to describe priests, interchangeable with *presbyter* above. There may certainly have been differences between these two terms at the time, but such distinctions, without documentary evidence, are impossible for modern readers to understand.

tigernos — The Celtic word for "lord," sometimes used to designate local lords, but believed by some scholars to have been combined with the word "vor" to produce the name "Vortigern," or "overlord."

vallum — A ditch, possibly holding a wooden palisade, used as both a defense and a boundary marker for monastical sites during the fifth century and onward.

Via Arturius — "Arthur's Way." A roadway or lane actually ran from Cadbury Castle to Glastonbury. It has become known as Arthur's Way. Two major Roman roads near Cadbury Castle were the Via Fosse and the Via Harrow.

Via Caedes — "The Killing Way." Obviously, this is a creation for the novel, but skeletons have been found along the main roadway entering Cadbury Castle. They were victims of an ancient massacre, probably at the hands of Romans and probably in reaction to the rebellions of Caractacus or Boudicca.

vigile — The Roman equivalent, in a sense, of both a policeman and a fireman. In Rome, they watched for fires as much as any crime.

Votadini (Votadinii) — A tribe residing in what is now northern England and into the lands of the Scots border as far as the Firth of Forth. One story of a chieftain named Cunneda (Kenneth) suggests that some of the Votadini migrated to northern Wales, but, according to Snyder, that possibility has been discounted.

Ynys-witrin — According to some sources, this was the early name for what is now Glastonbury. It is believed that a Christian community may have resided there during the Arthurian age.

Author's Note

As I like to point out, this is a novel. While I have done my best to adhere to elements of the actual time period as we know it, this is not intended to be history. No one knows exactly what life was like in the age of Arthur, but I have tried to give a flavor of what it may have been like as best we understand the evidence.

The story of Lauhiir killing three of Arthur's men tracks to one of the earliest Arthurian tales, the life of Saint Cadoc. As it is told traditionally, David, Teilo, and Dochu do play a part, but only as mediators along with the abbot. Such a story is interesting, but I've chosen to make it a nefarious plot to overthrow Arthur. Indeed, the story also gives a hint of how unpopular Arthur was in certain areas. The Welsh material, particularly, tends to paint Arthur in a far less sympathetic way than he is normally seen. Is this some hint of an Arthur less grand than he is depicted in the romances? Since nearly all written material was prepared by the clergy, it more likely is indicative of the attitude within the clergy toward Arthur.

Counterfeiting in the fifth century? Certainly. On the scale that I indicate? Probably not. Tin was mined extensively in western Britain even before the days of the Romans. But the departure of the Romans meant a reduction in the tin production. The exact date that tin mining resumed is elusive. But a ruling body, in the wake of the Roman withdrawal, would certainly have seen the profit in mining tin.

One method of counterfeiting coins included using tin and bronze with a silver wash. Others involved pewter, a mixture of tin and lead, with a silver wash. They were typically marked by a degradation of the original design and/or errors. In actuality, many early coin designs were copies of Greek and Roman coins anyway.

Patrick. The great saint himself told us in his *Confessio* that he had committed a horrible sin in his youth, a sin confided to only one person, and that that person had revealed his confidence to the church. It did indeed cause him problems, as many in the church were jealous of his fame. Some scholars point to Burnham-on-the-Sea in Somerset as the site of Bannaventa while others look farther north. A number of traditions at Glastonbury have it that Patrick is buried there; some even credit him as the founder of the abbey. And Patrick actually did request that no stone mark his grave, hence some of the confusion over his final resting place. Another likely grave site is Downpatrick in Ireland. But no one knows for certain where the old bishop's bones lie.

Pelagianism was a constant problem for the church, evidence their dispatch of Germanus not once but twice. Agricola was a British Pelagian attacked by Germanus. We know little of Agricola's life before or after this event. I've simply stirred all of these up and woven them into my story.

Glastonbury as Ynys-witrin. That's the earliest recorded name for the area. During the time of the novel, it really was something of an island. The Somerset Levels were flooded for much of the year. The Romans truly did have a wharf at the base of Wirral Hill, and it's believed that the Brue River was navigable by ships as far as Glastonbury.

The founding of the abbey is shrouded in mystery. There are no absolutely reliable records that date the abbey before the seventh century. But there is a mountain of tradition, folklore, and legend that carries it back to the time of the novel. Glastonbury Tor was almost certainly occupied at this date, as evidenced by archaeological digs. While the data suggests occupation by, perhaps, a Dark Age lord, it could also have been a hermitage site.

The cave where Malgwyn is imprisoned is Wookey Hole Cavern, a remarkable set of passages that run deep under the Mendip Hills not far from the lovely cathedral city of Wells. There have been, indeed, any number of skeletons recovered from Wookey Hole, including those of Roman soldiers. According to the tour guide, scenes from Kevin Costner's *Robin Hood* were filmed there and even J. K. Rowling has visited, seeking inspiration. For anyone who visits, the cave's potential as a setting for a story is obvious.

For the inevitable mistakes, I take full responsibility. A task of these proportions creates ample opportunity for error, but I have done my best to avoid as many as possible.